Dear Reader,

Cat Cantrell doesn't trust me farther than she
can throw me, but she can't deny the chemistry
between us. She doesn't believe that a city
slicker like me can take Wyoming ranch life.
When I tell her that I forgot all about New York
the moment I laid eyes on her, she laughs. But
when I kiss her, it's no laughing matter. You
see, ranching is in my blood, and so is
Cat Cantrell.

Garrick Drexel

Wyoming

MEN MADE IN AMERICA

SHARON BRONDOS
Special Touches

Wyoming

Harlequin Books

TORONTO • NEW YORK • LONDON
AMSTERDAM • PARIS • SYDNEY • HAMBURG
STOCKHOLM • ATHENS • TOKYO • MILAN
MADRID • WARSAW • BUDAPEST • AUCKLAND

To Joan Clark,
friend and former editor

 HARLEQUIN ENTERPRISES LTD.
225 Duncan Mill Road, Don Mills,
Ontario, Canada M3B 3K9

SPECIAL TOUCHES

ISBN: 0-373-45200-4

Published Harlequin Enterprises, Ltd. 1988, 1993

Printed in the U.S.A.

CHAPTER ONE

CAT CANTRELL TOUCHED the Jeep's brake with the toe of her boot. Although it was hard to be sure at this distance, she could have sworn she saw someone walking down the middle of the road ahead of her. She squinted, trying to bring the figure into focus. It could be miles away or only a few thousand yards, she mused. In Wyoming, space between objects was often deceiving.

Almost as deceiving as the wily horse trader who just a few hours ago had tried to trick her out of the ten thousand dollars in cash she had brought with her to purchase some quality animals. Cat gritted her teeth at the memory.

She slowed a bit more. The sky was cloudless and the intensity of the high-altitude sunlight created mirages, patterns that looked like pools of water on the two-lane highway. The air rippled over the blacktop, further distorting her view and making the object on the road shimmer. But the closer she got, the more certain she was that she was coming up behind a lone traveler. On foot. In the middle of nowhere. The nearest town behind was hours away; Lone Tree, her home, almost as far. What on earth was anyone doing hiking out here? she wondered. If the person's car had broken down, didn't he have enough sense to stay in it until someone came along to get help? What kind of idiot would abandon shelter of any sort during the spring when the weather could suddenly, almost without warning, turn vicious? Cat shook her head in disbelief.

It was a man. She could see him more clearly now, and he was quite a sight. He appeared to be wearing a business suit. A coat was thrown casually over his shoulder and she could make out the distinctive plaid lining of a Burberry—garb appropriate enough for Manhattan, but hardly suitable for an afternoon's stroll on a seldom traveled back road to Lone Tree, Wyoming. Cat touched the brake again and honked the horn.

The man didn't turn. He just stepped to one side and held out his thumb in the traditional gesture. A warning bell went off inside Cat's head. He ought to have turned to face her. He ought to have been overjoyed that someone had come along to rescue him. He ought not to have even *been* here. As she slowed the Jeep, she shifted position so that the revolver she always wore when driving alone was readily available. No sense taking chances, she told herself. The weapon was on her left side where she could draw it easily.

Deliberately, she continued to coast until the Jeep was about twenty feet ahead of the hitchhiker. Watching him approach in the rearview mirror, she grew even more apprehensive. He was a big man. The three-piece suit couldn't disguise the wide shoulders and broad chest. And he had a neck like a bull. Sunglasses masked his eyes. Cat took a deep breath as he opened the passenger door with a hand large enough to cover almost two of hers.

"Anywhere you're going," he said, tossing the coat over the seat and settling in. "I'm not particular." He slammed the door decisively. Then he slumped down, not looking at her. He leaned his head on the back of the seat and made a noise that sounded to her surprisingly like one of self-disgust.

"Buckle your belt," Cat ordered. When he didn't obey immediately, she repeated the command. "I don't drive people anywhere unless they're buckled in."

Now he looked at her. With his eyes hidden by the dark glasses, she could make out no expression. The rest of his face was deadpan. She studied the generous mouth with firmly carved lips and the broad forehead across which a dip of rich, thick hair fell. At the temples, his black hair was starting to turn gray. The haircut, she recognized, was an expensive one. Coupled with the suit that also looked costly and certainly had to have been tailor-made, her passenger was made even more of a puzzle.

"You always this bossy?" he asked. Not a muscle in his face moved that didn't have to.

"Care to keep walking?" Cat sat hard on her temper.

He seemed to consider that a viable option for a moment. Then he made a noise deep in his chest, sat up and pulled the belt across himself. Looking at her again, he said, "I guess you're the captain, Calamity."

"Very funny." She put the Jeep in gear. "That's not my name." The tires squealed as she started off.

"Could have fooled me." His voice was deep, but gentle in tone... almost a drawl over an accent she remembered from the past. "Fringed suede jacket. Jeans and cowboy boots. I thought I might have walked through some sort of time barrier and was being rescued by the great Calamity Jane herself."

Under the dry words, she heard a hint of humor. "Well, then," she replied. "Look at yourself. If you came through a time barrier, you must have crossed it while walking down Wall Street. Nobody dresses that way out here. Just how lost are you?"

"You didn't call me stranger," he said. "Darn."

Cat began to relax. He might be crazy, but he didn't seem dangerous. "All right, stranger," she twanged. "What brings you to these here parts? Got a broke-down nag or something?"

"A broke-down BMW," he said, his tone now bleak. "If there's a phone wherever we're going, I'll call Animal Control to put it out of its misery."

"You can't trash a BMW!" Cat slowed. "Where did you leave it? I know my way around machinery. Maybe I can—"

"Forget it." His voice was harsh now. "There's nothing about the car or where it came from that I want to remember. Just forget it."

A head case, Cat decided. She had picked up a lunatic. How he had gotten there was now a secondary consideration to why. And to what she was going to do with him. She glanced over and saw he was staring out the window. "Like the scenery?" she asked, hoping to learn more.

He shrugged, his shoulders stretching the suit coat.

"It is pretty monotonous along this part of the highway," she said. "Not many people go this way. The interstate's quicker."

No comment.

"Where are you from?"

"New York."

No surprise there. She would have bet good money on his being from a big Eastern city. "How did you get out here?"

"Drove."

"The ill-fated BMW?"

"Yeah." She felt him look at her again. "Ill-fated. That doesn't sound like cowgirl lingo," he commented.

"That's because I'm not a cowgirl, New York. I run a guest ranch just outside Lone Tree. I was over at a place in South Dakota seeing about buying some stock."

"No luck, huh?"

"Not this time. I was ready to pay top dollar, too. But I'm still battling a male-chauvinist conspiracy that won't seem to believe I can recognize good and bad horseflesh." She slammed her hand against the steering wheel as the frustration rose in her mind. "It just makes me so mad I could spit!"

He straightened and the glasses came off. "You trade in cash?"

"Of cour... No." She suddenly realized what she had been giving away. Where had her natural caution gone? Now she was in it! Unless the guy was entirely stupid—and a man didn't get clothes like that by being an ignoramus—she had just admitted to him that she was traveling with a sizable amount of cash. The pressure of the .357 at her hip was suddenly extremely comforting. "No. I was planning on making arrangements for a trade if I saw a few animals I could use. I never deal directly in cash."

"Liar." His voice sounded ominously silky now. Out of the corner of her eyes, Cat saw him slip his hand inside his jacket.

She didn't need to see his weapon to justify producing her own. The revolver was in her hand and pointing at the middle of his forehead as she carefully slowed the Jeep. "Take that hand out a millimeter at a time," she said, amazed that her voice didn't shake. "Then clasp both hands on top of your head. If you move otherwise, you're history. Make no mistake about it." As she didn't have enough hands and eyes to cover him, and drive at the same time, she pulled over to the side of the road.

Garrick Drexel obeyed without question. For the first time since he had sat down next to her, the woman had his undivided attention. She looked like a regular female Dirty Harry with the cannon aimed at him. He noted the long mane of blond hair, the wide blue eyes, the strongly carved features and the tanned skin. Hell, she looked like a lioness. "I think, miss," he said as carefully as possible, "that you're the one making the mistake."

"Sure I am." She unsnapped her seat belt. "And I'm going to keep on making it. Don't move!" She reached inside his suit coat. The muzzle of the gun didn't waver. She was, Garrick realized, quite at home with the weapon. A trickle of cold sweat ran down his side. It had been a long, long time since anyone had held him at gunpoint, and he found he didn't like it any better for all the years that had passed.

However, this was a far prettier antagonist than any he had encountered before. She was no beauty—her face was too strong to be called lovely. But it had something that pleased his aesthetic sense, even when he feared he wouldn't be around much longer to enjoy it. She had fished out his wallet and was studying its contents without taking much of her attention off him. "I'm Garrick Drexel," he said. "Innocent man. If you want my cash, go ahead and take it. I was going to offer to pay for the ride anyway."

"Maybe you were." She put the wallet back, her fingers slipping it deftly into the inner pocket of his jacket. Close up, she smelled of horses, suede and some vaguely flowery scent. "Maybe you were, but why the interest in my financial dealings?" Suspicion harshened her tone. "Don't bother lying. I could hear it in your voice. I'm very good at voices."

If it hadn't been for the gun, he would have shouted in exasperation. "I've been nothing but truthful with you," he said. "I was just curious about the horse business. I'm...I was in finance. It was only natural curiosity. Honest." He tried a smile.

No effect. She glared at him stonily. "Get out."

"Look, miss." He started to lower his hands, raising them quickly when she cocked the revolver. "Okay, go ahead! You might as well shoot me. It'll be quicker than dying of thirst and starvation out in this godforsaken desert!"

"You seemed happy enough trudging along before I picked you up." She gestured with the barrel. "Out."

"No." Garrick took a chance. He sat back, his hands still in the surrender position. "I'm tired and hungry. You can tie me up or something until we reach civilization—turn me over to the law if you want. But I'm damned if I'm getting out of this car!"

Cat regarded him. He meant what he said, she could see that. His mouth was set in a firm line, and his dark eyes challenged her. They were nice eyes, she thought inappropriately, long lashed and intelligent looking. Whatever else he was, she decided he wasn't simply a well-dressed bum. "All right," she said, thinking. "Since you insist. Turn around. Back to me." She handled horses far stronger than any man, and although this was a creature who could possibly outthink her, she didn't intend to give him a chance. Reaching onto the seat behind her, she grabbed a strap from a set of reins she had picked up in Rapid City. The leather was stiff, but it would serve. "Don't even breathe deeply," she warned.

Garrick gritted his teeth in frustration. She was actually planning to hog-tie him! Well, it was better than being shot or kicked out to hoof it on his own. He should never have inquired about the horse dealings. She must be carrying a considerable amount of money to be as skittish as she was, he mused. In the city he would understand a woman being this defensive. But out here people were supposed to be more trusting. Weren't they?

Trusting or not, she knew just how to use a rope. In a pinch he could probably break loose, he thought, testing the bonds by tensing his muscles. But since she seemed satisfied that he was helpless, it would best serve his purpose to remain tied up. He had no doubt that if he gave her the slightest excuse there would be a hole in him big enough for a bowling ball. But it took all of his self-control not to laugh in her face when she asked him in all seriousness if he was comfortable as she fastened his seat belt back across him.

"I'm fine, thanks. I appreciate your consideration," he replied.

"Mr. Drexel." She replaced the revolver in a holster on her left hip. "If I'm wrong about you, I will make it up to you in any way you want. You have to understand that it's foolhardy to take chances even out here. It may not be quite as dangerous as a city, but out in the wilds you'd be amazed how many people lose their civilized veneers." She eased the Jeep into gear and started off again. "Oh, not the locals, of course. Most of us can be trusted. We've learned to depend on each other."

"But not on the wily stranger?" He sounded bitter.

"I said I was sorry if I was wrong. But even you'd have to admit that you're a pretty intimidating guy. Are you into weights or something?"

Garrick swore. Now he was getting grilled about his private life. Well, he wasn't going to give her the satisfaction of responding. Retreating into the black emotional state he'd been in when she picked him up, he just glared straight ahead.

Cat drove on, already regretting her hasty action, but not certain enough to release the man when she was still so far from any help, should he turn out to be vindictive. Okay, he hadn't had a gun in his coat as she had believed, but with his size he hardly needed a weapon. She wasn't a small woman, however she had no illusions about her ability to deal with him without the advantage she had taken.

If only she didn't feel worse and worse about it the farther she drove with him trussed up beside her.

"Home on the range," he said after a long, uncomfortable silence.

"What?"

"The song. It promises a kind of paradise. What a laugh. I've never seen such desolate country. Or been treated with such creative hostility."

"What was I supposed to think! You probed around about my money. Then it looked as if you were going for a gun. Was I supposed to just sit, big-eyed and dumb, while you robbed me? Or worse?" Her face felt hot, and she wished she could shrug out of her jacket. Embarrassment warmed more than her cheeks.

"Oh, hell, I don't know. I guess I didn't have any business being out here in the first place. I'm damned if I know why I kept driving. I knew the car was on its last legs. Then, when it broke down, I just got out and kept on walking. Left all my stuff back in the car. Just said to hell with it all and walked. I don't even know how long I'd been going when you picked me up."

Cat stole a glance at him. Unless he was one of the best actors she had ever met, he certainly seemed to be telling the truth. She began to grow even more uncertain and uneasy about what she had done.

"Of course, you don't have any way to know whether I'm being straight with you," he said, changing his position on the seat. "I could actually be an insane roadside murderer working his way across the country. I could have planned to do you, take your car and drive until I ran into the next victim." He paused. "Why'd you stop to pick me up, anyhow?"

Cat swallowed hard. "It seemed like the thing to do at the time. You just don't pass a person on foot out here."

"Yeah," he said. "Right."

They drove in silence for a while. The landscape began to change as the Jeep climbed toward the mountains and Lone Tree. Now the wide vistas were blocked by low hills and great outcroppings of rock. Stunted pines grew in clusters, proclaiming that the forest waited up ahead. As they drew nearer to the town, Cat felt a combination of genuine relief and total humiliation. Perhaps, she thought, she ought to take the strap off his arms before they reached Lone Tree. She was still debating the issue when the Jeep declared itself dead with a wheeze and a clunk.

"Now what?" Her captive sat upright, straining the seat belt. "Is it my inevitable fate to be stranded? What's the matter with this thing?"

"Nothing serious." Cat unbuckled herself and got out. "It sounds like it just flipped a fan belt. Be patient. I'll have it fixed in a minute."

"Like I have a choice. Say, you know, you haven't told me your name." He raised a black eyebrow. "Not that I haven't been spending my time productively making them up for you, my dear."

She felt her face grow redder. "I'm Cat. Catherine Cantrell. If you're on the level and want to sue me or something, you'd need to know. I would have told you." She went to the rear of the Jeep and took down the toolbox.

"Ah. So now you don't think I was out to rob you. And you're starting to worry about the legal repercussions of drawing down on me and binding me against my will. Great. We're making real progress here, Cat."

"I don't like sarcasm." She moved to the front of the vehicle and raised the hood. The smell of torn and burned rubber assailed her.

"Too bad, Cat." He must have moved because the Jeep rocked. "I've been told I'm a master at the art of verbal repartee. And I'm getting crankier by the minute. You're really going to love me after another hour or so." The Jeep rocked again.

"Quit moving around." She bent over, working the broken belt loose. "I can't fix this if you jostle— Ah!" She broke off with a scream as the hood crashed down, crushing her arm beneath it and pinning her. The pain was an ocean wave drowning her and overwhelming all her senses. The edges of her vision darkened. She didn't pass out.

Garrick watched in horror as the accident occurred. For a terrible moment he saw her clearly as she screamed in pain. Then the golden-haired head dropped out of sight. Swearing through his teeth without being aware he was doing it, he struggled with the leather strap around his wrists. It gave at the same time the seat belt came out of its moorings. The skin on his wrists stung, but he barely noticed the pain.

He leaped out of the Jeep and ran to the front. She was hanging almost to the ground, blood running down her arm and onto the dusty road. Her eyes were open, a universe of pain reflected in their blue depths, and he was suddenly reminded of the only time he had ever hunted deer. Garrick felt a sickness rise inside him, which he pushed away as quickly as it had developed.

"Easy, there, Cat," he said softly. "I'm going to get you out of this." He put an arm around her and lifted her slightly, relieving the pressure on her trapped limb. She moaned. He hooked his fingers under the hood and raised it. Breath hissed through her parted lips.

"Cat, I think you've got a good, clean break there," he said, reaching over and supporting the arm. "Don't worry now. I've had some experience with emergencies. You're going to be all right."

She couldn't speak, but she heard the gentle, caring tone plainly. Part of the pain moved aside for astonishment. That he would help her wasn't that much of a surprise, although his having gotten loose was. What amazed her was the degree to which he seemed concerned. He continued talking while he carried her to the side of the road, his words soothing and comforting. He sounded as though he were speaking to a hurt and frightened child, and her eyes filled with tears that had nothing to do with her injury. It had been a long, long time since anyone had talked to her that way.

"I don't know if I can fix your car, or how far it is to a town," he said, laying her down on the hard, rock-strewn shoulder. "So I'm going to do what I can for you now. You're going to have to trust me, Catherine. Think you can do that?"

She managed a nod.

Garrick touched her cheek, made sure her arm was lying securely across her stomach, then went back to the Jeep to look for first-aid equipment.

There was none. Only a dirty blanket that smelled distinctively of horse. He discarded it immediately, wishing he had some place to wash his hands. Okay, he thought. Time to innovate. After pulling off his suit coat and vest and tossing the vest onto the seat next to his trench coat, he returned to the injured woman.

Her eyes reminded him even more of the deer now. The sick feeling returned, increasing when he bent down very gently to push up the sleeve of her jacket and examine the arm. The break was not clean and needed immediate attention—attention that was going to hurt beyond anything she had probably ever felt before. He slipped his suit coat under her head and stroked her hair.

"Listen, babe," he said. "I'm going to have to do a little work on that arm. It's not going to be a whole lot of fun for you, but I can't leave it the way it is. You're bleeding pretty badly. Understand?"

She nodded. "Don't call me babe," she whispered. "It's sexist."

Garrick smiled. She was going to handle it all right.

And he would have to, as well.

He unbuttoned his shirt, leaving it on for the moment but planning to tear it into strips for bandages. Then he took hold of her arm.

When the pain came this time, Cat almost choked trying to keep the scream from bursting out of her. Agony took her to the edge of unconsciousness but cruelly kept her from falling off into black relief. Her breath came in jerking sobs although no tears wet her cheeks. The man was talking, but she couldn't make out the words, only his tone, blessedly kind and tender. She concentrated on that, trying to force her body to ignore the torment it was suffering. It helped a bit.

Garrick wasn't entirely satisfied with the way he had set the arm, but he was unwilling to put her through any more. She was undoubtedly the bravest woman he had ever had the pleasure to meet. He knew from unpleasant experience how painful his ministrations had been. Taking off his shirt, he tore it up and proceeded to bind the wound. It wasn't particularly sanitary, but it would be effective in stopping the bleeding. While he worked, he was aware of her gaze on him.

Cat knew she was beginning to suffer from shock. Her skin felt cold and she shivered so much that her teeth chattered. That did not, however, stop her from noting the raw male beauty Garrick Drexel had revealed when he had stripped off his shirt. His well-muscled torso showed not a trace of softness or fat. His smooth, lightly tanned skin almost glowed in the sunlight. The pain in her arm was lessening now, and she began to feel a little light-headed. With her left hand, she reached up and touched his bare skin. It was warm.

The touch startled Garrick. He finished bandaging her quickly. Her body was trembling, and he knew he had to get her to professional help soon. "Can you tell me what to do to get the car going?" he asked, bending close so that she didn't have to strain to hear. "I'm afraid I'm not much of a mechanic."

"Fan belt," she slurred. "Can't miss it. Just slip it into the grooves."

"Don't tell me it's so simple a child could do it. I'll get terribly embarrassed. Don't move." He stood, dusted off the knees of his pants and went over to the Jeep.

A frustrating ten minutes later, he admitted defeat. He could see how the damn belt was supposed to go, could intellectually understand how to get it on, but try as he might, he couldn't get his hands to do what his mind was telling them. Finally, the belt, strained beyond its limited limits, broke. He went back to Cat.

She looked as if she was sleeping. Her closed eyes exposed long, light brown lashes that swept the tops of her cheeks. Her lips were parted, giving her a vulnerable appearance. Her whole face seemed softer and lovelier. But her color was waxen and her breathing shallow. When he touched her skin it was far colder than it should have been. Garrick felt an answering chill deep inside. It wasn't possible that someone could die from a broken arm—especially not a woman as obviously strong and healthy as this one. Was it?

Fuming at his own inadequacy and helplessness, he slipped his arms under her and lifted her to his chest, placing his suit coat over her. Without the car there was only one way to get her to help and safety. Holding her carefully to avoid jostling her arm, he took a deep breath and started walking down the road. If no other car came along, he would carry her until he reached a human settlement of some kind. Surely the wilderness couldn't go on indefinitely, he told himself. Surely someone would drive down this road eventually. Surely...

CHAPTER TWO

CAT DRIFTED IN AND OUT of a dream. She was helpless, an innocent maiden being carried along a jungle path by a brawny hero. In the dream her head rested comfortably against a wide chest, and she could hear the steady strong beat of the man's heart. She felt warm, safe, secure. It was lovely.

She allowed the fantasy to run wild because her mind recognized it for a dream. A dream could be whatever it wanted. It couldn't hurt her. She let it weave along its romantic path, accepting whatever happened.

Until, in the dream, a poisoned arrow struck her in the arm.

"What?" She opened her eyes and blinked against the bright sunlight. "What happened? Where..." Her question trailed off as she looked up and saw the man carrying her. She realized it was no dream.

"Take it easy, Cat," he said. "You just took a little nap. Not a bad idea under the circumstances."

"Put me down! I... Oh!"

"Don't move! I didn't splint the arm because there weren't any straight sticks around." Garrick continued to walk. He was tired, but not enough to justify a pause. "You don't want me to have to set it again, do you? I would think once was quite enough for anyone."

Her memory flooded back. "The Jeep? What happened to the Jeep?"

"Not much, I'm afraid." He grinned sheepishly. "I warned you I was a real dud with machinery."

"You couldn't get a *fan belt* in place?"

"Nope. And when I came back to you, you had passed out. The only thing I could think to do was pick you up and start walking. I hope we're going in the right direction. I am a bit better with my feet than my hands."

"If you're heading the way we were driving, we're fine." She lifted her head and looked around. "Good Lord! How long have you been carrying me?"

"I'm not sure. It's easier to travel under a load if you don't try to keep track of time. Not that you're too heavy for me, although I am beginning to regret that you aren't more on the petite side."

"Thanks a lot." She glanced at the scenery again. "But we're a long way from the Jeep. You can't have rested and gone this far. Put me down. You must be exhausted."

"No."

"What was your name again?" She relaxed against his chest. The heartbeat was the one she had heard in her dream.

"Drexel. Garrick Drexel. Someone once said my name sounded like a man walking on gravel in combat boots."

"It's a good name, Garrick. Strong. But I think you ought to rest. You don't have to prove anything to me."

"Sure I don't. If I hadn't been wriggling around, the hood wouldn't have come down on you. It's my fault you're hurt. I intend to get you to help as quickly as I can."

"You'll not be any good to either of us if you have a heart attack. Now, stop and rest. It was not your fault. What if I'd been alone?"

"If you'd been alone, you'd have been all right. I'm not stopping."

She argued pointlessly for a few more minutes, then shut up when the throbbing in her arm got worse. He was clearly not going to pay any attention to her, she decided. For that matter, he didn't really seem to be suffering unduly from carrying her. There was a slight sheen of sweat on his face and chest, but no labored breathing or lines of strain on his face. And that heartbeat was slow and steady.

Her silence made Garrick take his gaze from the horizon where the road met the sky and look down at her. She hadn't passed out again, and her color was much better. "How do you feel?" he asked.

"Foolish. While I'd love for someone to come along and give us a ride, I only hope it isn't someone I know. I'd never live it down if one of my friends saw you carrying me along like a sack of grain." Her lips curved in a slight smile.

He smiled back. "You don't look like a sack of grain. Not that I can recall ever actually seeing one."

"You're kidding."

"No. Except for a few memorable years when I was in the army, I've been a city boy all my life. My idea of seeing the wilderness is taking a day trip into New England. Until now, I'd never been in the West. I don't count California."

"Well?" She studied his face. It didn't look like the face of a city dweller. "What do you think?"

"About wilderness?" His smile twisted a bit. "I entered it with an automobile and a suitcase full of my life. Now, I don't even have the shirt on my back. Hey, I love it."

She couldn't tell if he was joking or dead serious. There was an almost antic quality to his expression. "What do you mean about a suitcase full of your life?" she asked.

"It's a long story, but—" he stopped suddenly. "Do you hear something?"

Cat strained her ears. The country was no longer flat, and it was impossible to see even vehicles that were nearby. "I think so," she said. "Set me down. You can flag it better that way."

In spite of the relief it brought his arms and back, Garrick felt oddly reluctant to carry her over to the side of the road and lay her down on the ground. She wanted to sit or stand, but he sternly warned her again about the arm. Only by lying on her back could she cradle her arm on her stomach so that no further movement of the bone would take place. When he was certain she was as comfortable as possible, he stood and moved into the center of the road.

He saw the approaching vehicle a moment later. It was a blue truck with two men in the cab. He waved, confident that when they saw him and noticed Cat, they would stop.

The truck nearly ran him down and kept going.

Garrick let fly a string of invectives describing the ancestry and parentage of the driver, adding a few choice phrases about the passenger. When he went back to Cat, he was shaking, he was so furious. "Another sterling subscriber to the idea of Western hospitality," he snarled, moving to pick her up again.

She put a restraining hand on his arm. "What do you mean by that? He must not have seen you."

"The hell he didn't. He looked right at me, then tried to make a grease spot out of me. You with your gun. That guy with his truck. Makes a man wonder."

"You can't possibly equate what I did with what that driver did! I was only trying to protect myself, Garrick Drexel."

"Maybe. We can argue later, after you're patched up." He slid his arm under her shoulders. "Come on. Up you go. I'd like to reach shelter and help before dark. It's starting to get chilly."

"Take your jacket back. I don't need both of them anymore." She tried to push his suit coat off.

"Don't. You still need to keep warm. And quit moving like that. You're going to jar your—"

Cat screamed. His warning came just as unbelievable spasms of pain tore through the muscles of her arm. She gasped and cried out again as he gingerly returned the arm to a secure position.

Neither of them heard or saw the tan four-wheel-drive vehicle that pulled up a few yards away. Not until an authoritative voice called out for Garrick to freeze.

Through a haze of pain, Cat saw him raise his hands over his head. Then a tall figure appeared behind him, gun in hand. She blinked, trying to clear her vision, and the figure came into focus. "Tom, no," she whispered. "He's trying to help me."

The sheriff's deputy didn't hear her. Keeping up a running commentary of verbal abuse directed at Garrick, he forced the man to go to his knees and cuffed him. "One wrong move, you pervert," he rasped, "and I'm liable to forget about your civil rights. Understand me?"

"About as well as I've understood anything in this ridiculous country." Garrick's tone was dry and resigned. "However, when you finish with the John Wayne stuff, I think it might be a good idea if you got the lady some help. That's a bad break she has."

Cat struggled to raise her head without moving her arm. "Tom, listen to me. He's a *friend*. He didn't hurt me."

Tom Hendry holstered his gun and knelt beside her. "Cat, you don't have to be afraid no more," he said. "I'll take care of you now. And I'm gonna put that animal away where he can't hurt you or nobody else ever again." His lean face was drawn into an earnest expression. Garrick made a derisive, snorting sound.

"Tom, clean the macho out of your ears and pay attention to what I'm saying," Cat snapped. "That man carried me for miles. He was helping me. Let him loose!"

The deputy looked puzzled. "He's half naked. He was touching you, and you was screaming."

"She gave me a ride. Her car broke down. She broke her arm when the hood smashed it. I couldn't fix the car. I used my shirt to bandage her arm." Garrick spoke slowly and clearly, as if he were talking to a not-very-bright child. "I did have a vest and a trench coat, but when we started out, it was warm and I didn't want to lug them along. Hence, my nudity."

"Um," Tom said.

"I screamed because my arm hurt," Cat explained. "Garrick probably saved my life. If it isn't too much trouble, would you mind giving us a ride to town? I'd sort of like to see Doc Turner before gangrene sets in."

Tom still hesitated, plainly convinced that some kind of crime was right under his nose. Cat glared at him, her temper kept in check only by the thinnest of threads.

"Keep me in cuffs if you want. Throw me in jail if that's what you think you ought to do. But get the lady to a doctor. That should be your first priority."

Tom said "Um" again. Then he looked closely at Cat. "Can you walk?" he asked.

Cat sighed. "No, Tom. I can't. Not because there's anything wrong with my legs, but I have to keep my arm still. You can't carry me. Let him loose. He can."

"You don't happen to have a first-aid kit in your car?" Garrick asked. "If I could splint her arm, she'd be able to walk and would be much better off."

"I got a kit," Tom replied, looking uncertain.

Garrick waited.

"I'll get it," the deputy said.

The kit had everything Garrick needed. Under the watchful eye of the deputy, he splinted Cat's arm and got her to swallow a few aspirin. "They won't help much," he told her. "But they might take some of the edge off the pain, make the ride into town a bit more comfortable."

Cat was sitting up. He had done a good job on her arm and it now rested in a sling. Looking down at it, she suddenly realized what a broken arm actually meant. She was going to be severely handicapped right at the time of year when she had the most work to do getting the ranch ready for the tourist season. Then she remembered the money.

"We can't go to town yet," she said. "We have to get back to the Jeep."

Garrick glanced up at the deputy. He was frowning. "Cat," Garrick said gently, looking down at her, "the Jeep will still be there a few hours from now. I'm sure that our friendly lawman will be happy to drive someone out to fix it and bring it to you. Right now—"

"Right now we have got to get to the Jeep," she insisted. "There's almost ten thousand dollars in cash in my briefcase!"

It took about fifteen minutes to drive to the place where the Jeep waited on the roadside. Cat sat, wrapped in a blanket in the back seat of the deputy's vehicle, and Garrick, now wearing his suit coat over a bare torso, was in the passenger seat beside the officer. Tom Hendry had apparently decided Garrick had committed no crime he could be charged with for the time being. Garrick took that to be a sign of progress, but Tom still didn't act as if he trusted the other man out of sight.

"Oh, no!" Cat wailed as they neared the Jeep. "Someone's been in it!" The door on the driver's side was wide open, and she distinctly remembered closing it before going to get the tool kit from the back. She waited, knowing the worst had happened, while Garrick and Tom examined the Jeep. When Garrick came back, he had a gloomy expression on his face.

"The only thing left is the piece of leather you used to tie me up," he said. "They even took my trench coat and vest. Your friend is looking for clues, but I don't think he's going to find anything." He glanced over at the Jeep. Hendry's rear end stuck up as he leaned over the front seat to explore the back. "That is not a quick young man," Garrick added in a softer tone.

Cat tried to smile, fighting the tears the loss of her money was threatening to cause. "He's really a nice person," she said. "And very conscientious."

"So I can see. But who had the nerve to give the man a license to carry a gun, for pete's sake?"

"His uncle's the sheriff. A very competent man. I think he hired Tom because he figured that was the only way he was going to get steady employment. And Nelson is quite capable of cleaning up any mistakes Tom makes. Oh, damn! How could I have been so careless? I can't afford to lose that kind of money. And with this arm out of commission I'm going to have to hire help." In spite of her resolve to face the situation bravely, tears began to flow.

"Hey, hey." Garrick got in beside her and pulled her head down to his shoulder. He patted her hair soothingly, thinking how nice and silky it felt—thinking how if he hadn't been idiot enough to let his own car die and then go strolling down the road, she would never have gotten hurt, much less robbed. She was crying softly, but he could sense the despair in her. "Hush now," he said. "Something will work out for you, Catherine." He would, he resolved, make sure that it did.

Tom finally finished whatever he was doing to the Jeep and announced that they were heading to Lone Tree at top speed. Cat continued to let her head rest on Garrick's shoulder. It was an illusory comfort, she knew, but somehow leaning on him made her feel better, more secure. As if she weren't facing an uncertain future in which she might lose the one thing she loved most in the world—her ranch.

And what would she do if that happened? Thinking about having to return to her original profession almost made her sick. But if worse came to worst, she might be forced to swallow her pride and principles and place a call to her former agent. Lord knew he'd called *her* often enough over the years since she had walked away. Perhaps she was still marketable. But she didn't want to have to find out.

"So, Mr. Drexel." Tom shouted to be heard over the banshee scream of the siren. "Where are you from and what are you doing out here?"

"New York," Garrick shouted back. "And I'm escaping."

"Huh?" Tom glanced back, making Garrick highly nervous. They were doing ninety.

"Keep it simple," Cat whispered in his ear. "Or you might end up handcuffed again."

"So? I was actually getting used to having my hands behind my back." He smiled at her.

Cat's breath caught in her throat. For the first time she was struck by what an attractive man he was. He was probably the most attractive man she had seen in a long, long while. Old instincts took over, and she found herself regretting the casual, unadorned way she was dressed. No makeup. Hair just there. He was from New York and was used to seeing hordes of beautiful women. He—

Angrily, she cut off that line of thought. She was long past being unsure of herself because of her appearance.

Long past feeling the need to impress men with her exterior. And long, *long* past letting a man's exterior impress her!

"I left the city," Garrick was saying to Tom, "because I got sick of it and of what I was doing for a living. That's what I meant by escaping." Tom seemed satisfied with that answer. He directed his full attention back to the road.

As they neared Lone Tree, Cat sat up, uncomfortable now being so close to Garrick Drexel. Her reaction to him told her that she still had the weakness, that she had not really learned her lesson about handsome men. Of course, it was unfair to judge him on the basis of the short time she had known him, and he had certainly behaved gallantly toward her in spite of the rude way she had treated him. Just because he was good-looking didn't mean he wasn't a decent human being, she reminded herself.

But he was strange, no doubt about that, wandering the highway without any idea where he was or how far it was to a town, saying he had left the city because he didn't like it anymore. Her curiosity was aroused, but his past was none of her business. Shortly, he would be gone. And she certainly had plenty of other matters to occupy her mind.

When they reached the town, the siren's noise brought people out of their houses and places of business. Cat wanted to tell Tom to shut the thing off, but she lacked the energy. So they drove, attracting a good deal of attention, to the little house where Doc Turner had his office. The only thing lacking, Cat thought wryly, was a marching band and two majorettes carrying a banner declaring: Cat Cantrell Busted Her Arm!

Well, everyone would know soon enough.

Doc Turner appeared in the doorway, his nurse, Sue Futrell, peering over his shoulder. Both gray-haired people gaped in astonishment as Tom and Garrick got out. Cat remained where she was, feeling even weaker now that she was about to be helped medically. Her arm throbbed almost unbearably. She was also miserably aware that she was near tears again and would be humiliated if she cried in front of her friends and neighbors. Once more, Garrick came to her rescue.

"Whatever it costs to patch Ms Cantrell up," he stated, loudly enough for the gathering crowd to hear, "I'm paying. She really saved my bacon this afternoon, and I'm deeply in her debt." Before she could protest, he had reached in and picked her up. As he carried her past the astonished doctor and nurse, several people started to applaud. Cat was too flustered now to even think about crying.

When he was certain that she was in competent, caring hands, Garrick bent over her and spoke softly so that only she could hear what he said. "I'm going to go out and find that sheriff, Nelson what's-his-name. If he's any good at all, maybe we can get your money back. I have a pretty good idea who took it."

"What? Who?" She struggled to sit up.

"You stay put." He gently forced her to lie down. "Those creeps who nearly ran me down, that's who. Nobody else passed us, and someone coming on the Jeep from the other direction wouldn't have known we were walking up ahead. They would have had to pass us. I think I can remember what the truck looked like."

Cat thought for a moment. "They might find your car, too. Do you remember where you left it?"

"It's safe. When it started fizzling out on me, I drove off the main highway and parked it behind a big clump of some kind of bush." He grinned. "I know I'm crazy, but I'm not insane. No New Yorker would ever leave an expensive car right out in the open, no matter how many screws he had loose. You be a good patient now. I'll get back to you." Then he kissed her on the forehead. And he was gone.

Cat lay very still, blinking and staring at the ceiling. Sue Futrell came over and warned her that something was going to sting a little. The needle felt hot and cold at the same time. Sue murmured words about Garrick Drexel being a fine figure of a man. Cat didn't respond. She closed her eyes and waited for the shot to take effect. As she drifted into dreamless darkness, she wondered just what effects all the events of this day were going to have on her future. She was glad when she was no longer able to think....

GARRICK HAD NO TROUBLE locating the sheriff. Nelson Hendry found him. When he left the doctor's place, Garrick noted that the curious crowd had left or been dispersed. Tom Hendry was still there, leaning on the fender of his four-wheel drive and regarding Garrick with a now-you'll-get-yours expression. The obvious reason for his confidence was standing in front of him, massive legs planted in a stance that undoubtedly came from years of fighting experience.

Garrick was big himself. When he was young, he had worked at it, but now he seemed able to maintain muscle with only the occasional workout or recreational activity. Ordinarily, he took his size for granted. At the moment, however, he was deeply grateful for what nature had allotted him. The sheriff was a huge man. From the top of his steel-gray, close-cropped hair to the tips of his enormous cowboy boots, he defied the normal limits of male dimension. His head was almost square, his features harshly carved, and his torso was a muscled rectangle from which tree-trunk arms and legs emerged. Garrick smiled, thinking that the very last thing he would ever want to do was make this lawman angry.

"You the dude who hurt Miss Cantrell?" The voice was strangely at odds with the body. It was soft and breathy, and would almost have been soothing if the words hadn't promised trouble. If he actually had hurt "Miss Cantrell," Garrick realized, he might just as well have bent over and kissed what was his goodbye.

"I was with her when it happened," he said. "But I didn't hurt her, and I did everything in my power to help her." Quickly, using as few words as possible, he explained how Cat had broken her arm, how his own car had died, and how two men had nearly run him down. The sheriff's expression darkened when Garrick described Cat's despair at her loss.

"I'm Sheriff Nelson Hendry," he said when Garrick had finished his recital. "You don't sound like some Eastern weirdo to me, Drexel." He glanced at his deputy. Tom seemed to shrink. "I'd like you to ride with me out to the scene of the crime. Give Tom here a description of that truck first, though. While we're out, he can post a bulletin on them boys." Garrick obliged.

Twilight was setting in when they started out of town, this time riding in Hendry's truck. It had a winch in back, and, the sheriff explained, enough power to haul back both wounded vehicles if need be. He planned, however, to try fixing Cat's Jeep. Garrick had no doubt that he would be able to do just that and possibly to fix the BMW, as well. The big man radiated competence and confidence.

He had loaned Garrick a shirt that was several sizes too large and looked absurd with the suit coat over it. But for the first time in a long while, Garrick didn't care what he looked like. He was, he realized, dropping the trappings of city life one by one like a creature emerging from an old, outgrown coating to a new, fresh life. "Sheriff," he said, glancing at his companion, "I hope you don't mind my mentioning it, but it strikes me you're fond of Cat Cantrell. Is she as remarkable a woman as she seems?"

"I'm real fond of her," Hendry replied. "Knew her ma and pa, and when Cat got her senses back and left that stuff she was doing for TV and radio and moved to Lone Tree permanent, why, my wife and me was tickled pink. She's a fine lady and a credit to the town. 'Course she don't actually live in town, but the ranch is near enough. We all like to call her neighbor."

"That's nice." Garrick considered what he had learned. So she wasn't just a local girl who had an unusual way of defending herself against strangers. Maybe she had learned the hard way that pulling a gun when she felt threatened was wise. He tried to remember if she had seemed unduly frightened. As he recalled, she hadn't. That made him feel better. He didn't like to think that at some time in her past she had been badly hurt by an assailant.

As for what she had been doing on television and radio, he would just wait and ask her himself. Information was far more worthwhile from a primary than a secondary source. Especially if the primary source was an interesting and good-looking woman. Garrick grinned to himself and felt the tense muscles in his shoulders start to relax. He felt happier at this moment, riding down a dark highway at the side of a throwback to the days of the Wild West and thinking about Cat Cantrell, than he could remember feeling for a long, long time.

CHAPTER THREE

CAT STARED at the outlandish figure standing at the foot of her bed and did her best not to laugh. She had spent the night unwillingly in one of the rooms Doc used to keep patients overnight for observation, and she had been complaining and demanding permission to return to the ranch ever since waking up. Doc had only smiled and promised her a verdict after lunch. Cat had glumly eaten a wonderful breakfast prepared for her by Sue, had called Jude Honeytree, her wrangler, to explain her absence and had settled down to await release with her temper growing more sour by the minute.

Then Garrick Drexel had come to visit.

"I think I found the only roses in the county," he said, presenting her with four bedraggled red blooms. "There's no florist here."

"You have to call over to Jackson," she explained, gathering up the pathetic flowers and inhaling their fragrance, which had not lessened any. "It was very thoughtful of you to bring me these, though. I really appreciate it, Garrick."

"Tell me how I look," he said, grinning broadly. "After I found the roses, I spent a little time in the clothing store. Thought I'd try to pass for a native."

"Oh, you pass," she said carefully. He was wearing jeans and boots, which looked all right. But he had topped the outfit with the most gaudy Western shirt Cat had ever had the misfortune to see and a cowboy hat that would have made John Wayne blush. Clearly, the proprietor of the clothing store had seen a golden opportunity to unload some genuine junk on a genuine greenhorn. "You look very dashing," she added, crossing her fingers under the roses.

"Actually, I think I look ridiculous," he said, still grinning. He took off the hat and tossed it onto a chair. "But it's better than pinstripes. Now, I want to talk seriously with you. Feel up to it?"

She cocked her head to one side, puzzled. "I don't understand. What could we possibly have to talk seriously about? Doc told me this morning that Nelson had found and fixed your car. I thought you'd be on your way by now."

"Well, I'm not." He hooked his thumbs into his belt. "And I don't intend to be any time soon. Yes, he fixed both cars. But we didn't find your money or the men who might have taken it. He's got the whole Rocky Mountain region alerted to the truck, but I'm afraid you are going to have to face the fact that unless those men are extremely stupid, you won't get your money back. That's what I wanted to talk about."

"What's to say?" she asked gloomily. "I lost ten thousand dollars. I've either got to manage without it or figure some way to earn it back."

"What was it you did before you bought the ranch?" He picked up the hat and tossed it on the small dresser, then turned the chair around and sat on it with his arms on the back. "Hendry mentioned television work."

Cat laughed. "That's making it sound much more glamorous than it was. I did commercial singing, Garrick. Jingles. You know: Buy X-brand bread like your mama said. I spent nearly ten years singing Madison Avenue into America's living rooms." She became serious. "And when I left, I swore I would never do it again."

"Why not? Doesn't it pay well?"

"It pays very well, thank you. I quit for personal reasons. I wasn't really happy away from Wyoming. Except for being worried, I am happy now."

He thought for a moment. "You've had a financial loss. It isn't any of my business how badly this stings you, but I doubt if anyone running a guest ranch can afford to sneeze away ten thousand, no matter how much one may have saved in the past. You won't be doing much work for a while with that arm in a cast. How much help do you have out there?''

She shrugged. ''Enough under ordinary conditions. During the winter, it's just me and my wrangler, Jude. At the end of May, when school lets out, two teenagers will be coming to help with housekeeping and any baby-sitting. It's not a big place. I've concentrated on offering a quality vacation opportunity, not on packing as many warm bodies as I can onto the property.''

''Wrangler? Isn't that some kind of jeans?''

''He takes care of the horses. Jude is an old-time ranch hand. He's a wonder with horses.''

''But not much else. Right?''

''Well . . .'' She began to wonder where all this was leading. It was the end of April, four more weeks before the girls would be able to live on the ranch. She could ask them to drive out after school and work for an hour or so, but that would eat into her budget—maybe not disastrously, but at this point, with no income pending until June at the earliest, she couldn't afford to risk stretching her finances. Perhaps Don Jeffers down at the bank would let her borrow a few thousand more to shore her up until tourist season. . . .

''Not much else,'' Garrick repeated, mostly to himself. This was probably the most insane thing he had ever decided to do. But since the idea had occurred to him late the previous night in the postage-stamp-sized motel bed, he had been able to find nothing wrong with it. ''What you need until you get back on your feet is an employee who can be trained to handle anything. In other words, my malleable self.'' He spread his arms wide.

''You?'' Cat couldn't help laughing. ''*You?* Garrick Drexel, you couldn't even replace a fan belt. Lord knows what you'd do with barbed wire. Probably enclose yourself.''

"You're probably right." He stood, walked to the foot of the bed and placed his hands on the footboard. "But you can change all that, Cat. I'm a quick study. Just explain to me how to do something, and I can pick it up almost immediately. I'm not trying to brag or impress you. It's just the way I am. Cars have always been a mystery to me because I've never had to learn my way around them. I've lived in the city where driving your own car is foolish. You must have spent time in New York if you were in advertising. You know how it is."

She shuddered slightly. "Yes. But you can't just drop all your plans and be stuck out on a ranch for a month. And I have no idea what to pay you...."

"Cat." He leaned forward, the expression on his face intent. "I *have* no plans. I was on my way no place. And I won't take one dime from you. I owe you, and in my mind, the best way I can pay you back is to help you through this. I'm not going to take no for an answer."

In the end, it was his determination that won out. Her weakened condition had drained Cat's usual will to battle an issue to the finish, and even though she was convinced it was the worst idea since polyester, she agreed to hire him on for no wages and no benefits except room and board. Room, she warned him, would be in the bunkhouse with Jude, a man not known for his hospitable ways. The prospect did not seem to faze him.

She got the first sign that her direst fears were going to be realized when they started for the ranch late that afternoon. Doc Turner had reluctantly given her freedom to her under the proviso that Garrick would haul her fanny back into town at the first sign of a problem. They had stopped by the sheriff's office for a few minutes and had learned that no progress had been made on the case of the stolen money and other items. Nelson Hendry had seemed so apologetic that she almost recommended he stop by Doc's for a checkup. But he regained his spirit when he described what he would do to those no-count cusses if they ever fell into his hands, so she held her tongue. Then they got into the Jeep with the BMW in tow by the rear hitch.

"Oh. Gosh," Garrick said.

"What's the matter?" Cat was in the passenger seat, having been forbidden to drive since she was still taking pain pills. "Don't tell me you can't—"

"Not a stick. I never learned to handle a clutch," he admitted dismally.

He did learn, although it strained her nerves to the shrieking point and probably damaged the transmission horribly. Once they were off and running, however, he managed the Jeep with no small skill. Cat began to relax as the familiar hills and valleys around her land appeared.

"No place like home?" Garrick asked, noting the expression on her face. She was, he decided, prettier than he had thought at first. She had the kind of looks that grew on you.

"No place like it," she agreed. The wind blew strands of blond hair across her face, and she brushed them away with her left hand. It was a long, slender, capable-looking hand, Garrick noticed, with short nails, a couple of scars and a calloused ridge on her palm. Hers were very different hands than those he had seen around the office and socially back East. He pondered the meaning of that difference as they drove along.

If Cat had had a career in advertising—commercials were certainly part of the advertising world—she would surely have been exposed to, if not part of, the high-powered business scene. That she had chosen to leave it and return to a simpler life out here meant she might understand what he was doing. She just might understand and be sympathetic to his need to find fresh meaning in his life, to make some sense out of his existence aside from an ability to make money. A man had to be worth more than that!

What he wanted to do, he suddenly realized, was to pull over, take her hand in his, look out at the magnificent scenery and unburden his mind and heart. But that was crazy. She had no desire to hear his life story, to know of the sorrows that had gradually leeched his days of pleasure, of the disillusionment and dissatisfaction that had finally made him come to the decision to leave behind everything he had known and worked for. If she ever asked, he wouldn't hesitate to tell her everything. For now, however, it was better that they were just two people who had been thrown together by chance.

"Turn left at the next road," she said. "You can't miss it. I put up a sign."

"What does it say? Ranch this-a-way?" he asked teasingly.

"Cute." She pointed. "There it is. Slow down."

He did, only making the engine protest for a moment. The sign was a rectangle of natural wood, hung by sturdy chains from a frame of logs with the bark still on them. It read: Cat's Cradle. Guest Ranch. A stylized cat's head was drawn behind the words. Garrick made the turn and started down a dirt road.

Cat shifted nervously. "Go slowly, please. This isn't the smoothest road, and I don't know how the Jeep's taking the combination of your driving and towing your car. I certainly can't afford repairs right now."

"Yes, boss lady. Whatever you say." He slowed. Then he stopped. "My God," he whispered.

They had driven around a low hill and were on a rim above a small valley. Below stretched out one of the most beautiful scenes he had ever seen. The floor of the valley was gently rolling and covered by a pale green carpet of grass, interspersed with a few stubborn patches of snow. Through the center ran a narrow stream that bubbled and rushed over rocks and boulders. Bushes with bright red stems lined its path. To the left of the stream was a long, low building made of wood with a stone foundation. Smoke drifted out of a chimney located at the rear of the structure. To the right were half a dozen cabins placed to take advantage of the view of towering mountains off in the distance. Beyond the cabins were several outbuildings and a stable with a corral built next to it. A few horses strolled within the fence, nibbling at bunches of straw on the ground and occasionally at one another. As he drank in the sights, Garrick felt a sense of peace like nothing he'd known before.

"It is something, isn't it?" Cat asked proudly. "Just a little bit of paradise."

"Yeah." He managed to slip the Jeep into first gear without taking his gaze off the ranch. "I believe that I'm going to be very happy here."

AFTER A WEEK under Cat's slave driving and Jude Honeytree's scorn, Garrick had to admit that if he wasn't exactly happy, he was far too busy for soul-searching, and too sore and tired to suffer from the angst that had plagued him for so long. It was as if the backbreaking work and the position of lowest creature on the totem pole had purged him and made him a new man. He'd been handed a fresh slate on which he was free to write a whole new life. Every so often, while grabbing a priceless moment of rest, he would reflect that that was not really the case. No one could actually leave a past self behind and start all over. But when he crawled wearily into his narrow bunk at night, aching in every joint and muscle and filled to his gullet with Cat's fantastic home cooking, he felt as close to being reborn as possible. With any luck, he thought muzzily just before drifting into dreamless sleep, the feeling would last.

Cat, after a week, wondered how she had ever managed without him. Not that he was much help yet. He required careful instruction and supervision for all but the simplest of physical tasks. But he was learning and didn't need to be told twice how to do something. It was more than his actual work that pleased her, however. He was unfailingly cheerful no matter how much abuse Jude heaped on him or how waspish she became when a task hadn't been done to suit her demands. He literally whistled while he worked, driving the lean old wrangler to declare the city boy was clean out of his head, but injecting a note of optimism into Cat's days. In spite of her financial worries and physical disability, her attitude was positive. In the mornings before sunrise, as she prepared breakfast for the three of them, she began to look forward eagerly to his appearance and pleasant conversation. She and Jude communicated primarily by single words and grunts. It was a real pleasure to have a conversationalist around for a change.

And Garrick did converse. But for the most part he talked about the countryside, the horses and what he was learning rather than his past. Once in a while, though, he would make mention of New York. She gleaned from his comments that he had been married—although she didn't know if he had been divorced—and as he had told her when she had drawn down on him, he had worked in finance. He'd been a stockbroker, to be exact. Since he tended to get a little short when his profession came up, she avoided the subject, thinking that as long as he behaved, as he was doing so far, his past had no relevance to the present.

Nor did his undeniable masculine appeal. Or so Cat kept telling herself. He treated her with unfailing politeness, and she reciprocated with good manners as often as she could. This served effectively as a barrier to anything more serious than a friendly exchange. But as the first week passed and the second one began, she had more difficulty turning off her thoughts of him at night when she lay alone in the dark.

The weather had warmed, and though a late snowfall was still a possibility, the sunshine was hot in the middle of the day. He had taken to working shirtless from around noon until three. He made an impressive sight, his skin tanned from the high-altitude sunlight and his already massive muscles hardened and defined by physical work. Cat kept telling herself there wasn't a thing wrong with appreciating his looks. As long as appreciate them from a safe distance was all she did. He was charming; he was handsome. She knew only too well the kind of pain he might cause her.

ONE MORNING Garrick woke before Jude could kick him out of a sound slumber. The wrangler was still asleep, judging by the breathy snores emitting from his bunk. The man was so thin that he barely raised a bump under his blanket.

Garrick grinned to himself, stretched and noted with wonder that nothing hurt. He must finally be acclimated, he thought with a special sense of accomplishment. It felt damned good.

He rose, dressed quietly and stepped out into the predawn air. It was cold, but the heavy flannel shirt Cat had brought back for him from her last trip into town was sufficient covering. Touching the soft material at his collar, he looked across the creek to the main house. A light in the kitchen window indicated that the boss was already up and working. Garrick decided to offer his help. While her cooking was exceptional, he had a recipe or two he wanted to try out to see if it was just the mountain air that made her food taste so good. Humming under his breath, he made his way agilely down the hill from the bunkhouse, stepped carefully across the rushing stream and started up to the house. A faint, sweet musical sound made him stop and change direction.

It was Cat singing, he decided. It had to be. Sirens were only found in legends and myths. But he was drawn as if by a siren to follow the sound up the path of the creek and over to a hill topped by a small grove of pine trees. As he neared and the sound grew more distinct, he was moved almost to tears by the sheer beauty of what he was hearing. He didn't recognize the melody or understand the words with his mind. But his heart seemed to be getting an exact translation.

He climbed the hill, approaching the grove from behind, not wanting to do anything to disturb that thrilling sound. She wasn't just singing. Every so often her voice would stop and the high, pure sound of some musical instrument would warble out into the lightening dawn. Garrick found himself shivering. It was an almost unearthly sound.

She was seated just inside the grove on a small rock that protruded a few inches out of the ground. Her blond hair was a wild, uncombed mass around her head and shoulders, and she wore her heavy shearling coat, a garment she had told him was warmer than any fur or down jacket. A

long, silver instrument he recognized as a flute was in her
hand. She sang, then raised the flute to her lips, balancing
it with her jean-clad knee. The notes she brought out were
few, but beautiful.

He sank down as silently as he could and listened. She
sang again, this time letting her voice trill along like bird
song. From the trees above and from the shelter of the
bushes along the creek came a chirp, a squawk, then a me-
lodious challenge from a meadowlark in reply. Cat started
to laugh.

Garrick clapped. When she turned and stared in obvious
embarrassment at him, he rose and went over to her. "I've
never heard anything so beautiful," he said, kneeling on one
knee in front of her. Putting his fingers on her chin, he made
her look directly at him. "Cat, you have no right to keep
such a voice to yourself. It must be shared." Then he bent
forward and gently kissed the lips that had made such sweet
sounds.

Cat was frozen with astonishment. For the last few days
she had been having silent, private dreams about kissing
him, but nothing had prepared her for the actual feeling of
his lips on hers, his fingers on her skin, his warm breath on
her face and the closeness of his body. The flute fell from
her grasp, and her hand went up to touch his thick, soft hair.
When her fingers twined into the warm silkiness, she could
feel a shudder go through him. His arms went around her,
and his kiss deepened. Cat yielded, opening her mouth and
pulling her cast out from where it was wedged between
them. As if of one mind, they stood, his arms drawing her
close, then closer until they were molded together, each
feeling, sensing, the desire in the other's body.

Garrick recovered first. He broke the kiss gently, although he kept holding her tightly. Gazing down into her
face, he smiled. "I've always been a passionate music
lover," he quipped, thinking it was probably a good idea to
handle any awkwardness she might be feeling with humor.
"Guess I got a little carried away." That was an understatement! The kiss and embrace had done far more to him than

he was ready to admit aloud. Any doubts he might have had about Cat's unusual beauty turning him on had vanished. Without feeling disloyal to his memories, he confessed in his heart that even with the broken arm her rangy body felt more womanly than any he had ever held before.

"I...I guess so," she stammered, still gazing at him with such soft passion that it was all he could do to resist crushing her to him again. If he had been more certain of her response, he knew that nothing would have prevented him from moving this strong physical attraction to a more interesting level. But he was still not sure exactly what made Cat Cantrell tick, and he didn't want to risk their budding friendship by overplaying his hand.

So he smiled and said, "If you really need the money, Cat, let me get in contact with some people I know. With the right PR and management you could make a pile in just a short..." He stopped talking when her expression turned hard and she jerked out of his arms.

"Who would manage me?" she snapped. "Who would handle the money? You?" Her eyes flashed with an anger as deep, if not deeper, than the desire that had glowed there moments before.

"Well, I am good at it," he said, puzzled by her sudden change of behavior. "And I'd do it—"

"What? For free?" She was shouting now. "You'd manage me just for the pleasure of my company? Oh, Mr. Drexel. Have I heard that one before!" She turned, grabbed up the flute and was running down the hill before he could recover. Garrick watched her go, wondering if the morning air had addled both their minds. Then, slowly, thoughtfully, he followed in her footsteps.

Breakfast was a painful experience. For the first time, she cooked badly. The toast and bacon were burned, the eggs fried until they were rubbery. At least the coffee was palatable. Garrick ate without comment, figuring he was the reason for her lapse. Jude grumbled, but a sharp look from Cat shut him up. After the meal, she announced in clipped tones that she was going into town for mail and supplies.

Did either of them want anything? They didn't. She left shortly without her usual goodbye.

Garrick worked with Jude in silence for a while. They had the unenviable task that morning of mucking out the stables, and the odorous job suited his mood perfectly. Then he decided to take a chance. The sparks between him and Cat had been real, and he wasn't feeling like just forgetting them. He straightened and addressed the wrangler.

"Jude, I know we haven't exchanged more than a dozen words, but I have to ask you something. I think it's going to take more than a monosyllable or a grunt to answer. Mind stopping for a minute?"

Jude quit shoveling. He eyed Garrick with sharp suspicion, and the lines around his thin lips deepened. "This about Miz Cat?"

"It is. I want to know why mentioning the combination of money and her singing makes her lose her temper. Can you shed any light for me?"

The old man thought for a moment. "Boy, you done gone and opened one hell of a can of worms. No wonder she tried to poison the two of us this morning." He cleared his throat, spat into a corner and told Garrick about Cat's ex-husband.

CAT MANAGED to control herself almost all the way into town. Her anger helped. What a complete fool she had been! Letting a kiss get her going like that, then reacting to his comment about her singing as if he were the devil himself. Tears stung her eyes, and finally she gave in and pulled over, fumbling for tissues to blot her waterworks.

Garrick Drexel was not her ex-husband, Benny Jones. Garrick had innocently walked right into her own private emotional swamp and been sucked down into the quicksand there. Cat cried harder. She *liked* Garrick. How could she be comparing him with Benny the Rat? Just because he was handsome, just because he was a financier didn't mean he had the same money-grubbing, mean spirit. She finished crying, blew her nose and resolved to apologize the moment she saw him again—apologize and, if she could, explain why she had gone so crazy. She smiled a little. The kiss had been wonderful. And there was no doubt in her mind that he had enjoyed it as much as—perhaps even more than—she had. With some talk and understanding, perhaps they could...

Flashing lights from Sheriff Nelson Hendry's truck interrupted her thoughts. He pulled in behind her and got out. She could see Tom sitting in the passenger seat, which was odd. They didn't usually patrol together. Nelson came over to her and took off his hat. He ran his fingers through his bristly hair.

"Cat, that Drexel fella still out at your place?"

"Sure," she replied. At least unless he's decided I'm really nuts and has pulled up stakes, she thought. "Why?"

Nelson looked unhappy. "Well, Tom was worried. Seems Drexel said something about escaping when he was talking to him that day you picked him up. Anyways, Tom pestered me until I wired to New York City and checked up on the man. Cat, your friend's wanted in questioning about some shady money deals. Seems some of the federal boys think he might be making dough illegal-like."

CHAPTER FOUR

SHE LISTENED with a sinking feeling as Nelson tried to explain Garrick's problem. His company was one of several under investigation for what the sheriff called "inside jobs." Cat translated that for herself as insider trading, or maybe one of the other financial crimes that was being prosecuted with vigor. While she was no longer tied to or interested in the goings-on in the big cities, she wasn't uninformed. If Garrick had indeed been undertaking illegal activities, then his running away from his old life made perfect sense. And what better place to hole up until the heat was off than an out-of-the-way guest ranch with a gullible boss lady who could be cajoled with a polite manner and a sweet kiss! Her anger turned white hot, then cold as ice.

"That's most interesting, Nelson," she said, hearing the tension in her own voice. "How reliable was the person you spoke to, if you don't mind my asking?"

"Pretty reliable, I guess." Nelson ran a hand over his bristly hair. "Guy by the name of Willis Kent. He's some kind of federal agent. SEC, I think. Say, Cat, what is that inside stuff anyhow? This Drexel any kind of threat out here?"

"No." She laughed bitterly. "Not in the sense you mean. Insider trading simply involves unethical practices in finance. I don't see him heading for town to stick up the bank." She didn't tell him that in her present financial state, she had an occasional fantasy about doing the deed herself. "It's not a violent crime, just a nasty one."

"Nasty, is it?" Nelson's expression turned thunderous. "Then I want his hide off your place, Cat. Don't care for the idea of you being out there with only Jude to watch out for you."

She took a deep breath. Never was she going to be able to convince males like Nelson that she didn't need a man to take care of her. They accepted her competence up to a point, but after that, the code of the West took over, and she was just another female critter. Most of the time, she was able to laugh about it. This morning, she was too emotionally stirred up by everything that had happened. "Nelson," she said tightly, "I appreciate your concern. But let me deal with this my way, please. The man has done me a great favor by working three weeks for only room and board. I owe him a chance to explain, at least."

Nelson sighed. "Well, you won't mind if Tom and I wander out later on to see how you're doing, would you?"

"No, of course not." As if she could keep them away.

Dropping the subject of Garrick, they gossiped for another minute, and then Cat begged off, saying she had things to do in town before heading back for a confrontation with Garrick. Nelson said goodbye and lumbered back to his truck. As she drove off, she could see Tom in her rearview mirror. He was plainly grilling his boss about her reaction to the news.

She was still mad by the time she returned from her errands, but the emotion was no longer fueling her energy, but making her weak and dangerously close to weeping. She understood that once again she was resurrecting old feelings to apply to the present. If Garrick was a financial crook, it was a problem only for the people who might have lost money by his dealings. She herself was in no way harmed. So why did she have this sense of deep betrayal that could only have come from the old pain caused by her ex-husband? It just wasn't fair for her to feel that way; it wasn't fair to her or to Garrick. No amount of reasonable thought, however, could keep her from wanting to cry.

She covered it by pulling to an abrupt stop by the corral where Jude and Garrick were repairing a section of the fence and imperiously demanding the latter's presence in her office as soon as possible. If she could conduct the interview with all the psychological and territorial advantages on her side, she might not break down and reveal the weakness she felt. It was a good plan, but when Garrick entered the pine-paneled room and grinned at her sitting behind her oak desk, she experienced such a rush of affection that the tears sprang in spite of her best intentions.

Garrick saw only an angry, beautiful woman seated in the power position. Recognizing the office-and-desk ploy from his own days as a boss, he realized that he was in for some kind of dressing-down. Was she still so mad about his suggestion that she sing again? Or was it the kiss? Either way, he figured he could jolly her out of her mad with a few well-chosen words of apology.

"I stand before you, figurative hat in hand," he said, smiling what he believed to be his most winning smile. "I did a little research today and found out why you have no love for managerial types and why you're probably going to share your singing gifts with the birds and trees for the rest of your life. I want to apologize, and beg innocence out of ignorance."

His words caught Cat entirely off guard. "J-Jude?" She stammered. "Jude told you about my...what I did before?"

He nodded, his smile fading as a look of sympathy came over his face. "You wouldn't be the first country lady with talent who got fleeced by a good-looking, fast-talking guy, Cat. And I didn't realize how important you must have been in the industry. When Jude told me some of the jingles your voice made, I—"

"Forget about my voice, jingles and any problems this country lady might have had with slick city types, Mr. Drexel. I'd like to hear about anyone, lady or otherwise, whom you might have fleeced in your business dealings." She stood, pressing both palms flat on her desk. "Because this ranch isn't so hard up that we have to harbor a crook!"

"What?"

"You heard me. Nelson Hendry stopped me on the way to town today and told me some man from the SEC is looking into your practice. I believe the operative phrase was 'insider trading.'"

Without asking permission, he reached behind him and pulled a chair over. He sat down on it heavily.

"The way I see it," she said, coming out from behind the desk and standing in front of him, "you were on the lam. Maybe too frightened to make serious plans. Then I happened along conveniently with just the right—"

"Catherine Cantrell." He stood, speaking softly and glaring at her with a dangerous glint in his eyes. "I have never deliberately misguided a soul when it came to money, nor have I ever had to cheat in order to gain a dollar. I didn't *need* to. I'm as good as they come. I'm only forty years old, and if I never did another lick of work in my life, I could manage quite comfortably on the investments I've made. And whether you choose to believe this or not, I worked even harder for my clients. Worked *honestly*."

Cat swallowed. There was no doubting his anger and indignation. He sounded sincere enough, as well, although she knew better than to trust her judgment on that. "But what about the report Nelson got from New York?" she countered, trying to match him glare for glare. It wasn't easy.

"I don't know," he admitted, suddenly looking less sure of himself. "I certainly didn't leave under a cloud, even though no one seemed to understand how I could just pick up and go." He turned away, running a hand nervously through his hair. "I can't imagine why anyone from the SEC would be interested in me."

"Nelson said his name was Willis K—"

"Son of a— Willie Kent." Garrick laughed harshly. "Well, there's your answer, Cat. Kent hates my guts. Has ever since I was called in as an expert witness in a fraud case and helped get the *innocently* accused off. He's a little weasel. Probably did this just out of spite." He held out his hands pleadingly. "I haven't done anything wrong. I wish I could make you believe me."

The tears that had subsided during the confrontation returned to Cat's eyes. "I wish I could, too," she almost whispered.

"Aw, Cat." Garrick moved toward her, intent on taking her in his arms, but she stepped away. Her face was averted, and he could tell she was in the grip of some strong emotion. What amazed him was the fact that he seemed to be the cause of it. "Maybe," he said gently, "you just need to know more about me. We haven't really talked all that much since I've been here. I do have a history, and I think it may explain to you just why I've left the past behind and why I'm so happy here pitching manure and getting splinters in my hands."

"What can you tell me?" She crossed her arms and stared out the window. In the distance she could see the snow on the high peaks. Late in June she would take riding parties up there and let them wonder at the sight of wide meadows filled with wildflowers. For now, the mountains were just grand and forbidding. "I know you were in finance. I gathered you didn't leave any family, since you haven't made any calls, or to the best of my knowledge mailed any letters. All I know for sure is you must have had a compelling reason to drop everything and run away. It does jibe with the theory you were leaving a personal mess of some sort."

"I did leave some family. I was married."

Cat turned. "You bastard! How could you run off and leave—"

"*Was* married." His expression was neutral, but sadness shone from his eyes. "I've been a widower for five years, Cat."

"Oh!" Shame flooded her. "I'm so sorry, Garrick. I should never have jumped to a conclusion like that."

"It's all right." He held out a hand again. "Come on, let's go someplace friendly and neutral and I'll tell you about myself. This office is your territory and, frankly, you are a little intimidating in here. I feel as though I ought to be bowing and scraping and tugging at my forelock."

She laughed, warming his heart with her smile.

They went outside to sit on the back-porch swing. The view of the valley and the hills beyond was definitely friendly, neutral and, most important, soothing. Garrick had felt a surge of anxiety when he had promised to tell her of his past, but the sound of the wind in the pines and the burble of the stream, combined with the beauty of the scenery, put him at ease. What an incredible land this was, he mused. It had restorative powers. He could testify to that. He still held Cat's hand, and the feel of her warm skin and calloused palm seemed just as restorative.

He began, "After I finished college—"

"No," she interrupted. "Before that. I want to know everything."

Garrick grinned. "Are you always this greedy, Miz Cat?"

"Almost always." She couldn't smile. Not with him holding her hand like that and his face so close to hers. Her heart began to pound as she remembered how his lips felt on hers that morning.

But he didn't repeat the kiss. For a breath-stopping moment, it looked as if he was going to, then he seemed to shake himself loose from some spell and sat back, letting go of her hand as he did so. Garrick Drexel began to talk.

Cat learned he had been born and raised in the city. His father had been in banking and his mother in society. He had gone to school at Columbia, graduating with a degree in economics and heavy-duty grooming to follow his father's footsteps. But he had chosen instead to join the Marines, where he became a medical corpsman. He glossed over his military career in a sentence or two, but she could sense he had grown up during his time of service in a way that could never have happened had he stayed in familiar surroundings. It also explained how he had known what to do with her arm. She wondered what other experiences he had lived through while wearing a uniform and performing a job totally unrelated to his vocation. He was not forthcoming on the subject, and she cautioned herself to keep still. He was already exposing so much of himself.

When he finished his time, he returned to school to get an MBA. It was while he was at Harvard that he met and married Ann Norton, a woman he described as lovely, delicate and frail. He was not to know about the last trait until years later.

Ann had a weak heart, the result of a childhood bout with rheumatic fever brought on by a case of strep throat. She had kept the condition secret from her husband almost until the time she died. Garrick's voice took on a husky quality as he told Cat of his emotions: the guilt he had felt for not knowing and making her take better care of herself, the bitterness of grief and self-reproach. It had taken the ministrations of a friend who was also a doctor and a professional counselor to make him see that Ann had chosen her own life, and that to have kept her wrapped in cotton batting, however loving, would have been far more cruel than to allow her to spend the time she had as she wanted. When he had emerged from his grief and guilt, he was a far stronger person with a great love for his departed wife, but no longer chained to her memory. He felt only gratitude for what little time he had been able to enjoy with her.

It took great control for Cat not to break down and cry as she listened. Her throat tightened and her eyes stung, but she knew that to cry would be to tarnish the moment for Garrick. He wasn't asking for pity, only understanding.

He turned to the subject of his work. Without bragging, he explained in some detail about his success. He had a natural sense of the market, Cat realized; an instinctive grasp of economics that had enabled him to rise far and fast in Wall Street circles. But while his work had kept him going in the first years after Ann's death, lately he had felt his existence to be hollow and without purpose.

"I wasn't excited anymore," he explained. "I was nervous. The city that had been home to me for so many years was beginning to make me frightened and anxious. Sights that would have been easy for me to ignore only months before were branded into my brain, and I'd feel sick for hours after seeing a bag lady lying in filth on the sidewalk with hundreds passing by as if they didn't see. It was all getting to me."

"I know the feeling."

He looked at her for a moment. "You knew where to come for healing. Out here. I was just lucky. Lucky you happened along. That's something to ponder, isn't it?"

"You mentioned family," she said, suddenly self-conscious. "Your parents? Do they know where you are?"

"My father died not long after he retired. Stress, they said. Mother is living in Palm Beach, having a fine time bringing culture to the hinterland. She seems happy. I do feel sorry for my dad, though."

"Why is that?"

Garrick waved at the far hills. "I doubt if he ever sat on a porch swing on a warm spring day and watched a view like this." He grinned. "Of course, he might have been bored out of his mind. I suppose we each have our place and niche in life. For me, my old one didn't fit anymore." He glanced at her. "Maybe I've found the new one."

She had no direct answer to that, but it seemed highly unlikely a man with the kind of wealth and power he said he had would be content for long working as an unskilled hand on a guest ranch. No, she decided, happy as he was or claimed to be now, sooner or later he would long for the challenge only New York could give him. He was forty and alone. It was a mid-life crisis.

"I do still have a sister-in-law living in New York," he said. "I bet she'd like a few days out here."

"Your wife's sister?"

"Yes. Janet came to work at the same firm I was in a few years after Ann and I were married. She's a real financial fireball, that woman. Quite different from Ann. Harder, aggressive and highly successful." His praise rang a bit false to Cat's ears, and she wondered how much his feelings for the sister-in-law might have affected his decision to leave. Was he afraid of romantic leanings that might seem improper to him? He seemed to be making too much of a case about the differences between the sisters.

But then he turned to the most important issue—the accusations against himself. He was adamant about his innocence. "As a matter of fact, disillusionment with the way some of my colleagues were handling their business was a factor in my deciding to seek a new profession," he stated. "The field is full of fine, ethical people, but the rotten apples are giving us all a bad name. It used to be that the client, hell, the *government* trusted stockbrokers. Not anymore. I bet Willis Kent is just carrying out a personal vendetta as far as I'm concerned, but if he isn't, it's because no one, no matter how fine their reputation, is safe from suspicion."

"Especially if they are successful?"

"Exactly."

He talked for a little while longer, obviously doing his best to convince her of his innocence. And he did a good job. If she hadn't been so cynical, Cat reflected, she would have bought his story, no questions asked. He seemed earnest to a fault. Finally, she decided, she just couldn't throw him out on the basis of a second- or even third-hand rumor. She would find out for herself whether he was telling the truth, then do what was necessary.

Garrick finished his recitation, fully intending to ask her to give him equal time to learn details of her story. It didn't take a mind reader to know that much of her emotional reaction was caused by pain from the past, and his growing fondness for her was making him more curious than he could ever remember being about a woman. He wanted to *know* Cat Cantrell.

But as he began to frame his lead question, the spare figure of Jude Honeytree ambled around the side of the house. The wrangler didn't look at them, didn't say a word. He just carried his bony shoulders at an angle that screamed weariness and pity-me. The load of firewood in his arms looked as if it weighed a ton, plus. After dumping his burden onto the pile beside the porch, he sighed, turned and made his way slowly out of sight. When he was gone, both Garrick and Cat started to laugh.

"I believe I was just delivered a complaint," Cat said.

"The boss shouldn't show favoritism." Garrick stood. "It's one of the cardinal rules of running a smooth operation. I'd better get back to work."

"Garrick, I—"

"Give me the benefit of the doubt, Cat." His tone was both pleading and demanding. "Let me do some investigating and see if I can get to the bottom of this mess. I can make some calls—I have a credit card, so you won't be charged. I can ask Janet to find out what Kent is up to."

"You don't want to go back and do the investigating yourself?" It would be the best excuse in the world for getting out of his promise to work for her. The best excuse in the world to go back and gather up all the power he had turned his back on.

"Hell, no." His grin was wide. "I haven't been so happy, so content in years." He gestured toward the valley. "I love getting up with the sun and smelling fresh air. My lungs haven't felt so good in decades. You couldn't drag me back in chains."

Still wondering about his motives despite his words, Cat agreed to wait and let him handle the matter his own way. When he left her side to return to work, he was whistling merrily.

She spent most of the afternoon riding the trails, noting where winter storms had caused trees to fall across the paths and where new game trails created possible hazards for inexperienced riders. One small deer bolting out in front of a trail horse whose rider was barely managing to stay in the saddle could spell disaster. She or any other employee who led the riders would have to be ready to flush wild animals before the guests even got to the trails. It was part of her code to take every precaution to make certain her guests were safe. It was one of the special touches Cat's Cradle offered vacationers. So far, she hadn't suffered the embarrassment and expense of an injured guest, thanks, she believed, to her diligence and foresight.

But she wondered just how much foresight she was showing in her dealings with Garrick Drexel. He wove in and out of her thoughts all afternoon like a friendly phantom. She wanted so much to believe him, to accept his declaration of innocence. Yet, in spite of all she now knew about him, he still remained a mystery. He was a puzzle that didn't quite fit.

Her horse, a little bay mare named Fat Chance, picked her way gingerly along the trail, avoiding the occasional spot of unmelted snow. Fatty was a persnickety beast who liked to do as little work as possible. She'd earned her nickname by stubbornly resisting the exercise that would wear off the winter's accumulation of poundage. Fatty, however, was one of Cat's best dude horses, putting up with all kinds of abuse from unskilled riders, patiently making her way along the trail without paying the least amount of attention to whoas and giddaps. It was in the hopes of finding other mounts with such placid temperaments that Cat had made the fateful journey to South Dakota. The result: no horses, no money, but the addition of Garrick to her life. She sighed. What a bargain! Fatty whoofed in disgust, her way blocked by a snowdrift. Cat smiled and let the animal pick her way through the pine trees around the barrier. Without the extra horses—and all hope of buying them was gone with the stolen cash—Fatty was liable to be working her broad tail off this summer. It wouldn't hurt to pamper her while she still had leisure time.

Fatty stumbled over a root while getting back to the trail beyond the drift, and Cat lurched forward, hitting her cast on the saddle horn. Her arm throbbed briefly, and she thought longingly of the time when the bone would be healed and the damned clumsy cast gone. That brought Garrick back. When she was whole again, would he choose to go back to New York? Or just move on? Though she had managed to keep from dwelling on the kiss they had shared that morning up until now, it burst on her consciousness with an undeniable force. She had been kissed plenty in her time, but no one had reached immediately to that special place where she could feel almost at one with the man caressing her. Usually, it took a long time for her to trust enough to be that open. And, hell, she didn't even trust Garrick! So why the reaction? She had no answers, and the question continued to bother her for the rest of the day.

GARRICK THREW HIMSELF into the physical labor of chopping wood and hauling it off to fill the log boxes by the cabins. He worked with a will that had nothing to do with a desire to finish the job before nightfall. The harder he worked, the more he sweated—and the less he thought about what Cat had told him. How the devil could anyone be accusing him of illegal trade dealings? It was so fantastic it was almost funny. Almost. It set his teeth on edge to consider even the possibility of having his reputation stained. Not that he was considering going back and depending on that reputation ever again. It was strictly a matter of pride, and he knew he had that in spades. Nearly to a fault. Finally, it was the pride that made him determined to ride the situation out on the basis of his past performance and good name. Janet would let him know just what was going on, and he would ask his lawyer to take care of the problem. Sheldon Sheridan was a friend as well as a business associate, and Garrick could trust him, just as he could trust Janet.

Between the time when the shadows were long enough for Jude to call a halt to the day's work and suppertime, Garrick commandeered the ranch's one phone, located in Cat's office. He had quickly showered off the sweat and dirt and dressed in clean jeans and a white oxford-cloth shirt from his supply of "Eastern" clothes, as Jude had snidely termed his old garments. He didn't wear them much now, but calling Janet seemed to demand he put on at least a little of his old life. She answered on the second ring.

"Janet," he said with a heartiness he didn't feel. "This is Garrick, calling from the heart of the old West. How are you?"

There was silence for a moment, then, "Garrick? Is this a joke?"

"No, dear sis-in-law. I only wish it was. Listen, Janet, I've heard some fairly disturbing rumors. Someone says Willis Kent is sniffing around, saying I've run some dirty deals. Know anything about it?"

"W-Willis Kent? Garrick, where are you? Nobody could believe you'd just left everything and taken off. Pratt won't let anyone move into your old office. He's treating it like it's some kind of *shrine*, for God's sake."

"I'm working at a little guest ranch called Cat's Cradle. It's heaven. Tell Jamison he might as well start selling tickets to my office if he wants to get any use out of it. I ain't comin' back."

"Garrick, are you in trouble?" Her voice held an odd tone, but he couldn't read it over the phone.

"Not that I know of. But apparently someone thinks so. Would you do me a big favor and check into this Willis Kent thing for me? It'd be a big load off my mind to hear he was just after my behind because I wasn't there to defend it. If you have any trouble, let Sheldon Sheridan know. He's handling my legal interests."

He explained and cajoled for a while longer, finally getting her promise to see what was going on and to get back to him with the information. He hung up, satisfied that she would do a good job. Janet was uptight and compulsive, but when she did something, it was *done*. He thought about Ann for a moment, but it was Cat who was on his mind when he left the office and entered the kitchen, starved for dinner. To his surprise, then pleasure, Nelson and Tom Hendry were also seated at the table. They had arrived while he'd been on the phone, and Cat informed him they had agreed without hesitation to stay for dinner when she had offered. Garrick's sense of well-being increased. He could use the time to explain to the two lawmen what he was doing about the shadow on his reputation. Dinner, he decided, was going to be a fulfilling experience in more ways than one.

CHAPTER FIVE

JANET NORTON GLARED at the telephone. She wrapped her arms around herself, trying to control the shaking that had begun when she had heard Garrick's voice. She hadn't been sure she would ever hear it again.

But she had schemed and hoped. By allying herself with Willis Kent, she had made it inevitable that Garrick would have to come home. Home, where he belonged, instead of traipsing around the countryside, forgetting about his wife.

His wife. Janet gazed at the picture of her sister that rested on the long table as though on a shrine. *Oh, Ann, if only you hadn't married him.*

But she had, and now he had an obligation to stay near her. To tend to her grave. To pray.... Tears filled Janet's eyes, and hatred grew in her heart. He had no right to run away!

But she would get him back. She would drive him back!

It was time to sit at her desk and plan. Plan how to best accomplish her goals. Her mind hummed along as she wondered how Garrick's spotless professional reputation could be gradually dirtied, made questionable enough for him to have to return to defend himself. It wasn't easy—he had been a faultless record keeper. But with the access she had to his files as a member of his firm, and to his personal papers, thanks to the key Ann had given her in secret before she had... Well, it was going to be possible to lay a paper trail that would shadow Garrick Drexel forever. She worked far into the night, knowing that work would keep her ghosts at bay.

"SO I PUT MY COLLEAGUE and sister-in-law on to the situation," Garrick explained between bites of dinner. "She'll find out what's actually going on and sic my lawyer on whoever's responsible. Be straightened out in no time."

"Sister-in-law?" Tom looked outraged. "You married?"

"*Was* married," Cat said, repeating Garrick's words from earlier. "He's a widower, Tom."

"Oh. Sorry." The younger man began to study his plate seriously.

"It's okay," Garrick said. "I loved her, and I still miss her from time to time, but life's for the living. I expect I'll fall in love again someday." He glanced at Cat. Their eyes met for a second, then she started to give her plate the same studious attention Tom was bestowing on his.

"I hope your sister-in-law has better luck with your case than I'm having with Cat's," Nelson commented. "I reckon those old boys who took your stuff and her cash are down Mexico way by now. I got reports of a truck matching the description you gave passing through Colorado and New Mexico. Cat, even if we caught 'em now, I doubt we'd get any of your money back. I'm real sorry."

She shrugged, depressed again. "I shouldn't have carried that much cash around, Nelson. It was an expensive lesson, though."

Garrick shifted in his seat. He could offer to loan her the cash. Hell, he would love to outright *give* it to her. But guarded conversation with Jude had warned him not to dare. Cat's pride was equal to, if not greater than, his, he realized. She'd hand him back his offer with a succinct description of where to put it. Damn, but this was a touchy situation.

"Say," said Tom. "Mr. Drexel here must have some money he can spare. Why don't you let him help you out, Cat?"

Garrick swallowed half a mouthful the wrong way and had to down a glass of water to keep from choking.

"Tom, Mr. Drexel has problems of his own," he heard Cat say sweetly. "I can take care of my own money problems. There's no need to bother anyone else with them. How's Abby?"

When the tears cleared from Garrick's eyes, he saw Tom was back staring at his plate. But now he was blushing and grinning like a fool. Abby must be someone special, Garrick decided.

The only other mention of money and Garrick's expertise with it came from a surprising source. He and Jude were walking back to the bunkhouse, and the wrangler, who hadn't said two words all night, stopped just after they crossed the creek. He looked up at the sky, and Garrick could see by the bright moonlight that the little man was deep in thought. The lines in his face seemed dug deeper, and gave him the look of a worried gnome. "Seems to me," he said around the frayed toothpick that had been his companion since dessert, "that when a boss's got a top-notch hand with horses, the boss oughta assign that man to the horses." He looked steadily at Garrick. "Know what I mean?"

"Jude, you aren't telling me to loan Cat money?" Garrick pushed his hat back on his head. "I thought that you all but said I'd be out of my mind to try. And she made it quite clear that she doesn't want a loan."

"Ain't saying you should loan her nothing. Just saying if you're half what I hear them say you are, you'd be better riding the books than the ponies. That's all." He removed the toothpick from his lips and pitched it away in the darkness. "Think about it, son. Come on, let's get some shuteye. We got a hard day ahead."

Garrick followed, shaking his head and wishing that someone around Cat's Cradle would speak clearly and directly for a change.

He had no opportunity to do anything about Jude's advice over the next week, however. Cat rode both him and the wrangler harder than ever before, clearly determined that the ranch would be a showplace by the time the guests arrived. Jude was spared housework, Garrick decided, because Cat knew the limits of her Captain Bligh act. Jude was outdoor help. Garrick was more flexible.

He didn't mind the extra work, however. In fact, he found a perverse satisfaction in standing back like an army private while she inspected the cabins he'd cleaned. He would grin inwardly when she could find nothing to criticize. Now and then her expression softened as she watched him, but for the most part, she was all boss lady, letting nothing personal emerge from behind her businesslike facade. One night, he allowed himself the luxury of some mild complaining when he and Jude were alone in the bunkhouse.

"She's working us like slaves," he said, easing off his boots. "Reminds me of a drill sergeant."

"She's scared." Jude lit up one of the hand-rolled cigarettes he always smoked before going to sleep. "We got less than two weeks to June. She ain't got two dimes to rub together."

"How do you know?"

"She ain't never asked me to wait for my weekly pay." The wrangler leaned back on his bunk. "She did today. Told her it wasn't no problem."

Garrick swore. He stood and rubbed the back of his neck. Then he made a decision.

IT WAS ELEVEN O'CLOCK, and Cat still sat at her desk. She'd been working on the books since nine, and the figures refused to budge one iota. The ranch would go under as soon as the next set of bills arrived. She couldn't survive.

That afternoon she had experienced one of the more humiliating moments of her life when her supposed friend, Don Jeffers, the bank manager, had refused her any further loans. If she'd had the new horses she had intended to buy, he had explained, she could use the animals as fresh collateral. As it stood, everything she owned was in hock.

She held her head in her hands and fought helpless tears. She had tried her best. She had worked hard, harder than ever before in her life. She had denied herself everything but the most necessary items. It had been years since she had bought a new article of clothing other than jeans and boots.

But she had been so happy. The ranch meant everything to her, and now she was about to lose it due to her own carelessness. She had long since ceased to blame or be angry at the thieves. They had only behaved according to their own natures. It had been her fault entirely. When the tears came, she was hardly aware she was weeping.

The front door was partly open, and Garrick entered quietly, some instinct warning him not to knock. The light in the office located Cat for him, but when he got to the door, he wondered briefly if he ought not to slip away just as silently.

She was sitting at her desk, crying. Not as if her heart would break, but as if she had already lost hope. The tears were large and rolled down her cheeks to fall and stain her blue work shirt. She didn't sob or sniffle; she just wept. His heart ached for her.

Through her tears, she saw him standing in the doorway and wasn't the least bit surprised. "Oh, Garrick," she whispered. "I've failed."

The emptiness in her tone galvanized him. "The hell you have!" he almost shouted. He strode into the room and planted himself in front of her desk. "No woman who can pull a gun on me and live to tell about it can ever fail. Come on, Cat. Are you just a transplanted soft city lady, or do you really have the backbone you pretend to have when you're kicking my behind all over the place?"

She smiled weakly. "Nice try, pal. But it won't work. I even crawled to the bank today to try for a few thousand to see us over to June. No go." She shut the ledger slowly. "It's all over."

"No," Garrick said. "It isn't." He rounded the desk, pulled her roughly out of her chair and into his arms. For a moment, he glared down at her startled eyes, and then he kissed her with all the feeling that had been building up in him since the first time they had embraced.

Cat felt caught in a force beyond her control. Had she not already been feeling so helpless, she realized, she might not have slipped as easily into his arms and let him press the length of his body so closely against hers, or allowed the sweet intrusion of his tongue into her mouth. But she was helpless. And it felt wonderful to be held. Her arms encircled his neck, and somewhere in her mind she marveled at how much stronger his shoulders had become since the first time she had touched them. Not much of her mind was operational, however. Most of it was just crying out how wonderful he felt, and how much she needed him to care for her, to want her.

Garrick continued to kiss her passionately, but he forced himself to control his need. Sex was not what Cat needed tonight. She needed to know he cared. She needed to know he could help. He *would* help, no matter how much she might protest! He eased back on the kiss slowly, then broke it.

Her face was flushed, her eyes shining, and she looked more beautiful than he had ever seen her, or any woman look. His resolve slipped, then recovered. "You *matter* to me, Cat," he said fiercely. "This place matters to me, and I can help you. I'm *going* to help you."

Cat blinked. She had been certain they would end up in her bed—that she would share one night of love with him before she had to let both him and Jude go, before she had to turn the ranch over to the court. What he was saying made little sense to her. "Garrick, I don't—"

"Let me have a go at the books," he said, loosening his embrace so that they could step apart. "One day, Cat. If I can't find a way out, then you can get all desperate. But promise me that day. I may be able to surprise you."

She laughed weakly. "You've already managed that a time or two. All right. I guess one day can't hurt." Her expression saddened. "But don't give me false hopes, Garrick. I don't think I could stand that. I'm a realist. If you can find a way out, fine—no, wonderful! But I can take it if this is the end. I've been down before and got up. I can do it again." She lifted her chin slightly.

The sight thrilled him. "That's the woman I know! Come on. Let's go into the kitchen and get some warm milk." He put his arm around her shoulders. "I don't know about you, but when I get wound up, that settles me down better than anything."

Cat wasn't exactly sure she wanted to be "settled down," but she let him lead her to the kitchen. She sat while he heated the milk and listened to him chatter away about his boyhood, well aware that he was trying to take her mind off her troubles.

To a certain extent, he succeeded.

He painted a cozy picture of a way of life she'd been unaware of during the years she had lived in New York. He talked of wintertime walks with his parents to the skating rink at Rockefeller Center and of hot-chocolate drinks that warmed their chilled bodies afterward. There was the magic of Manhattan at Christmas, and a small boy's wonder at window-shopping.

Warm milk and memories. By the time Cat had drained her cup she was so drowsy, she could barely keep her eyes open—in spite of her worries.

"Okay, Sleeping Beauty." Garrick took her cup and placed it in the sink. "Time for the sack. Tomorrow is another day, and there be dragons beyond. Get plenty of rest, because if I'm on the books, Jude's liable to expect you out in the corral."

"Of course," she said, hearing the words slur. "I was planning on it. The tack still needs work, several of the horses haven't done the trails yet and I haven't even begun to clean out the quarters for Abby and Ellen. Lots to do."

Garrick didn't ask who Abby and Ellen were. He assumed they were the teenagers she'd once mentioned. If he wasn't able to find a solution to Cat's prime problem, it wouldn't matter who they were. Abby and Ellen wouldn't have jobs to come to, and their quarters could just stay dirty.

Then he remembered how Tom Hendry had reacted to the name Abby.

He guided the sleepy woman into the living room, but didn't dare follow as she waved and headed in the direction of her bedroom. She was so soft and sensual right now that he didn't trust himself for one minute longer in her presence. Not even the awkward cast on her arm detracted from her desirability. Smiling cheerfully though he felt far from cheerful, he blew her a good-night kiss and left, breathing in the cool night air as if he had been running for a mile.

When he returned to the bunkhouse, Jude seemed asleep. But after Garrick had undressed and pulled the blanket up to his chin, he heard the other man make a grunt that sounded strangely satisfied and approving.

Meanwhile, Cat was lying in her bed, wide awake, dazed but unable to drift immediately into slumber. Her libido was still racing at an all-time high, and she wasn't sure just why Garrick hadn't taken advantage of her obvious willingness.

He wanted her, she would bet on it. But he had taken care of her instead, had nurtured her with tender loving care, warm milk and stories. What was with Garrick Drexel?

She wondered about that until she had exhausted all possibilities without reaching an answer that satisfied her. Forcing herself to drop him from her mental marquee, she substituted the faceless thieves who were probably now enjoying themselves at her expense. Gritting her teeth, she hoped they were having a hell of a rotten time!

"HERE'S TO MISS Catherine Cantrell!" Norm Runge lifted his bottle of Carta Blanca high. "May she enjoy good health and wealth."

"Yeah." His brother, Bob, giggled and drank. "And may she leave some of that wealth on the road again so's we can just pick it right up." His laugh turned mean.

The two brothers were celebrating at a Mexican cantina in a small town about a hundred miles from the U.S. border. Norm, the cleverer of the two, had insisted they sell the truck and head south to avoid any possibility that the law might have sniffed out their trail. It was unlikely, Norm counseled, that anyone would connect them to the robbery except the big guy they almost ran down, and he had looked weird as all hell, standing there in the middle of the road with no shirt on, so he was probably a loony. But it paid to be careful. And they were happy with the little Volkswagen they'd practically stolen, from the guy who'd bought the truck. What a deal!

Bob burbled into the ample bosom of one of the girls who frequented the cantina, and Norm grinned happily. They were two lucky dudes, all right. And they owed it all to Catherine Cantrell of Lone Tree, Wyoming!

THE NEXT MORNING Cat rose to mixed emotions of anxiety and excitement. She was anxious to know if what she remembered from the previous night was just a dream—if Garrick's promise and his passion had been only her overheated imagination at work—and excited at the prospect that it had all actually happened just as she remembered. One look at his face when he and Jude stomped into the kitchen for breakfast confirmed the latter. Her heart soared.

Garrick had already explained to Jude that he was turning in his lariat, which he still couldn't use, and his work gloves, which were almost worn through, and would be "riding the books" for a while. The wrangler's expression hadn't changed, but when he had performed his ritual morning hawk-and-spit, the corners of his thin mouth had turned upward for a second. Garrick knew he approved.

Cat was as nervous as her feline namesake. She managed breakfast without any serious disasters, but her hands shook as she poured coffee and her smile refused to stay in place without trembling. Not even as a raw girl, out for her first major audition, had she had a case of nerves like this. She tried controlling her breathing, thinking of pleasant scenes, getting angry. Nothing worked.

Until she and Garrick were closed up in the office alone together. "I want to get one thing straight," he said in a firm, businesslike tone. In keeping with his new job he had worn a white shirt and a herringbone-patterned sports coat over his jeans. "One thing," he repeated as Cat turned with a puzzled look on her face.

"What?" His lips provided the answer. This kiss was nothing like the powerhouse caress of last night, but it did confirm the reality of what had happened, and it did serve to seal something between them. Cat knew she was probably out of her mind, but at the moment there was no human being on earth she trusted as much as she trusted Garrick Drexel.

"That," he said after he pulled away. Her lips this morning tasted like sweet water and sunshine, and it took far more willpower than he cared to let on to break contact. "Now. I need to see all your records for the last five years."

"Five years?"

"Five. It's the minimum the IRS would ask for. I assume your accountant has told you that."

"I don't . . . I don't have an accountant. I've done all my taxes myself."

Garrick groaned. This was going to be worse than he had feared. "All right, Cat. Don't worry about it. Just give me what you have on hand."

What she had on hand was just about what he needed. It was poorly organized, of course, and a financial examiner's nightmare, but he was up to the task. He was liable, however, to need more than one day to tackle the mountain of paperwork. Cat agreed numbly that he was to take all the time he needed. She wasn't going anywhere, after all.

She left him to it and spent the morning working three of the horses who had been allowed to laze around while the rest of the preparations for the season had been seen to. One big black gelding named Sam Spade gave her a particularly hard time, actually tossing her onto the hard, dusty ground of the corral twice before she made him understand playtime was over and work time had begun. Once settled, he was a delightful mount with a comfortable gait and decent manners. He just had to be reminded about them.

Lunch was a silent affair between herself and Jude. She had called Garrick, but he had abstractedly asked to be served in the office. When she'd brought a tray with soup, sandwiches and coffee, he hadn't even looked up. Her office had looked like a hurricane was living in it and she had set the tray down, gulped and turned on her heel to flee the sight.

Cat spent the first part of the afternoon cleaning out the cabin where her teenage helpers would live—if Garrick could work a miracle. She wasn't feeling hopeful, but it was hard work and it took her mind off the situation. Abby Springer and Ellen Futrell, nurse Sue Futrell's granddaughter, had been her summer hands since they had turned twelve five years ago. Starting as baby-sitters, the two had gradually taken on more and more responsibilities until now Cat couldn't imagine handling a summer without them. They were almost younger sisters to her. Her eyes misted a bit as she smoothed the cover on one bunk. Her own family, consisting of one brother who had a ranch in eastern Colorado and a sister who worked down in Casper as a medical technologist, would help her out if they knew of her troubles, but she could never ask. This was her battle, and she could hold her head up if she failed, but not if she failed and brought others down with her.

Her arm started hurting after a while, and she decided it was time for a break. Moving to the small porch of the cabin, she kicked a chair into position and sat down.

The afternoon had turned hot. Smells from the earth and the burgeoning spring vegetation rose under the sun's rays. A haze of dust from the horses' hooves stirring the dirt on the corral floor drifted by on the warm air. Cat sneezed, then blinked against more tears. *Damn,* she thought. All she seemed to be doing lately was bawling. It was the strong sense of her place, she realized—the sounds and sights and smells. Giving it up would be like giving up a beloved.

But if she had to, she could. She firmed her mouth, fighting the tremble of her lower lip. She was an experienced manager and ranch hand. She could always get a job.

So she wouldn't be boss. Was being boss everything? Was it really so great? Wouldn't it be nice at night to just mosey over to a bunkhouse and curl up in bed without any worries?

Sure it would.

She kicked at the planks on the porch floor. They gave off a hollow sound, and she reminded herself to have Jude check under all the cabins for varmints. All she needed was one skunk family to set up housekeeping under—

Who was she kidding? She *loved* being boss. Loved the rhythm of management, of knowing all the details were taken care of; loved testing herself against the challenge of each new season. She beat the fist of her good arm on her thigh. She was going to miss it all!

The honk of a horn interrupted her unhappy musing. Standing, she saw Tom driving down the road in his own four-wheel-drive vehicle, a Bronco. Beside him was redhaired Abby. Cat waved when they stopped and got out of the car.

Tom spoke first. "Uh, we just drove out to see—"

"Cat, we heard about the bank," Abby wailed, throwing her arms around her. "What're you gonna do?"

Cat patted Abby's shoulder. "I don't honestly know. Last night, Garrick offered to take a look at my books. I suppose if anyone can find an out, he ought to. But he's been at it since sunrise and I haven't heard a word from him."

"Here he comes." Tom pointed. Garrick had a handful of papers and a odd expression on his face. When he reached the trio, he nodded to Tom and Abby, but spoke to Cat.

"You've been in business for six years?" The question was clipped.

"Yes. I bought it from—"

"Yeah, I know all that." He raked his fingers through his hair, causing it to stand up in places. "Six years, and this is the first time you've been in trouble?"

"Well, I haven't exactly been turning a sizable profit. But yes, this is the closest I've come to having to give it up."

Abby started to wail again. Tom hushed her. Garrick didn't seem to notice. "So what you're saying is that you've been solvent until now."

"Yes."

"Good." He turned and headed for the main house.

"Garrick!" Cat ran to catch up with him. He was striding so fast she had to run to keep up. "What's going on? Did you find anything? Is there a way out?"

He paused and smiled at her. "Maybe. I wouldn't wish your system of record keeping on my worst enemy, but you've been honest to a fault in your bookkeeping and there's no question your business has been an economic asset to the area. With Jackson Hole taking in the big tourist bucks, any that can be persuaded to fall on this side of the pass is that much to the good. I think we have a case."

"A case?"

"Yes." A light gleamed in his dark eyes. "Cat, I think you've gone into the red at just the right moment in history. The economy of this region is in trouble because of oil and gas prices, right?"

"Sure. That's common knowledge. But what's that got to do with a struggling little guest ranch?"

"Everything." He spread his arms out. "Cat, tourism is this state's salvation. I've got a call in to the governor's office. My dear lady, I think I'm going to be able to get you a bleeding-heart hardship loan!"

CHAPTER SIX

AS THE HOURS PASSED, the telephone became a kind of living, breathing entity, taunting, teasing and tormenting them with its silence. After Garrick's announcement, Cat had undergone a series of conflicting emotional states, ranging from embarrassed outrage at the prospect of having to take a state handout to gratitude toward the man with the ingenuity to think of the possibility. Finally, she reasoned that she had given much to the state and would continue to do so. Therefore, it wasn't really so shameful to ask for help temporarily. Deep inside, however, she cringed at the knowledge that she had been ready to give up all her dreams without a fight. It had taken this city-bred Easterner to provide the way for her hopes to survive a little longer. It made her question her own backbone, and that was a most unpleasant thought.

Garrick was acutely aware of the feelings his tactic had raised in her. Cat Cantrell wasn't exactly the ideal candidate for government aid, unlikely as she was to enjoy playing the grateful games that would be expected of her. He would have to run interference if it worked out. Watching her sitting behind her desk, her silence and her tapping fingertips betraying her nervousness, he thought that there was quite a bit about her business that could use his interference.

After he had announced that he'd called the governor, he had seen a new side of Cat—an uncertain and indecisive side. She had quietly asked for an explanation of the terms, which he'd been unable to give her, although he'd assured her they would undoubtedly be most favorable. She hadn't seemed too sure of that, but had given him no real argument. She had invited the two young people to stay for supper and seemed relieved when they declined, leaving after wishing her the best of luck. For the rest of the afternoon she had hung around the house, plainly anxious about the telephone call. In spite of her abstraction, however, dinner had been delicious, a hearty meal without flaw. She was, Garrick realized, capable of being a good hostess under the most trying of circumstances. It was as a businesswoman that he found her lacking.

From the living room he heard the snap and crackle of the fire she had made after dinner. Jude was in there, pretending to read the paper, but obviously waiting as anxiously as anyone else. He had a stake in this, too, Garrick mused. Jude's relationship to his boss was one of the gentle mysteries of the ranch, and someday, Garrick thought, he'd like to unravel it. Tonight was not the time.

The hours he had spent going over her books had been an accountant's nightmare. He had seen some "creative" methods of bookkeeping in his time, but Cat's system defied logic. There was a method in her madness, however, and once he'd discovered that she tended to file items under people's names rather than categories, he'd been able to make some sense of her books. After he secured the money for her, he would redo her entire business operation. It was no wonder she never made a sizable profit; her system put personal considerations above business ones. Jude, for instance, had for several years received his pay in odd doses— nothing one week, then several months' worth the next. His salary was back on a normal schedule now, but there had been a while there—

Cat pushed away from the desk and started pacing the room. "Are you sure they said they'd get back to you tonight?" she asked. She was cradling her broken arm in her good hand, and Garrick wondered if it was hurting her. A wave of tenderness swept through him. She seemed so tough, so competent. In reality she was just as flawed and vulnerable as the next person, her strengths balancing weaknesses, too—

"Well?" She was staring at him, waiting for an answer. Her eyes were wide, her mouth soft, as if she was having difficulty not crying.

"I'll be called tonight," he said. "Trust me, Cat."

She turned toward the window and gave him a look over her shoulder that said, among other things, "Fat chance, buster, until I hear the phone ringing." Garrick started to smile. Then the grin froze on his lips.

She was backlighted by the lamp on her desk, a silvery aura around her blond hair. Her slim figure was straight and her shoulders were squared. Her gaze lingered on him a moment more, bathing him with her unique combination of sophisticated skepticism and dreamy hopefulness. By the time she turned away, Garrick was wondering if he was in love.

None of it made any sense. She was truly the antithesis of the kind of woman he was attracted to, notwithstanding her undeniable charms. He had expected to grow fonder of her as they spent time together—probably even to have a mutually satisfactory affair. But love?

He knew enough about himself to recognize the difference between lust or infatuation and the real, genuine article. He was no inexperienced youth, ready to be bowled over by a pretty blonde whose legs went on forever and who could sing like an angel when the mood struck her. She kept books that would make a saint curse, she ran her ranch like Ghenghis Khan on an off day and she lacked many of the feminine touches he was used to in women. He couldn't possibly be in love with her.

But was he? He ached with desire for her, but far more than that, he ached to make her world right, make it safe and secure and just the way *she* wanted it to be. That was the key. He wanted what she wanted more than what he wanted. Garrick groaned softly and shook his head. This, he hadn't banked on.

"What's the matter?" Cat turned and saw an anguished look twist Garrick's features for a split second. It was an expression of such raw openness she felt embarrassed at having caught it. But it was replaced so quickly with his usual cheerful grin she wasn't sure exactly what she had seen.

"Just a touch of indigestion," he said, rubbing his midsection. "I guess I'm more serious about this than I realized."

"Well, you shouldn't—" The phone rang, and Cat dived for it.

Fifteen minutes later, she hung up, dazed at her good fortune. Garrick, who had sat quietly through the conversation, raised one eyebrow. "We're still in business," he said with no emotion in his voice. Cat stared at him for a moment. Then she let out a whoop of joy and threw herself into his arms.

"You are a wizard!" she cried. "That was Jacob Howard, special economic assistant to the governor. He practically *begged* me to take the loan. How did you manage to do it?"

"I just told the truth." He closed his eyes, absorbing the feel of her. Lust for her had been fun. This was far sweeter and far more painful. He had no idea how to act, how to further the relationship in the direction he was now plunging.

Cat felt his tension and realized something elemental was different between them. She pulled away slightly and once more caught an unguarded look of pain on his face. To her mind, the message was clear: he had done his best to get her out of a jam he felt partly responsible for. Now he was trying to decide how to tell her it was time for him to move on—perhaps to return to New York and straighten out his own problems. The ache in her heart made her catch her breath, but she was determined not to stand in his way. He had accomplished a miracle for her. She could only hope he'd accomplish the same for himself.

"You really are a wonderful man," she said softly, stepping back and touching his face with the palm of her hand. "I'm always going to be grateful for what you've done. I'm never going to forget—"

"Never going to forget what?" His voice had turned harsh, and when she looked, she saw anger in his dark eyes. The deep emotion and quiet fury startled her, but she wasn't frightened. Instinctively, she knew Garrick would never knowingly hurt her. "Never going to forget how I looked, walking down the road like an idiot? Or my expression when you pointed that cannon at my nose? Cat, don't you know what's happened to me over the past few weeks? I've found a new life! You sound as if you're saying goodbye. It's going to take the armed forces to get me out of here. I'm *home*."

His vehemence astonished her. "Well, of course you are. As long as you want a place, there'll always be one here for you. I just thought—"

"Do me a favor." He spoke softly, but with a forcefulness that silenced her. "Don't think you can think the way I'm thinking. At least not yet. Just remember this whenever you're tempted." His hands gripped her shoulders, and his lips covered hers.

It was different. Cat nearly cried out in surprise in spite of the fact that her mouth was warmly muffled by his. She dug her fingers into his arms, trying to sort out the feelings surging through her. He had shown passion in the past when he had kissed her, but this was much more. She was swept along by waves of emotion not entirely her own, and she felt herself rising to a new level of awareness. Garrick Drexel didn't just like her, didn't just want her. He seemed to be trying to give her something she had never received from a man before. Part of her heart and mind knew plainly what it was and acknowledged the preciousness of the gift. The rest of her, the part that still dominated, refused. No man could and no man would, she still believed, be entirely unselfish when it came to a woman he desired. Still, she clung to him.

The sound of Jude rudely clearing his throat broke the spell. They stepped apart, both looking at the wrangler, who was leaning against the doorway to the living room. "Just wondered if I still had my job," he said, lighting a cigarette stuck between his thin lips. Cat could have sworn he was using the gesture to hide a smile. "Guess I'm in luck a while longer. See you in a bit, Drexel." He turned and was gone.

"I guess we're all in luck," Cat said. Her heart raced wildly in spite of her orders to it to calm down. "And I'm sorry for what I seemed to be saying. I don't want you to leave. Not unless you're ready to go. But I won't stand in your way, ever. Please believe that."

"I do." He touched her cheek gently, and she saw disappointment in his eyes. Once more, she had spoken the wrong words. Only it was too late to take them back. "I believe you want everyone to have their freedom," he continued, "no matter what it may cost you. You're a very special woman, Cat. I'm glad I was able to help you."

"You've done far more than just help," she murmured. But the moment was lost. His expression was friendly, but closed. For a few minutes longer, he discussed some possible financial plans with her, then said good-night, leaving without kissing her again. Cat felt a vast emptiness open around her when the front door closed.

She walked slowly around the house, turning off lights, setting dishes in the sink to soak and checking the doors, although she didn't bother locking them. She wandered like a sleepwalker into her bedroom and undressed, tossing her clothes onto the floor rather than picking them up and placing them in the hamper as usual. She dragged on a cotton nightgown and, not bothering to wash her face or brush her hair, crawled into her bed. There she turned out the remaining light and began to cry.

She cried for all the lovely dreams of love she had once enjoyed and now believed she was no longer capable of dreaming. She wept in bitterness at the greed and betrayal that had robbed her of the innocence necessary to respond to what Garrick seemed to be feeling. She was only in her early thirties, and she was already as hard and tough as an old range widow, unable to think beyond her own selfish needs and survival.

Oh, she had once been so soft, so vulnerable, so trusting. She had taken her God-given talent and . . .

Just who was she trying to snow, anyway? She turned over, half nauseated at her own attempt at self-pity and deception. She'd been no wide-eyed country girl, going pure and innocent to the big, wicked city. Hell, no! She, Catherine Cantrell, age twenty and full of her own self-importance, had journeyed to New York, fully intent on getting her slice of Big Apple pie. She had wanted money and fame just as much as the next person. And she had gotten them, only to be outsmarted. *Don't give me that poor-me stuff,* she thought, furious. Maybe she had gotten only what she had deserved. Maybe she had never been a very nice person.

Her tears stopped with that sobering thought. She still didn't know the whole truth about Garrick, but from what she had seen, she would have to say he certainly had been acting like a good man—a virtuous man, to use an old-fashioned expression. Sure, he had kissed her with plain passion—maybe more—but he hadn't pressed her to have sex with him. She rolled over and punched her pillow. He was acting more like the hero in an old Western movie than a slick villain from back East. If it wasn't for the cloud of innuendo hanging over him, he would be almost too perfect to be true. Deep down inside herself, she gave a little prayer of thanks for that flaw. It made her own petty nastiness a bit more tolerable.

Sleep was long in coming, and her dreams were filled with unpleasantness.

The next morning, Cat found it impossible to be cheerful, though she managed to avoid taking out her bad temper on Garrick or Jude. But the looks they gave her at the breakfast table told her she was fooling neither of them with her forced politeness. Jude seemed unmoved by her attitude, but she could tell Garrick was upset. To avoid a confrontation with him that might lead to an embarrassing explanation, she took off early for town, pleading the need to be at the bank when the check from Jacob Howard came through. Garrick seemed to accept that. He was going to work in her office.

As she neared Lone Tree, her emotions swung back into balance. She had the wherewithal to keep on going until the ranch began producing income in a few weeks. She had two loyal employees, one of whom was willing to work without hope of pay for a while and another who was not only willing to work free, but was capable of finding financing for her. Never mind what else he might be thinking about or needing from her: he had quite literally saved her dream.

So why did she let thoughts of him upset her so much? Pulling into the parking lot in front of the bank, Cat made herself ask the questions she had avoided all night and most of the morning. Was she falling in love with Garrick? Had he fallen for her? And what did it mean for the two of them if the answer to either or both questions was yes?

That, she decided quickly, would depend on a number of factors, and now was not the time to dwell on them. Now, she needed to get her financial house in order. Emotional disorders could follow when there was time.

Don Jeffers, the bank president, was annoyingly pleasant, considering that the last time they had spoken he had left her without much dignity and even less hope. She was determined, however, to remain calm and businesslike, and she even politely refused to consider a new bank loan in the light of her windfall. She needed no new debts. Don was plainly disappointed in her attitude, but he dutifully accounted her with the money from the economic-assistance check. When Cat left the bank, she felt almost smug.

Her mood improved as she shopped for groceries at the town's general store. Once summer arrived, and she had to prepare food in bulk, she would order from a wholesaler, but for now, she preferred patronizing the local merchants when she could, and it was clear they appreciated it. Fred Cosby, at the butcher stand, sliced off two extra steaks and wrapped them up without adding their price on her meat package. At the cash register, his wife suggested she try a bunch of the new green grapes that had just come in. After all, there was no charge. Cat walked out practically humming.

The morning had been chilly, though sunny. Now, near noon, it was hot. She shed her jacket after stowing the groceries in the back of the Jeep and decided to run into Sal's Café for a cup of coffee and a muffin before heading home. Doing so would give her a chance to catch up on town gossip and provide the best possible means of broadcasting the fact that Cat's Cradle was still in business. Sal was better than a communications satellite for spreading the word about almost anything. And Cat wanted this particular word spread far and wide.

The café was set back from the Western-style wooden sidewalk that ran the length of Main Street. A trio of wooden steps led up to the front door, which boasted one of the few screen doors in town. Sal was originally from the South, and she didn't hold with the native tolerance of insects during the short summer months. Besides, Cat thought as she pulled open the door and stepped inside the restaurant, it lent a homey touch, slamming as it did with a thin thud whenever a customer entered. It certainly beat those annoying little bells.

"Hey, there, Cat," Sal called from behind the counter. "Nice to see you. You been such a stranger lately."

"Getting ready for the tourists." Cat grinned and sat down on a stool at the counter. Sal, with her keen interest in people and her ready, barbed wit, was one of her favorite folks. The older woman was thin and angular, red-cheeked from daily ministrations over a hot grill, but always ready with a smile and a personal inquiry. No one remained a stranger to Sal for long. "You know as well as I do that I'll have my hands full from now on until the end of hunting season," Cat added. "I can't be hanging around gossiping and expect to make a living, too."

"Heard a word or two 'bout that." Sal set out a cup of black coffee and a date muffin without asking what Cat's preference was. "Seems you ran into some problems a few weeks ago."

"I did." She sipped the coffee. It was hot and rich. "But that's all behind me now. I'm in great shape and looking forward to June."

Sal pursed her lips, clearly dying to ask more details. Cat let her stew for a moment, then she said, "I was able to get a hardship loan from the state, Sal—one I don't have to pay back until I'm absolutely able. And there's no interest. It seems they don't want people like me going under because of a financial crunch that will pass once guests start coming and paying."

"Whew! Ain't you the lucky gal." Sal shook her head, the gray curls under the hair net catching silver from the sunlight. "You got somebody special lighting candles for you? There's small businesses all over the place going under. How'd you manage that loan?"

"I know someone who knew the right buttons to push." Cat took a bite of the muffin. Chewing on it, she began to frown. She had hardly given Garrick the full amount of credit and she certainly hadn't shown him how truly grateful she was. Her reaction to his strange behavior had rattled her more than she had thought, she realized. It took sitting here, talking about it, for her to acknowledge how special he was and how special he had become to her.

"Might that somebody be that big, good-looking dude I hear you got stashed out at your place?" Sal kept her expression neutral, but Cat could see the wheels turning in her head. So there was speculation around town as to Garrick's relationship with her. Well, good. Now was the time to set everyone straight.

Even if she wasn't certain of the correct answer herself.

"Garrick Drexel is working for me," she said casually. "He's assisting Jude and helping me with the books." Not exactly true. He had taken over the books. "He knows a lot about money. He used to work on Wall Street. Like I said, he knew which buttons to press."

"Any of those buttons yours, honey?" Sal's tone was kind, as if she understood some of the turmoil Cat was experiencing. Cat hesitated, unsure of how to reply, of how much to say. She was saved by the banging of the screen door. A group of women came in for a coffee break, and Sal's attention was redirected. Cat knew the others, but she only nodded hello rather than going over and joining them. She wanted to be alone with her thoughts for a little while. Directing her attention back to the muffin and coffee, she tried to sort through her feelings about what had happened the previous night.

She and Garrick had met by accident, but his staying on had been no accident. It had been a deliberate, free choice on his part. He had said he was leaving behind an old life that no longer meant anything to him. He was also leaving behind troubles. Troubles he seemed unwilling to deal with. He spoke of work at the ranch as if it was a born-again experience for him. He certainly was cheerful and enthusiastic most of the time—she could hardly fault him on attitude. And he had feelings toward her. No man could kiss like that and not mean something by it.

But just what did he mean? What strange alchemy had he dipped into to make her feel so... cherished when he kissed her last night? What was storming around inside of her that had made her so prickly this morning? None of it made any sense, nor did she work up any answers.

But she did know one thing: even if he was guilty as sin of cooking books on Wall Street, he was a good man at heart. No accusation from any federal agents would change her opinion on that matter. Before they had even known each other a scant hour, Garrick had shown extraordinary kindness and tenderness in caring for her when she had broken her arm. A blush stained her cheeks as she remembered being carried in his arms and nestling against his bare torso.

"A penny for *that* thought." Sal's voice interrupted her musings. "It must have been a doozie!"

"Just recalling an embarrassing moment, Sal," Cat lied. "The muffin was great, as usual. I'd better be getting on. I've got groceries in the Jeep."

"Don't kid me. You just want to get on back to that cute dude of yours." Sal chuckled. "Hear you actually picked him up, hitchhiking on the highway."

"His car broke down. I offered a lift like anyone else would." Cat couldn't decided whether to be annoyed or not. She had known Sal would want to gossip, but talking about Garrick made her feel raw. "He . . . he stayed on to help after I busted my arm." She managed a weak grin. "He works, but he seems to enjoy it. Funny, isn't it? Having a dude work on a dude ranch."

"A laugh riot." Sal eyed her speculatively. "So, there ain't no romance between you two? Least not one you want to talk about?"

"Sal, he's going through some kind of life crisis. He is big and handsome. He's also a hard worker, a delight to have around, always cheerful and, quite honestly, the reason why I can still open the ranch next month. I'm not entirely sure how he did it, but the loan I got was his idea. Apparently, he found the right things in my records and said the right things to the man in Cheyenne. I like him—I'd be crazy not to. But there's no romance. Sorry."

Sal removed the empty plate and cup. She ran a cloth over the counter in front of Cat. "Abigail Springer was in here last night with that Tom Hendry who's sparking her so heavy. She said your friend was sweet on you. Leastwise, that's how it seemed to her."

"Abby is seventeen, Sal. I have to go."

"You're blushing to beat the band, Cat Cantrell." Sal was clearly enjoying herself. The other women in the café had stopped chatting and were listening with undisguised interest to the exchange. Cat hurriedly dug in her jeans pocket for cash to pay for her snack. She put two dollars down on the counter and told Sal not to bother getting change. "Your money's no good here," Sal stated, pushing the bills back to her. "Just you promise to recommend my place to your guests, as usual. That's all the payment I want."

Cat heard the screen door slam again, but didn't turn to see who had come in this time. Sal had never hesitated to take money from her before, and it made her feel like a poor relation to have the café owner doing so now that it was common knowledge her finances had been shaky. "Sal, I appreciate your kindness, but I can still pay my own way. Please take the money." Suddenly, the generosity of the grocers seemed insulting, too. She wished she had the nerve to go back and ask them to charge her for the steaks and grapes. But too much time had passed, and it would seem doubly insulting to them if she tried. No, the only place her pride was likely to be salvaged today was here at Sal's. "Take the money," she repeated.

"Can I help you, mister?" Sal was looking beyond and behind Cat. She ignored the two dollars.

Cat turned. Standing directly behind her, observing the scene with Sal, was a tall, thin man dressed in a gray business suit. He had pale skin, pale blue eyes and pale blond hair. His narrow features were set in an expression of arrogant know-it-allness. Cat disliked him on sight.

"You Catherine Cantrell?" he asked, eyeing her as if she were some sort of insect. "Owner of Cat's Cradle?" His lips seemed to sneer out the name of her ranch.

Cat bristled and started to answer sharply, but Sal came out from behind the counter and planted herself in front of the man. "I asked if I could help you, mister," she said, her tone heavy with warning. "This here is a café. You want something to eat, fine. Otherwise, take your business elsewhere."

"My business is with Miss Cantrell." The man reached into his inner coat pocket and took out a leather folder. Stepping around Sal, he flipped the folder open in Cat's face, showing a badge and identification photo. "My name is Willis Kent, Miss Cantrell. I'd like to ask you some questions about a man named Garrick Drexel. He's a suspect in an investigation I'm conducting."

CHAPTER SEVEN

CAT STUDIED THE BADGE. It looked genuine enough, and the man's name was the one Garrick had mentioned when he'd spoken of a federal officer with a grudge against him. But nothing in her experience had prepared her for the sense of outrage she felt at the situation. The man was speaking to her and regarding her as if he thought she was the criminal! All the frustration and anger that had been building up in her before she'd gotten the loan surfaced. Cat was ready to do serious damage to the sneering face in front of her. Her short fingernails dug sharp crescents into her palms as she framed a reply.

"Garrick Drexel is my employee and friend," she said stiffly. "Any questions you may have about him should be asked in his presence. That's my opinion. I'm sure any good lawyer would back me up. Goodbye, Mr. Kent."

She started to brush past him, praying her control would last long enough for her to get out the door and down the street to her Jeep. Kent's hand reached out and slapped a hand down on her right shoulder, jarring her arm. Cat gasped in sudden pain.

Almost immediately Willis Kent realized he had made a serious mistake. He hadn't actually meant to hurt her, only to frighten her into cooperating. Cooperation was in short supply around this two-bit cowboy village, and Willis was sick and tired of having his queries answered in unsatisfactory monosyllables or not at all. It had practically taken a court order to find out that the woman Drexel was living with was in town for the morning.

Now, staring into her furious blue eyes, he was heartily sorry he had found out anything about her at all. Stepping back, he instinctively threw up both hands—one to ward off a blow and one to strike back in response. If she chose to hit him with that damn cast, he was liable to get hurt, and Willis disliked personal discomfort of any kind.

But she didn't strike. Instead, she looked startled, then frightened, and then she was crying out for someone to stop. Willis didn't hear all her words. A powerful force spun him around, a fist connected with his chin and then the floor came up and hit him in the face. After that, all he heard was the sealike sound of semiconsciousness.

"Garrick, Garrick!" Cat cried. "He's a cop. You don't hit cops, for God's sake!"

Garrick scowled and shook his sore knuckles. "No one's ever deserved it more, boss. He hurt you. If I didn't think the sheriff here'd try to stop me, I'd paste him again." His voice was low and held a dangerous edge. He was, Cat realized, holding himself in check by a thread.

"You got your lick in," Nelson Hendry said gruffly, stepping from behind Garrick and toeing Willis Kent experimentally. The blond man groaned but didn't move. "Can't say I saw much, though. Think he kind of tripped and hit his head. Any you folks see different?"

"Not a thing, Sheriff." Sal had moved behind her counter. "Clumsy fella. Fell against Cat, then kinda stumbled backward. I'd say he tripped when the big guy there touched his shoulder." The other customers chorused ready agreement.

Tom Hendry was hovering behind his uncle, and the older man instructed him to bundle the agent down to Doc Turner's to make sure he wasn't suffering from more than grogginess and a sore jaw. After checking with Cat to make sure she wasn't really hurt, he turned to Garrick. "Now, listen," he growled in a low tone, "I let you have him this once 'cause of what he did to her, but don't get the idea you can run around my town laying out anyone who don't please you."

"I understand, Sheriff." Garrick looked properly repentant, he hoped. Inside, he was still seething at Kent and still surprised at the overwhelming rage that had seized him when he had seen the man roughing up Cat. Loss of control was a rare occurrence with him. "It was just that I . . ."

"I know, son." Nelson clapped him on the shoulder. "I know. Don't let it happen again. I can't be covering for you next time."

Cat, still dazed by the speed and turn of events, finally found her voice. "How did the three of you manage to show up right at the same time?" she asked. "Garrick, is something wrong at the ranch?"

"Nothing's wrong." He grinned. "In fact, everything's more than a little all right. I got some more good news today, and I couldn't wait until you got back to tell you. I was out looking for you when I ran into Nelson here."

"That Kent fella busted into my office a little while ago," Nelson explained, "wanting all kinds of information about you. Fact is, he was downright insulting." The big man reddened. "I came close to decking him myself. Tom and me was looking for you to warn you about him when we ran into Drexel. Just happened to come in at the right time, I guess."

"I guess." Cat was now simmering with curiosity about Garrick's news, but she wanted to wait until they were alone to hear it. A premonition warned her that his idea of good tidings might not exactly jibe with hers. While she was grateful for all he had done so far, it made her a bit nervous to be relinquishing so much control. Once the bills were paid and the books rebalanced, she decided, she would tactfully find a way to take back management.

The sheriff told them to head on home, that he would have a personal chat with Willis Kent and explain the realities of law enforcement in the West. But he did warn them that the agent might continue to be a nuisance. He didn't ask Garrick if Kent actually had reason to be. Cat doubted if that oversight had been caused by courtesy. Rather, Nelson Hendry's instinctive judgment had probably told him that Garrick was not guilty of any wrongdoing. If Nelson had thought otherwise, he would have promptly taken Garrick down to the jail for a thorough and unpleasant grilling. Hendry was a lawman first and a friend second. And that was comforting. Cat wasn't yet ready to trust her own judgment, muddled as it was by emotions.

Her emotional stability wasn't helped by Garrick's big news item. They were seated in her Jeep when he told her.

"It looks as though somebody in heaven is watching out for you, Cat," he said cheerfully. "There's an ad company you used to work for that's ready to turn inside out if you agree to come back and do one little commercial spot. Your money worries are over!" His enthusiasm was clear and unfettered.

She was speechless for a moment. He talked on, giving her details that she didn't hear. One spot. One spot and she could probably bring in thousands as a future hedge against the kind of bind Garrick had just bailed her out of. One spot. A few weeks. A month at the most.

A month away from Cat's Cradle just when the tourist season was starting.

"I can't, Garrick. I'll call them back tomorrow morning. It was sweet of them to think of me, but I just—"

"Can't? Or won't?" His expression had turned stern. "Catherine, think about it. This is a big financial opportunity. I don't see how you can refuse."

She took a deep breath, feeling sudden tears at the back of her throat. "No, I don't suppose you can. Money is everything to you, isn't it? Well, it isn't everything to me. I have enough to manage now, and that's all I need. You'd better get on back to your car. I've got to get these groceries home."

"But..." He looked angry and flustered. And hurt.

"Go on, Garrick," she said gently. "We can talk this over later. I've got frozen stuff in the back."

He regarded her for a long moment out of eyes that showed a kaleidoscope of feelings. Then he growled, "Yeah, I know," and got out of the car without a further word or glance at her. As he walked away, she could tell by the set of his shoulders that he was furious. She started the Jeep and backed out into the street.

Well, she thought, driving past him. He could just be furious. It was her life, her ranch, her talent and she would use all of them the way she wanted, not the way some hotshot from Wall Street dictated. She had gotten along before she had met him, and she would get along after he had gone. She was driving much too fast, fueling her anger against him, when she heard a honk, and his BMW sailed past her as if she were standing still. She thought she could see him making a rude gesture at her. Cat slowed and started laughing.

Why was she getting in such an uproar? The man had only been trying to help. He had saved her business, punched out a guy who had shoved her and when he had happily brought her good news, she had practically spit in his eye. Lord, she thought. She was getting far too serious about life and everything connected with it. Deciding to give him an apology when she next saw him, she began to whistle softly.

Music was still important to her. She itched to have her right hand free again so that she could play her flute properly. She looked forward to nights around a camp fire when she could lead in singing the old favorites. There was the community event in July at the Pioneer Festival when, with her singing, she would reach almost celebrity status for a few days. Music would always be a part of her life. But never again her *life*. And never again would she allow herself to be manipulated and exploited because of it. Garrick would understand when she sat down and explained this to him calmly.

But when she arrived at the ranch, he wasn't around to listen calmly. The BMW looked as if it was still smoking, and she could find no sign of either man. Shrugging and assuming they had taken off on some mission, she unloaded the groceries and made preparations for a late lunch.

By two, when there was still no sign of them, she began to worry. Looking around she found that one horse, the Roman-nosed pony Jude preferred to ride, was missing. No other clues to the men's activities or whereabouts turned up. Cat fretted for a few minutes more, then made up her mind.

She saddled Sam Spade. He was faster and more reliable on the trail than Fatty, and she wanted a good mount beneath her. Sam flared his nostrils with excitement when she attached the rifle sling to his saddle. Memories of hunting trips surfacing in the depths of his equine brain, she realized. "No, Sam," she said softly. "It's only for protection or emergencies. And I'm praying I don't have to call on it." She holstered the old Remington that had belonged to her father and led Sam out of the corral. After tethering him to the hitching post in front of her house, she went inside and loaded a first-aid kit into a saddlebag and, as an afterthought, added wrapped sandwiches and a down jacket. Then she set out.

She was a fair tracker, but with the spring earth so moist, it was difficult to tell which way Jude had gone. Only a fresh pile of manure on the trail reassured her she was heading in the right direction. Equally fresh, but not as odoriferous, was the breeze blowing down from the peaks. She had thrown her sheepskin jacket over her shoulders as a matter of habit, and now she turned up the collar. She would be warm enough no matter what the weather did.

So would Jude. She knew he wouldn't go out without proper clothing. But Garrick? She could only hope they were together.

That hope faded when, after an hour of following Jude's trail, she met the man himself. He rode silently down the wooded trail toward her, not a line of his face telling her what had happened. He said nothing until they were close enough for the horses to touch tentative noses. Sam snorted and laid his ears back. Cat scolded him automatically.

"Dude's gone," Jude said. "Can't find hide nor hair of him."

"Tell me what happened." A sinking, sickened feeling came over her.

Garrick had arrived home in what Jude colorfully described as a real, old-fashioned snit. He had growled something to the wrangler about going for a walk to clear his head and had taken off into the trees. Jude had shrugged, gone back to work and hadn't thought anything more about it until he'd felt the wind starting up. "Gonna storm," he said.

Cat nodded. Her skin crawled with anxiety and frustration, but she knew trying to rush the old man wouldn't help. She'd learn what he knew in good time. Not before.

"Figured you'd be back soon, and it wouldn't take no time to find him." He shrugged. "I was wrong."

Cat frowned. "He's strong, and if he was walking quickly, he could have gotten quite a ways by now. What direction did he take?"

A ruddy color appeared under the bronze of Jude's skin. "Didn't notice and can't find a trail. He wasn't wearing boots, just those damn tennis-shoe things. Don't hardly make a dent in the ground 'less it's pure mud."

"All right." Cat shut her eyes for a minute. It was one of her worst nightmares—losing a guest in the wilds. At least Garrick was no soft city dweller anymore. His weeks in her employ had hardened an already hard body. He also wasn't stupid, in spite of the idiocy of charging off into the forest by himself, and to judge from the way he had handled other matters, he was not the kind to lose his head when in danger. She and Jude would find him, or he'd make his way back by himself. There was no reason to panic.

Jude cleared his throat. "Saw some tracks up in the high meadow. Where the snow's still hanging around."

"What kind?"

He told her, and her blood chilled. Cougars weren't often found down near the ranch, but it happened—especially if game was heading down in anticipation of a bad storm. Cat wished she had paid more attention to the weather report that morning, but her mind had been on

other matters. Money matters. She remembered the taunt
she had flung at Garrick about caring only for money.
Would money have sent him off in a temper when it couldn't
even bring him back to New York? She had been grossly
unfair. Now it was likely he would pay for that.

"Go back," she ordered Jude. "Let Nelson know what
we're up to. He'll tell the ranger service. Load up on am-
munition and supplies and meet me back in the upper
meadow. We'll hunt on our own until dark." Jude nodded
and set off down the trail, squeezing his horse past Sam,
who nickered warningly.

"Shut up, Sam," Cat said, kicking the big black animal
in the ribs. "We've got our work cut out for us, and I need
you to be on your best behavior." Her hand automatically
slid down to the rifle scabbard, and she checked her weapon.
A cougar wasn't likely to distinguish between his natural
prey and a man on foot. Or a woman on horseback. She
rode on upward into the increasingly chilly wind, which was
now cutting sharply even through the densest parts of the
forest. . . .

GARRICK WAS LOST, cold and mad—no longer mad at Cat,
but at himself. He had acted like a hotheaded kid, first
slugging Kent, a satisfying but highly stupid move, then
flying off the handle at Cat's reaction to his good news. And
dumbest of all was thinking he could take a stroll out here
in the middle of nowhere and think through his problems.

He had done fine at first. The sun had been high and hot
enough for him to take off his jacket and sweat a little. The
air smelled so good, full of fresh pine scents and earthy
odors, that his mood had lightened considerably by the time
he'd gone only a short way. But he had been moving quickly,
and his rapid pace had soon taken him into totally unfamiliar territory.

He tried peering through the trees and looking for the big
mountain off to the west of the ranch, but he found to his
surprise that it was not in sight. While he had been walking, clouds had rolled in from the direction he thought was

west and all the upper slopes were obscured. When the wind started to dry, then cool him, he began to worry.

Years ago, while in the army, he had taken field training, and his instructors, while impressed with his physical ability and his quick mastery of the medical skills required for his job, had despaired of him in the field. *Keep Drexel with you,* they had explained to the others in his unit. *If he don't get lost, he may save your butts.*

If he don't get lost.

He wandered around for a while, debating the best course of action. He could follow a stream down. If he could find a stream. There was something about moss growing on the north side of trees that he remembered from boyhood adventure tales. But there didn't seem to be a whole lot of moss on these Western pines, and it seemed to grow wherever it could get a grip.

Finally, he made what amounted to a command decision. He sat down. The trees were thick around him and provided adequate shelter from the wind—at least for the moment. It seemed to be blowing harder all the time. And getting colder. No matter how mad she was, he trusted Cat to come looking for him. She would find him eventually, and if he got a little cold and hungry while waiting, well, it was his own damn fault. Teach him to lose his temper twice in one day.

He never lost his temper, damn it! Garrick leaned against a tree trunk and thought. He had been considerably ticked off and emotionally moved time and time again in his life, but never as an adult had he acted so childishly as he had today... the past few days... the past few weeks.

"Maybe you're losing it, old buddy," he muttered to himself. "Maybe this is a mid-life crisis you'll never come back from. You'll starve to death, freeze to death out in God knows where all because you didn't have the sense possessed by one of those pigheaded horses of hers." He thought about that for a while.

They were *her* horses. This was *her* ranch. It was *her* life, and as far as she knew, he was just a ship passing in his own dark night. She didn't know how he felt. He knew. But she did not.

More thinking. About the time he decided to get up and try walking again, a snowflake fell lazily through the tree branches and hit his temple. Garrick swore and looked up. There were more coming.

He swore some more and tried to remember how to make a fire in the wilderness. Rubbing two sticks together was the ticket. He got up, dusted off the seat of his pants and started hunting sticks.

CAT AND JUDE met in the meadow and set out on a converging concentric search pattern. It was painfully methodical, but it insured all ground was covered. From time to time they called Garrick's name, but it was possible he had fallen and was lying injured and unconscious, unable to hear them. Cat didn't like to contemplate the ramifications of that. She tried to keep calm, but as the hours passed and the weather worsened, she grew more nervous. Every shadow in the trees was the cougar. Every branch that cracked under Sam's hooves was the first report of Jude's rifle. And every inert lump large enough to be a hurt or dead man was Garrick.

In her anxiety, her heart and mind were finally meeting on the matter: she really cared for him, crazy and self-defeating as that was. She might even be in love with the big idiot, truly insane as that was. Each time she and Jude crossed paths, she tried to control her expression, but when she was alone, the ache twisted her features and the tears stung her eyes. If anything had happened to him, she was never going to forgive herself.

It had been his temper, but her actions that had led them to this pass. If she had been a little gentler with her response, if she had listened and not flown off the handle herself, he wouldn't have taken her rejection of his idea so badly. He would have waited calmly to discuss the issue, as she had decided to do herself on the slow drive home. She was the culprit and he the victim.

And she had to find him.

The snow started at about four-thirty. Jude, when she passed him, commented laconically that tracking would be easier when a dusting of the white stuff covered the ground. At least they would see Garrick's footprints plainly. Cat said nothing. The weather wasn't bitter yet, but it was likely to be, and he was wearing only a wool sports jacket over his shirt and jeans.

If it had been fall or winter, she would have called a halt shortly after the snowfall started, but with spring well advanced, light would continue for some hours yet. They could still find him on their own. If not, she would call out the search-and-rescue unit immediately upon arriving back at the ranch. Doubts rushed around in her head as she wondered if she shouldn't have done that to begin with. She had been so sure they would find him after a short while. Hunger rumbled in her stomach, but that was the least painful of the aches she felt.

Jude, for his part, was obviously growing more concerned as time passed. Now, when they neared each other, the wrangler would begin talking, almost chattering, continuing on about subjects that had nothing to do with the situation. She also heard him calling Garrick's name more frequently, as if he needed to hear the sound of his own voice for reassurance. Her arm ached, her heart ached, and hearing the noise of their voices did nothing to soothe her.

The snow began to fall in earnest and the daylight they would ordinarily have been granted faded. One last pass, Cat decided. Then she would have to admit defeat and hope the S-and-R boys would have better luck with their dogs and helicopters in the morning. They wouldn't be able to start until first light, but thank God that would be early. If only Garrick had sense enough to find shelter of some kind, he would probably only suffer some temporary discomfort from hunger and cold. Probably. She tried to put thoughts of the big predator out of her mind.

THE BIG PREDATOR, however, was very much in the fore-front of Garrick's mind. He had caught sight of the animal while looking for sticks, and now he and it were playing some horrifying kind of game. The cat didn't seem especially interested in finishing him off at once, but was moving cautiously closer with every step it took. Once, it stopped and made a kind of growling sound that had a surprisingly human quality to it.

"Don't like the after-shave?" Garrick asked. "Hey, fella, I *bathe* in the stuff. I'm practically basted in it. You'd hate the flavor. Honest."

The cat seemed to consider that, then continued stalking.

Garrick looked around for weapons, uncertain how aggressive to be under the circumstances. If the cat charged, he stood little chance, but if he could bluff, there might be hope. He found a place between the roots of a tree where some stones had collected and picked up the largest of them. Keeping his back to the tree, he addressed the animal loudly and obscenely and hurled one stone. It seemed to shock the beast. It stopped and backed up, giving a low growl.

This is not good, Garrick thought, sweating heavily in spite of the cold. *My mama didn't raise me to be a cat burger. There's got to be a way out!* He yelled at the animal again. This time, it seemed to have more effect. The creature sat back on its haunches and regarded him in a thoughtful manner. Garrick tried again, calling on his army experience in order to curse as creatively as possible. The cat seemed fascinated.

"DID YOU HEAR THAT?" Cat stopped Sam. Jude, following right behind, pulled his horse up short, but not before its nose touched Sam's tail. Sam kicked out, but Cat didn't scold him. "Listen," she said.

"I hear it." Jude sucked in his breath. "Sounds like a man cussing to beat the band. Over that-a way."

"Let's go." Cat dug her heels into Sam's sides. The big horse leaped off the trail and crashed through the woods. Jude was right on his tail.

Garrick and the cat heard them at the same time. The animal crouched, snarled, then screamed. At the same instant, Garrick yelled out for whoever was coming to beware. The sound of Cat calling his name was the sweetest and most terrifying noise he'd ever heard. "Don't come any closer," he hollered. "There's a lion here, big as a house!"

About that time the "lion" decided reinforcements were not what it wanted to deal with. With one last yowl, it gave Garrick a strange, fathomless stare and ran off into the forest. Garrick's muscles gave out and he sank to the ground just as Cat thundered into view, reins in her teeth and a yard-long rifle in her left hand. She looked like a Valkyrie with her long hair flying and her eyes wide, looking for the enemy.

"He bugged out when he heard the cavalry," Garrick said weakly when the noise of Jude's arrival subsided. "Guess he figured he could handle a city boy, but when the real cowboys arrived, it was too much for him." He started to laugh.

Cat rammed her rifle back into the scabbard and jumped from her horse's back. Running over to Garrick, she took his face in her hands. "Are you hurt?" Tears filled her eyes when he didn't answer immediately. "Garrick, are you all right?"

His grin widened. "I am now," he said. "I sure am now!" It was on the tip of his tongue to blurt out that he loved her, but he wasn't certain if it was truly love he was feeling coursing through him at the moment or just plain old-fashioned joy at still being alive.

CHAPTER EIGHT

CAT FELT the starkest kind of relief, then anger. "You were an idiot to come out here on foot by yourself," she snapped, trying to pull him to his feet.

He got up slowly. "I know. I lost my temper and wasn't thinking clearly. I'm better now."

He sounded so humbled that she found it difficult to stay mad at him. But she managed to put on a show until they were back at the ranch. Leaving the taciturn Jude to manage the horses, she ordered Garrick into her house and ministered to him with hot soup and cocoa. It was clear he was suffering from a mild case of hypothermia and possibly shock. She bullied him into taking a hot bath and accepting the use of her bed for the night. She took the couch, but kept the bedroom door open in case he needed help. He fell asleep as soon as his head hit the pillow and hadn't stirred by the time she checked him later before turning in herself.

He was still sleeping when she rose before dawn to help Jude with the animals and assist in clearing some of the heavy snow off the roofs. When they finished and came back to the house, Garrick was up, looking bright and cheerful and making breakfast for them. Again he expressed his heartfelt thanks for his rescue.

"I would never think of letting someone unfamiliar with New York go wandering off alone. I shouldn't have done it here. A jungle is a jungle, whether it has concrete or pine needles on the ground."

"You were upset," Cat conceded. "First the confrontation with Kent and then..."

"With you," he finished, a gleam in his eyes.

Jude bent over his plate of eggs and bacon, clearly attempting to ignore the conversation.

But peace lasted until the dishes were cleaned and put away. The wrangler left to attend to chores, and Garrick turned to tend to Cat. "Just how much thought have you given to what I told you yesterday?" he asked, his voice businesslike. "Have you had a change of heart?"

"No." They moved into the office. His clothes were rumpled and he hadn't shaved yet, but he exuded an air of authority and power that astonished her. *My God*, she thought. *He is the boss. He always will be, no matter where he is.* The thought made her suddenly frightened for all that belonged to her. Including her heart. "I haven't changed my mind," she said with emphasis. "Have you?"

His expression warmed, and his long fingers tapped the side of the desk. "I'm making up my mind about a thing or two," he said. "I'll let you know when I've reached my final conclusions." He paused. "Look, you know the only reason I get upset with you is because I care about you. If I didn't, I wouldn't trouble myself. I still have plenty of problems of my own, you know."

"I know." She looked away, remembering his encounter with the agent. He had compounded his problems when he had struck out to defend her. Everything he had done had been with her welfare in mind. "But, damn it, Garrick, you have no right to dictate to me."

"I'm not dictating. Only pointing out that you ought to think about getting some extra capital, even if it means—"

"That I should go back to a city I hate and a job I despise? I don't need *that* money. Thanks to your efforts, I have enough."

"Enough? You have enough to make ends meet. Barely. *If* you don't go doing something typically financially irresponsible, like giving Jude a month's wages in advance. I like the guy a lot, don't get me wrong. Hell, I guess I owe him my life after last night, but—"

"Listen, you Scrooge! I gave him that extra money during a time when he had a sick sister to take care of. She died, and Jude's all alone in the world now. I don't expect he'll be hitting me for early wages anymore."

"Oh." He seemed to shrink inches.

"Yes. 'Oh.' You can't run this place like an investment firm." She went over and put her hands on his shoulders. "You run it like a family. And that means you don't usually get any monetary return worth shooting at. What you get is love, respect and satisfaction. Happiness, if you will."

Garrick said nothing for a moment. Then he shoved the hair from his forehead. "I can really be an ass, can't I," he said. "I wonder if I'll ever understand you and your ways, Cat Cantroll."

"I don't know, Garrick Drexel," she said, suddenly misty-eyed. "I guess all you can do is try."

"Sounds like a good idea to me." His arms went around her, and they clung together, all differences and misunderstandings temporarily forgotten by the pleasure the closeness brought. But when he kissed her, his desire seemed suppressed, leading her to wonder what was going to happen next.

What happened was that he continued to hold her tight. "This is heaven," he murmured. Then laughed. "If you hadn't found me when you did last night, it might actually *be* heaven. That lion had my name on his menu card."

"Actually, it was probably a her lion. And as long as you faced her and didn't run, the probability of her attacking was small. Unless she was very hungry or feeding cubs."

"Well," he said, releasing her, "she *looked* damn hungry close up. Do you get many of those things around here?"

"No. And they're usually more afraid of us than we are of them."

He grinned. "That makes them different from the predators where I come from, doesn't it? I'd just as soon stay away from either kind." He turned from her to the desk. "Now, let's go over these accounts."

Cat blinked. Just like that he could put aside personal matters and delve into business. She sat with him for a while, trying to understand the sophisticated mind he was bringing to bear on her holdings. Not fully following everything, she was nevertheless impressed. If she did want to let him organize the whole shooting match, he could probably build her quite the empire. Only when she began to realize how annoyed her gentle refusals to accept most of his suggestions was making him did she beg off, saying that Jude undoubtedly was feeling put upon doing all the outdoor chores himself. When she left him, he said absently that he would join them soon, and he turned back to her books.

Eventually, he did come outside, but he did his work without his usual cheerful conversation and she often saw a scowl darken his handsome features. Clearly, he was involved in some kind of inner struggle, she decided, and she left him alone with his thoughts.

The next few days brought relief in a number of ways. The sun rose high and hot, causing the snow to start melting in streams and rivers. Garrick was like a kid with a fascinating new toy, delighting in the sights and sounds of the late spring thaw, and superficially, his good temper returned. Nelson Hendry called, informing them that Willis Kent had fled town, appalled not only by the unseasonable weather, but by the fact that Garrick could assault him with apparent impunity. He was, Nelson speculated privately to Cat, afraid of the bigger man.

Also, Cat was able to begin serious preparations for the onslaught of paying guests. With Garrick watching her closely, she regained control of the management of the ranch. At least, control of most of it. He still insisted on starting a set of his own books to run in conjunction with hers. It was not a good sign.

Furthermore, he made no more romantic overtures, which began to bother her as time passed. How could he, she fretted, just turn himself on and off like that? It wasn't human!

So while on the surface things were better, underneath they seethed and tumbled. Both she and he were mired in unspoken feelings and opinions about their two ways of looking at life, which were almost diametrically opposed to one another.

For his part, Garrick was doing some serious soul-searching. Cat's almost medieval management techniques drove him crazy. She was so conservative and unwilling to open her mind to new concepts that he set her, in his imagination, back in a feudal and paternalistic society. She would have done just fine, he believed, running a manor or estate in tenth- or eleventh-century Europe. The way she dealt with her employees bothered him, too. She was a strong boss, but overly flexible when problems arose among her staff—willing to sacrifice the capitalistic bottom line of profit for the greater good of her employees. This became abundantly clear when the girls arrived on the scene. Garrick had never witnessed such a strange and, to his mind, silly relationship with a boss and workers.

Except maybe his own relationship with his "boss."

Abby Springer and Ellen Futrell started working for a few hours after school the last week of May. Working, that is, in the sense that they showed up, frequently ferried in by Tom Hendry, and began to organize their belongings in their summer quarters. The rest of the time, Cat tutored them for their final exams. He just could not get over it. *She* was paying *them* a quarter an hour over the minimum wage for her to help them with their studies!

She even had the temerity to ask him to assist with algebra. He did, but without good grace and totally without understanding why he let her talk him into doing it.

It was clear, however, that the girls adored her. They transferred some of that affection toward him when he unbent somewhat, but Cat was still their idol. Wisely, he kept his mouth shut about the matter, but stored it up for future arguments about her methods.

She had also turned the singing job down flat. While she'd sounded nice as pie on the phone to her old agent, she had left no doubt that she'd sooner walk barefoot over live coals than spend any time in New York. Garrick could imagine the agent wincing as he hung up. It would be a cold day in the nether regions, undoubtedly, before the man would call this particular ex-client again.

In short, nothing about her met with his approval at the moment. Except Cat herself. His heart twisted with a pain he began to recognize as love every time he saw her or heard the sound of her sweet voice. It fell on his ears like the most exquisite music, and he longed to hear her sing again.

Her smile started his mornings. The touch of her hand would start his heart beating rapidly. He was a mature, successful man who was falling as crazily and sweatily in love as a sixteen-year-old. She would near, and his palms would dampen. He fantasized about making love with her.

This got him in trouble more than once. As was typical of non-horsemen, Garrick trusted the animals even while he feared them, and would occasionally daydream while working around or on one. Twice he had ended up on his behind in the dirt. The big black horse known as Sam Spade seemed to take particular delight in nailing him with a well-placed hoof when his attention was less than focused.

The frantic pace of work just prior to the opening week in June, however, left him no time to work out his emotional problems. Not only were he and Cat busy from dawn to well after dark, but his problems at the other end of the country were apparently escalating. He tried to keep them out of his mind as much as possible, believing he had enough difficulty with the situation at hand, but they intruded.

Willis Kent had returned to New York with a renewed attitude of vengeance, it seemed. One afternoon Cat came out to the barn where Garrick was working. With a worried expression on her face, she told him he had a long-distance call from his friend and lawyer, Sheldon Sheridan.

"Gar," the attorney said, his resonant voice booming across the miles. "What the hell have you been up to? You've got this SEC guy after you who's as hot as a pack of hounds on the trail of the last of the great foxes. It was all I could do this week to keep him from confiscating your personal records.''

Garrick swore. He had given Sheldon power of attorney for him while he was on the road ''finding himself.'' If Sheldon was worried, matters had clearly gotten far out of hand. ''Hasn't Janet contacted you?'' he asked.

''Janet? Your sister-in-law? Not a word. I haven't seen her in ages.''

Garrick thought. ''She was supposed to talk to you. I heard weeks ago that Kent was on my tail about some imaginary faulty dealings. I asked her to check on it for me. Since I hadn't heard from you or her, I assumed she found nothing to be alarmed about.''

''But didn't Kent contact you?''

''Sure did. He was out here two weeks ago on a harassment binge pure and simple, Shel. He and I had a run-in, and he left town. Nothing more.''

''Would I be bothering you if it was nothing more? He's in court right now, alleging that you bribed local law enforcement to cover you, that you assaulted him and that your 'flight,' as he puts it, was to avoid just the sort of in-depth investigation he wants permission to do.''

''I haven't done anything wrong. Even if he does investigate, he won't find a thing.''

''If he does investigate, you stand to lose a lot of money, my friend. You still have people buying for their portfolios because of advice you gave them. That'll stop, and that'll be cash out of your pocket—to name but one simple instance of how this could affect you. Then there's the matter of your reputation, your good name. You can't be planning to stay out there in the boonies forever, Gar. One of these days, the novelty will wear off, you'll get it out of your system and you'll come home. It would be nice to have a job and clientele waiting, wouldn't it?''

Garrick paused. Then he said, ''I might not ever be back, Sheldon.''

"Oh, for...! Listen to me, Garrick. You're forty. You lost the wife you loved. You've just gone off on a tangent. It's understandable, but not a permanent condition. Not for a man like you. You *need* the challenge and excitement of the Street. What could ever take its place?"

Love could, Garrick told himself. But he said nothing about his feelings to Sheldon. They talked for a while longer, arguing about his unwillingness to return to defend himself and his unreasonableness in stubbornly remaining at the ranch where he couldn't possibly be having a satisfying professional experience. Garrick had to admit to himself there was truth in what his friend said.

Some truth. But not all of it, by a far piece. It was time, he decided, to see just where these feelings he had for Cat would take the two of them.

Cat noticed a big change in Garrick after the phone call. She had expected him to be drained and discouraged, since she was certain the call had something to do with his business problems. Instead, he seemed as cheerful as when he had started to work for her. Frequently, he would say things to make the girls laugh and even Jude would smile at his jokes from time to time. Toward her, he was affectionate almost to the point of being sexually aggressive, although he seemed to be deliberately holding back on that score.

It didn't help her keep her mind on ranch business.

He acted as if they were conducting a secret affair—a particularly torrid one no one else knew about. His eyes would gaze at her from across a room, and delicious shivers would rise from deep inside her. He went out of his way to touch her, but gently, fleetingly, maddeningly. Just enough to drive her absolutely crazy with desire for him. And she knew it had to be her overheated imagination, but he seemed to be getting handsomer every day. In the afternoons when she and the girls were working at their studies at the kitchen table, she would wander over to the open window and watch him. The sun had bronzed him Indian-dark by now and had added reddish highlights to his graying black hair. He worked with Jude for at least half the day now, and his muscles were hard and well-defined under skin impossibly smooth for a man his age. He was forty. He looked thirty at the outside—until one saw the experience and wisdom in his eyes, which made Cat's insides flip right out of control.

Her marriage had not been unsatisfying sexually, and she had not remained a woods-bound old maid since her escape from the city. But no man had ever promised her with a single, smoldering glance what Garrick Drexel promised every day, almost every time he *looked* at her. Cat was going out of her mind with suppressed sexual need.

Abby and Ellen didn't take long to start teasing her about him. They weren't unkind, but their frequent references to her "boyfriend" kept the matter uppermost in her mind when they were around. And after they had successfully passed the exams allowing them to become seniors, they were around all the time.

She settled them in as employees in earnest—much to the obvious approval of her "boyfriend." But with both of them maturing young women, and with Abby's relationship with Tom becoming more serious, Cat didn't take their teasing as just kids heckling an adult. They were seeing something quite intense developing and were reacting to it with embarrassment covered by jokes. What they were seeing was far more intense than anything they had witnessed before, Cat realized.

It was far more intense than anything she had experienced, as well. Garrick was still capable of spending the morning hours with her in the office, all business on the surface. But the volcano under the surface was as plain as the fact that he was making important improvements in her operations. Her groceries were now going to come in by truck over the pass from Jackson Hole, ensuring more regular delivery, since the drivers could stop at her place before heading down to Casper and then Denver. This eliminated hassling with the dealers down in Denver, who were less than eager to make her ranch an end run. Other changes involved purchasing feed and livestock supplies from a wholesaler. This one she fought.

"I don't like cutting out the local merchants," she said.

"Then talk to them about giving you a deal. With the wholesaler, you'd save over fifty percent during your busy season. It makes no sense to pay twice the price, Cat. It's simple arithmetic." His tone was kind, but firm. "Look. You could take the savings you'd accrue and apply them to making improvements around the place. Couldn't you justify doing that by employing local workers? They need money as much as the merchants. Maybe more."

His logic was painfully inescapable. Reluctantly and somewhat resentfully, she finally gave in. It was like this every day. Conflict over business. Underlying unity in mutual desire. That was almost a tangible thing between them as they sat in the office each day, the early summer sun sparking gold off the dust motes in the air.

ON THE WEDNESDAY before the Memorial Day weekend and the arrival of the first summer guests, Cat declared a holiday. It would be the last opportunity any of them would have for free time and personal business until the season ended. Jude, Abby and Ellen fled the ranch like birds freed.

She thought surely Garrick would imitate them, knowing he needed to check on his personal situation—he had confided some of what his lawyer had told him. But when she went to the corral to catch Sam for a ride up to the high meadows, Garrick was waiting for her.

"Jude said you were probably going up to the meadows," he said, grinning. "Don't you think it's time you showed me the high country, boss?" He was dressed for riding in jeans and a denim jacket, with proper boots on his feet.

Cat's heart did a giddy kind of lurch. "I figured you'd be spending the day on the telex," she said nervously, using her left hand to take down the lightweight saddle she'd used when she had to handle Sam alone. "Don't you want to use my phone?"

"I don't want to use any phone." He took the saddle from her. "And put this thing away. Jude said it's much too dainty for the Black Marauder." Before she could protest, he had captured Sam and outfitted the annoyed animal with the proper tack. She mounted before he could offer help. Then she watched in surprised admiration as he prepared a mount for himself, choosing a big, rawboned red mare with little sense and a trainload of patience. The mare, aptly named Grace, was a wise choice for an inexperienced horseman, and Cat felt further approval when he indicated that she should lead off. He understood the pecking order of trail horses. Sam would no more have stood for following the mare than he would have flown to the moon.

They rode wordlessly, each enjoying the sights, sounds and scents of the high country on the perfect summer morning. A soft breeze stirred the pines. Birds called. Squirrels and other mountain rodents scolded and piped. The horses blew air through their nostrils occasionally and plodded along. The sway of their slow gaits was soothing.

Cat, however, did not feel soothed. From Garrick's rearward position, he had an excellent opportunity to study her at will, and she could almost feel his gaze caressing her. Had he stayed behind and come along with seduction in his mind? If that was the case, would she care? Would she welcome it?

There were still so many problems: his attitude toward her business style, his willful disregard for his own problems, his obvious dance of romance lately. What was it Garrick really wanted from her? She suspected she would find out part of the answer this very morning.

They halted at a meadow where snow still lurked under the pines. High enough to offer a clear view of the magnificent Tetons in the distance, the meadow was a window to another world. Soft, green grass was already springing up out of winter's dead yellow mat. Here and there the stems of what would be an unbelievable profusion of flowers were starting to push up. Cat took a deep breath of air so pure it had practically no odor. The creak of saddle leather and a long, low whistle indicated Garrick had pulled up beside her. Sam didn't even lay back his ears at the mare.

"The vestibule to paradise." Garrick was staring at the scenery.

"That sounds like one of my old commercials. Just wait. It gets better."

"I don't see how it could." His tone was hushed. Awed. "Maybe for the first time I'm beginning to see things clearly...." The sentence trailed off and he looked down at the ground.

"What is it, Garrick? What's the matter?" She had expected romance, but she was suddenly getting the feeling that the man was deeply troubled.

Finally, he looked directly at her. "I have a request, Catherine," he said. "A request and a confession."

CHAPTER NINE

"A...A CONFESSION?" She was absolutely certain now that she was about to hear a farewell speech. All the emotion she had thought he was showing by his looks and touches over the past days meant nothing—worse than nothing. He had been indulging in flirtation knowing it would come to nothing!

"I've made some mistakes in my life," he said. "I've hurt some people I didn't mean to, though some I did. All of that I regret. But I'm basically not a bad guy. In fact, I flatter myself occasionally that I've done positive things for people from time to time." He paused, now glancing over at her. "I told you I did love my wife. In a way, I even cherished her."

"Yes." The words stuck in her throat. *Here it comes,* she warned herself. *Keep a stiff upper lip!* "I know."

"But I've been thinking lately I made one major mistake, been traveling in one disastrously wrong direction. I've based almost all my existence, my security on a poor foundation, Cat. I've made money my reason for being. In spite of my caring, my love for others, it's always been more important for me to be financially secure. You were right when you accused me of thinking only about the bottom line. You were right to say that money was everything to me. I was raised that way, and I've lived that way. I don't know how to change. Or if I can—or even if I really want to. But I think I *ought* to." He sounded absolutely miserable.

She was silent for a moment, digesting what she had just heard. It wasn't what she had expected at all. Deep inside, a fluttering of hope, of excitement, started. "You can't blame yourself, Garrick. We are both products of our environments and upbringings.''

"To a certain extent." He sounded more assured. "But we *can* change if we want or need to badly enough. At least we can try to modify ourselves. I've done it before. I can do it again. And I have to believe this is one reason I left New York. I was looking for something, and I think I may have found it. You heard the confession, Cat. Ready for the request?''

"I suppose so." She was surprised enough by what he had already said to be ready for anything now.

"Good." His gaze was hard on her now. "I've never known anyone like you. At least not well. You don't care about that bottom line. You care about the place and the people. If you never made a dime profit, I think you'd be perfectly happy. It's the experience that turns you on, not the security it might represent." He pointed to the far peaks. "For all we know, a storm off those things could kill us someday. But I don't think you'd care or mind, just as long as we had this view today.''

She couldn't look at the view. She was glued to his every word, his every nuance of expression. That is, as far as she was able to see. Her eyes were filled with tears.

"I need to know how to be like that," he said with such intensity she almost gasped aloud. He loosened his horse's reins and reached out to touch her arm with both hands, gripping her tightly enough for her to feel the pressure through the cast. "Cat, I know I came out here for a reason. Something or someone guided me to you. I love you. But more than that, I admire you. Show me how to be secure with nothing but the air and the trees and you.''

"Garrick, I—''

"Don't say anything yet." His arms went around her and lifted her from the saddle. "Just kiss me.''

How they both landed on the ground she would never know. In her memory, they floated together to the soft grass, but of course that was impossible. With his strength and love surrounding her, however, the realities of gravity, an awkward cast on her arm and the wetness of melting snow on the ground seemed as nothing.

He kissed her, caressed her and spoke words of endearment until she was wild with desire. No one had ever raised her to that level of excitement before, and the intensity of it almost frightened her. He removed none of her clothing, but his hands were so sure and skillful she might as well have been totally naked to his touch. Crying out his name, she arched to him, winding her fingers through his thick hair.

Garrick felt he'd found paradise for certain. Fulfillment of his own desire was the farthest thing from his mind as he caressed her. He sought only her pleasure, and as he realized how much he was giving her, his heart nearly burst with joy. *This must truly be love!* he thought in wonder. She tasted both sweet and salty and smelled of her own unique perfume—woman, flowers, leather and horse. Never in his life had he experienced such feelings for another human being.

When finally her soft cries told him she had received all he could give her, he drew away slightly, still holding her, but allowing her to regain some composure without the embarrassment of his observing the process. He had taken her by storm, he realized. And Cat was not a woman who was likely to consider that normal behavior in a lover. He shifted his hips, grateful for the constraints of his jeans. In loose clothing he would have lost control of himself entirely.

"What's the big idea," she said abruptly, her voice still husky with passion. She hoisted herself up on her good elbow and stared down at him.

"Huh?" He stared back. Surely, she'd been able to tell what the "big idea" had been. He *knew* she had been pleased.

"I said, what's the big idea, buster." Her words were clipped and tough, but she was smiling gently. Lovingly. "You've just gone all out for me and left nothing for yourself." She touched him with the fingertips of her right hand. "Does the cast put you off?"

"No, of course not."

"Then what? I always felt this kind of thing ought to be a two-way street. You know, with both parties enjoying it." She frowned. "Unless there's something wrong."

"Nothing's wrong. I just didn't feel I had the right to take you beyond what I just did." He was beginning to feel highly embarrassed by her frank questioning. Didn't she see he was only trying to be a gentleman?

"Garrick Drexel." She sat up, laughing. "I'm thirty-four. It's been a long, long time since anyone could look my way and say, 'Hey, there's the last virgin in America.' You were so sweet to do what you did for me. It was wonderful. Now, I'd like not only to return the favor, but to make it a mutually enjoyable experience."

He sat up gingerly. "Here?" He looked around. The meadow was empty except for the two horses, both of which had moved a decorous or disgusted distance away and were cropping the new grass. "I mean, wouldn't you want to wait until we could be indoors? In a bed?"

Her laughter pealed again like a sweet bell. "Afraid of getting sunburned on your buns?"

He blushed. Then his embarrassment fled. "No. And maybe it won't be *my* buns that get burned." They reached for each other.

The rest of the day they made love in the high meadow. The only hunger they had was for one another, and nothing seemed to slake it. Her fire and passion were equal to his, and if she didn't speak the words of love, as he did, it didn't matter. Her actions and touches spoke louder to him than any words. Cat Cantrell might not realize it yet, he believed, but she loved him, too.

Cat reveled in the wildness and freedom she felt with him. His declarations and demonstrations of love released any inhibitions she might have had, and her body rewarded her mind and heart by giving her more pleasure than she had dreamed possible. In tandem with him she rose from one height to another, spiraling down into warm valleys for what seemed only moments before rushing upward again into crests of delight and joy. Although they were lying beneath the sky on damp earth with grass crushed under their bodies, it seemed as if they were soaring beyond the natural realm into an otherworldly one. It was a lovers' dream of a day.

But all dreams end, and this one had its curtain drawn by lengthening shadows and a setting sun. Cat felt the air start to grow chilly and reached over to prod her dozing lover. "Hey," she murmured. "Time to head back."

"We have to ride?" He didn't move. "I thought they were sending an ambulance."

She prodded him again, this time less gently. "Ambulances can't get up here, sweetheart. A search-and-rescue helicopter, maybe. But I'd be pretty mortified if the guys found us like this. Could you at least attempt to get dressed?"

"As in clothes?"

She leaned over and kissed him. Both had swollen lips from hours of caresses, so she was careful. Even so, he groaned and put a hand to his mouth.

"You've gone and branded me, woman," he said, opening his eyes and looking up at her with all the love he had tried to express with his voice and body that day. "I'm yours forever, I guess."

She kissed him again without responding, and suddenly her mood became bittersweet. What lay in the future was a mystery. She would hold their wonderful, precious day forever in her memory, but she would not hold it over his head. He wasn't branded any more than she was. He was as free as a bird. "Come on, big guy," she said. "I'm starved, and no one's at the ranch to start supper for us. We have to fix it ourselves."

He sat up, galvanized. "That's right. No one's home. We have the place to ourselves."

"Garrick." She picked up her underwear and started dressing. "What happened here today was wonderful. Unbelievable. If anyone told me two people could share themselves like this, I never would have believed it. But the ranch is primarily a place for families to vacation. You and I can't—''

He got up and kissed her cheek. "I know that, love. I know. I understand you're still the boss, too, and I'm still the hired hand. That hasn't changed. I wouldn't jeopardize your reputation or your business. Surely you know that."

"I guess so." She couldn't meet his gaze. It would never be the same again between them. They could never recapture the glory of the day, nor could they pretend nothing had happened. What was she going to do? No, what were *they* going to do?

Garrick watched her. She had retreated into herself, and that hurt. He tried to understand. She needed time and space—she needed to think and to believe in his love. He would do his best to help her. "This is behind us," he said, pulling on his own clothing and trying to hide his feelings of disappointment. "We'll go back and behave as if nothing has changed. Today was a holiday, as you announced this morning. Once we hit the ranch, it's business as usual. I have no problem with that, boss."

"Good." Her heart sank.

"But don't think that every time I'm near you or see you across the yard I won't remember in detail the time we spent here." He took her chin in his hand, lifted her face and stared into her eyes. "Don't think that at the next opportunity, I won't try for another day or night like this, Cat. I want you and I love you. Nothing can change that."

Her spirits rose again. Perhaps they could work it out. Maybe they were meant to be lovers. Maybe he was right about having been led to her, crazy as it sounded. He certainly had saved her and had made her feel things she'd never known before. "Okay," she whispered, and they kissed softly.

They rode back to the ranch and spent a quiet evening eating dinner and talking about their pasts. Garrick had already shared much of himself with her, but now she found out why Willis Kent was so afraid of him.

"I told you I was in the service," he said as they cuddled on the sofa in front of a fire that was hardly needed in the mild weather, but romantic nevertheless. "Well, this sergeant got ahold of me because of my size and taught me more about boxing than I had already learned in high school and college. I was good. I became company champ, and a target for every fast gun in the division."

"That's very Western talk for an Eastern dude," she teased.

"I'm working on it. Anyhow, my last fight was a terrible experience. The guy used weighted gloves. Broke my arm before I figured out what was going on. That's why I knew so much about the pain you felt, love." He patted the cast affectionately. "Personal experience."

"But why would that make anyone afraid of you? You were injured."

"Oh, yes. I was injured. But you should have seen the other guy. I lost my temper and nearly killed him with my good arm. No charges were brought because I had been wronged, but it's all in my service record. How do you think a little wimp like Kent feels after being attacked by someone with that in their background?"

"I'm certain he will stay as far from you as possible," she said, glad to have another mystery about him cleared up.

"But if you had been seriously injured, God help him," he muttered darkly, and Cat shivered.

For her part, she revealed the whole shameful business with Benjamin Jones, her ex-husband. Benny had been a charmer in the right place at the right time. He had succeeded in winning the trust and love of the successful but lonely transplanted cowgirl with a talent for making money with her voice. Unable to see beyond the fact that the man seemed to worship her, she fell in love and married him without much thought. It was a mistake she had lived to regret bitterly.

"He sounded so sure of himself," she explained, "so confident about money that I just let him take over. I accepted everything he told me about himself at face value. I never checked on a thing. He seemed competent, optimistic, and was unfailingly cheerful and loving. I never saw the man frown or get upset about a thing. He seemed the perfect business manager."

"Why does the parallel make me uneasy?"

"There's no parallel, Garrick. If you don't think you were checked out by Nelson down to the brand of underwear you prefer, you don't know the man. You may be in some trouble back in the city, but not here. Nelson believes you."

"And you?"

"I believe you're innocent of any wrongdoing. I think you have a problem with other people believing that."

"Tell me more about Benny." He didn't seem eager to pursue the subject of his troubles, so she let it drop. For the time.

"I learned after the divorce proceedings began that I was only one of a string of victims." She blushed at the memory of her stupidity. "He was a pro, siphoning off savings and investments, and when he had bled me dry financially, it was bye-bye, sugar."

"And he couldn't be touched legally?" He rubbed her hand between his own.

"That's right. We were married. I had willingly given him the job of managing my money. His losing it didn't give me the right to bring charges against him. He was a money junkie, who got his kicks out of gambling in the market and commodities." She laughed. "I'll never have to worry about a man like that again, because I'll never be rich enough to attract one again."

"There's rich, and then there's rich." Garrick pulled her closer. Her animosity toward profit was now clear. If you didn't make it, she believed, then no one could steal it from you. When he considered it, he was amazed she had trusted him enough to let him into her house, much less become her lover. With his background and attitude about business, he surely represented much of what she had hidden from for years. Turning to kiss her, he felt himself brimming with love for the wonderful, complex, vulnerable human being that she was.

But deep down he wondered if he was strong and unselfish enough to give her what she needed—if, indeed, he was supposed to be the one to fill her life and her heart. It was a thought that brought him much disquiet.

THE NEXT DAY guests began arriving. Cat had slept like a log, having said good-night to Garrick reluctantly. They had agreed not to spend the night together. Doing so would have tempted them to make love again, and that was out of the question. While there was no reason to keep the romance between them a dark secret, it would have been inappropriate to make it obvious how far that romance had already taken them. But limiting themselves to looks and touches after the day in the meadow was almost worse than nothing at all.

Cat coped by expending her energies as she usually did this time of year. She knocked herself out to make her guests comfortable and happy. With the group in residence, it wasn't too difficult a task.

"Miss Cat? Miss Cat!" Two childish voices rang out across the yard early Saturday morning. Looking out the kitchen window, Cat waved at the Tanner twins. The tow-headed boys and their parents were regular visitors to the ranch. The kids had ridden their first horses under her careful tutelage and now, at nine years of age, the boys were excellent horsemen, almost ready to go out on trails by themselves. Almost. Cat had a ride planned for them later that morning. Clearly, the youngsters were eager to get going. She signaled they could come into the kitchen, usually off limits for guests.

They tumbled in, bringing a rush of fresh morning air with them. "Can I have Sam, Miss Cat?" pleaded one boy. She thought it was Roy, although not having seen them for a long time, she found it nearly impossible to tell them apart. Only their behavior differentiated one from the other, Roy being the more aggressive youngster. She set two cinnamon rolls on the table and indicated they could help themselves.

"I think we'd better give Sam to your dad," she said, smiling as the rolls disappeared. "They're both kind of large, and Sam works better under a heavy load, don't you think?"

"Dad ain't as big as your new guy," Troy or Roy commented around a mouthful of roll. "Where's he come from? He talks funny."

Cat stifled laughter. It hadn't occurred to her that Garrick's New York accent would sound strange to ears that had only heard local talk. "Mr. Drexel comes from back East," she explained. "He's out here for... for his health."

"He don't look sick to me," one of the twins commented. Then the conversation returned to the more important topic of who would get which horse for the trail ride.

Breakfast was a confused, fun affair. Cat had fallen into the rhythm of cooking for a dozen or more with no trouble. Since it was her policy to have employees and guests mingle at mealtimes, this morning the long table set up on the enclosed porch off the kitchen was jammed. In addition to Garrick, Jude, Abby and Ellen, there were the four Tanners, a young couple from South Dakota named Madison and a family of five from Colorado. The Tanner boys eyed the newcomers warily, clearly intending to make certain the other kids understood this was *their* ranch. Cat spent the meal playing diplomat, and peace was established. The kids went off together to explore the barn for kittens and undoubtedly to swap tall tales.

When Cat went into the office, Garrick was waiting for her. "You handled that potential bunch of tiny terrorists like a pro," he said, grinning.

She shrugged. "All I did was defuse a notion or two. The Tanners are understandably territorial about this place. They've been coming here since they were four."

"The little devils sure gave me the once-over last night." He chuckled. "I'm afraid I've never been much good around kids. I think they scare me."

"But didn't you want children?" she asked, hearing an odd note in his voice.

"Yes. But Ann never tried. I know why now. It would have killed her sooner."

Cat came around behind him and started massaging the muscles of his shoulders. "Well, from now on, Mr. Drexel, you've got kids. I'm making you the official kiddie wrangler here, in charge of and responsible for anyone under five feet tall."

"Cat!"

"Trust me. Just remember how much more energy they have to use foxing adults than we do looking for it. You'll do fine."

"Cat." He was almost whining, stopping only when she kissed him soundly. He left the office still complaining that he was certain he was about to make a complete fool of himself.

But she proved correct. After some initial sparring, he established who was a kid and who was the kid wrangler. However, he made no effort to conceal his ignorance from the Tanners, and asked their opinions whenever possible. By trail-ride time, he congratulated himself on having won some grudging respect.

It wasn't that easy.

"You're going to ride that big old fat red horse," one of the boys sneered as Garrick prepared Grace, his preferred mount.

"I'm riding this horse," he said defensively, "because I like her. And if she doesn't like me, she's kept it to herself. I like that in a lady, don't you?"

The boys just looked at each other, then Garrick. He realized he had lost whatever ground he had gained that morning.

But by the end of the weekend, he felt more secure in his new role. Cat did, too. "You were a smash, Mr. Drexel," she said fondly. "The Tanners like you."

"News to me." He was smiling.

"The heck it is. Listen, the boys are coming back in two weeks after their school is out. I'm going to put them in a cabin with you."

"In with *me!*" He took her shoulders in his hands. "Cat, what are you trying to do to me?"

"Cheer up. They can't do your ego much damage in a week. Besides, it'll do you good to commune with kindred souls. Last night after supper, I heard them trading trail treasures with the Lincoln kids. Money changed hands. The three of you have lots... Awk!" She broke off just as he lunged for her. Spinning and sprinting, she raced barely out of reach into the barn. He caught up with her, as she had intended, toward the back and next to a pile of fresh hay.

He trapped her with his arms. "Do I detect something deliberate about the route taken and the destination gained?"

She put her arms around his neck. "I've missed you so," she whispered. "Being so close, it's so hard."

"Not yet." He chuckled and nuzzled her neck. "But I'm working on it."

"You!" She aimed a kick at his shin, then yelped as she was pulled off balance and down onto the springy pile of hay. "You," she said yearningly. "Garrick, I've never felt like this before."

He managed to control the leap of hope in his heart. Nudging her to move back so they wouldn't be visible to anyone casually entering the barn, he said lightly, "You can't mean I'm your first hayride, boss."

"Don't tease." She laughed and threw hay at him. "I mean I really like you, Garrick—in addition to feeling other things, of course. I like you," she said in the same dreamy tone he would expect another woman to use for the words he really wanted to hear.

"I like you, too," he whispered, lowering his body slowly onto her. He could wait, he thought. He could wait until she was ready to say and mean it when she told him she loved him. He could wait.

Couldn't he?

CHAPTER TEN

"OH!" CAT GROANED WITH RELIEF as the last of the splintered cast slid off her arm. The exposed skin was sickly white and wrinkled, but it felt wonderful to be free of the hated encumbrance. She wiggled her fingers.

"Now, it's been six weeks," Doc Turner told her. "You take it easy with that wing for a while longer, and you'll be good as new."

"Don't make me any promises, Doc," Cat warned, grinning. "I stopped believing in the tooth fairy a long, long time ago. Am I really back in one piece?"

"You're healed, honey," he assured her. "You'll have a tiny scar and the arm may be prone to breaking again because the structure has been weakened. But if you stay off unreliable horses and let those two men of yours do the heavy lifting, you shouldn't have a problem in the world. Might twinge you a bit when it rains, but that doesn't happen often enough around here to matter, does it?"

Cat agreed.

It was actually a week past the scheduled removal of her cast. The ranch had been so busy she hadn't had a chance to escape into town until today, and Doc had kindly fitted her in. Not only was she occupied with regular, reserved guests, but the number of drop-ins was way above what she usually expected so early in the season. The extra income made Garrick happy, but she was feeling the strain of not having a moment to herself. While she was pleased with the opportunity to pay off a string of debts—she'd even managed a partial repayment of her state loan—she had been growing increasingly dissatisfied with conditions at the

l schedule didn't allow for the
ustomed to. She felt her treat-
ng. And it had not been a good

l shared that wild time in the
than a stolen kiss, furtively
em. While she agreed with her
ot exactly the most romantic of
igs, dust, seeds and the occa-
that time was burned into her
t would keep her tossing and
ely bed. How she yearned for

Sue Futrell had come into the
noticing. ''I've got a little list
nurse said, smiling.
he paper, on which was out-
uld take with her arm. ''I was
n so busy out at Cat's Cradle,
''
Sue didn't sound as if she be-
n time was what Cat had been
ourself too hard, now. It's not
d with that.
the first thing she did was un-
o the sun. The sooner her skin
r she was going to feel. Glanc-
had suggested an application
d adjusted to light. That made
idewalk toward the drugstore.
had everyone else. Hers was
suffered. Tom and Abby had
day afternoons, and then only
dates, Abby would sulk and
tting everyone know how dis-
tion. Cat had plain run out of
so busy was such a great thing.

Well, maybe it wasn't. She entered the drugstore, registering the pinging of the little bell the owner had installed above the door. Maybe she ought to put out a No Vacancy sign to discourage extra customers when they had enough guests to deal with comfortably, she mused. It was definitely not a good idea to work her staff—or herself—to death.

"Hi, Cat," Theo Fisher, owner and pharmacist, called out. "What can I get you?"

"Sunscreen." She held up her bare arm. "Doc cut me loose this morning, and I don't want to fry it when I go out on the trail for the first time."

"Got just the thing for you." Theo bustled out from behind the prescription counter and led her over to a shelf with skin preparations on it. Handing her a jar of cream, he extolled its virtues until she laughingly agreed to purchase it. She was standing at the cash register when she heard the voice.

"Miss Cantrell?" Low, well-modulated and female. Cat turned.

The woman was elegant, groomed to a fault, with perfect makeup and the kind of hairdo that required at least two visits a week to a stylist. In spite of the heat she wore a suit, obviously custom-cut for her trim figure. Automatically, Cat glanced down for the briefcase, and sure enough, the woman clutched one in her left hand while her right one held the strap of a smart little purse.

"I'm Cat Cantrell," Cat said, certain she was confronting someone from Garrick's past. The woman looked as out of place in Theo's drugstore as Garrick had so long ago out on the highway. "What can I help you with?"

"Possibly nothing." On the surface, the woman didn't seem contemptuous, only polite. But scorn was glowing deep in her green eyes—green eyes that looked quite striking with her dark red hair. "I'm looking for Garrick Drexel and was told you might be able to assist me."

"He works for me." Cat tried to keep a pleasant expression on her own face. "He's out at the ranch right now."

"So I understand." Once more, Cat saw that look betraying inner disgust. "But when I called there, the young lady who answered the telephone told me Mr. Drexel was...busy."

"I expect he is." Cat smiled. "You see, we have an unusually large number of guests right now and..."

"Her *exact* words were, I believe, 'He's up to his behind in rug rats.'" The disgust and contempt were not hidden now.

Cat wasn't sure whether to laugh or to be alarmed. "He's the kiddie wrangler," she explained. "And we're overloaded with young guests this week. My phone was answered by one of two seventeen-year-old girls who are currently working a dawn-to-dark shift. They tend to be a little short-tempered. If you need to talk to Garrick, I'll see you get the chance." She congratulated herself on her diplomacy and ability to keep cool. Something about this woman disturbed her deeply.

"That would be most kind of you," the other woman replied glacially. "You see, I'm his sister-in-law, Janet Norton, and I'm afraid I've some very bad news for him."

GARRICK WAS NOT only up to his rear in kids when they found him—he was up to his eyebrows in straw, dust, sweat and kittens. When Cat had arrived at the ranch with a silent, tight-lipped Janet Norton by her side in the Jeep, Ellen had informed them that the kiddie wrangler was in the barn with his charges, looking for kittens. He had, it seemed, formed a plan for population control among the fecund barn cats. Ellen hinted that the project was primarily designed to occupy the children while their parents were off for some high-country fishing with Jude, but that Garrick also intended to use the opportunity to instill a sense of teamwork in the youngsters. Curious, Cat led her reluctant companion to the designated building. What she saw when they got inside made her nearly double over with laughter.

Garrick and ten children, including the Tanner twins, were chasing and carefully capturing barn kittens. The kids were laughing and shrieking, the kittens mewing and occasionally spitting. Garrick was keeping up a running commentary about how they were going to keep the boy kittens away from the girl kittens. At least for a little while. "Until they're older," he said, making a dive for a particularly speedy little black cat, "and know what they're doing."

"They already know," yelled one of the twins. "Ain't that why there's so darn many of them?" He had three squirming kittens in his arms.

"Yeah, I guess." Garrick stood, the sable trophy held gently in his hands. Then he saw the women standing in the front of the barn. "Janet?" he said. The kitten jumped free.

"Hey," another child cried. "You let it get away!"

"It's okay, kids." He waved a hand. "Go ahead and play with the little guys gently. I don't think my idea would have worked very well, anyway." He brushed a hand through his hair and only succeeded in making himself look worse. "Hello, Janet," he said, coming toward them.

Cat watched. Janet Norton just stared at him as if he had crawled out from under a rock. He smiled, wiped his hands on his jeans and held one out to her. She didn't take it. "What in the hell are you doing, Garrick Drexel?" she snarled. "You really have lost your mind, haven't you."

Garrick looked as if he had been kicked. "I admit this isn't exactly Wall Street attire, Janet, but—"

"But you don't even look *civilized*!" Janet looked from her brother-in-law to the woman standing next to her. Neither one of them looked like decent people! The blonde was plain, with no makeup on and crow's-feet around her eyes. And that ugly, ugly white arm. Could she really be the reason Garrick had stayed away for so long? It made no sense. Then he caused a cold chill to rise in her heart when he went over to the creature and put his arm around her shoulders. She seemed to lean into him possessively.

"Maybe I'm not so civilized anymore, Janet," he said. "But I am happy. Happier than I've been for a long, long time. Can you understand that?"

She understood in a flash that almost made her gasp with pain. He had forgotten! He had already forsaken Ann's memory for this...this bitch in heat! Janet felt dizzy. No wonder her little scheme to lure him back to New York had failed.

"Janet said she had some bad news for you," Cat interjected, feeling thoroughly uncomfortable. She would have thought anyone who had known Garrick in New York would have laughed herself silly at the sight of him now, not dressed him down in such scathing tones. Clearly, something was amiss.

"I need to speak to you alone," Janet said, addressing Garrick as if Cat were hardly worth noticing.

He bristled. "Anything you say to me can be said in front of Cat."

"It's okay." Cat moved away from him. "I have to get lunch going, anyway." To Janet she said, "I'm sorry we're all booked up, otherwise I'd be delighted to offer you a cabin. In any event you are more than welcome to stay for lunch. It's on the house for relatives of the help."

"Thank you." She sounded more polite and in control. "I rented a room at that little motel on the edge of town. I wouldn't dream of putting you to any trouble. Garrick can clean up and drive me back after we've had our little talk."

"No, he can't." There was a decided edge to his voice now. "Cat needs my help at lunch. I'll take you back afterward." Sensing the potential for an unpleasant argument, Cat gathered the kids and shooed them out of the barn on the excuse that they had to wash before lunch. A few still carried kittens.

Garrick waited until she was out of earshot before turning to Janet. "That was quite a display of bad manners," he said, folding his arms across his chest. "This is one heck of a nice place and she's one heck of a nice lady."

Janet called on all her inner strength. Her aim was to get him back home, in his rightful place. Someone had to. "I'm sorry," she said. "But I'm upset. I have been so worried about you. And every day it looks as though they're going to indict you. Garrick, you must come back and defend yourself."

"No." He set his jaw. "I haven't done anything wrong, and I won't waste my time listening to lawyers argue with each other. Willis Kent cannot concoct a case against me. I am confident of that."

She started to cry. "I'm the only one putting flowers on Ann's grave now. Her apartment is so empty. Like a deserted tomb."

Garrick felt a shock of surprise. "*My* apartment? You've been in there?"

"She gave me a key before she died—when she was so sick, remember? You're her husband. You have to come home!" She was sobbing now.

Garrick put his arms around her and stroked her hair comfortingly. He may have gotten over his grief, but clearly Janet had not. What was so amazing was that he had never realized he represented some kind of link to her dead sister. No wonder she was exaggerating his problems. She would do anything to get him back to the place where she could still imagine Ann waiting for him every evening. "Janet," he said. "I know how you're feeling. I felt that way myself for a long time, but I got over it. You can get help."

"I don't need help." She stopped crying and pulled free. "*You* do. I'm sorry I got a little out of line there. I care for you, and it breaks my heart to think of you throwing away everything you and... you ever worked for. If you don't come back, your reputation will be irrevocably tarnished."

"Sheldon Sheridan indicated the same thing." Garrick grew thoughtful. Maybe there was more to all this than he had cared to think.

"Don't listen to Sheridan!" Janet's eyes grew wide and she grabbed him by the arm. "It's a conspiracy, don't you see? Sheridan, Jamison Pratt, others in the firm. I'm your only ally, Garrick. You must listen to me!"

"Sheldon Sheridan and Jamison Pratt in a conspiracy to discredit me? Don't be ridiculous, Janet. They are two of my oldest and dearest friends. I just won't believe anything against them." He glanced at his watch. "Anyhow, it's time for me to clean up for lunch. Why don't you look around the place while you wait? Or you can go inside and talk to Cat. You might find more to her than meets the eye. I know I have."

Janet picked the latter choice, less to find out about Cat Cantrell than to avoid walking on ground where dust and worse could ruin her shoes. Although she felt herself building to an emotional explosion because of Garrick's attitude, she maintained a calm exterior with the Cantrell woman.

"Garrick does seem quite happy here," she commented, leaning against a counter in the kitchen. "I honestly couldn't believe my eyes out there in the barn. He used to *hate* children."

Cat was busy assembling sandwiches. "I can't believe that. He's one of the kindest people I've ever known."

"Well, he just couldn't stand to have them around when he was married to my sister. That's why they never had any, you know."

"No." Cat carefully chopped lettuce. "I understood your sister had a heart condition and that was why—"

"My sister was perfectly healthy before she got married. It was the strain that finally..." Janet looked away, and Cat decided it was time to change the subject.

"Would you like to do something around the ranch this afternoon?" she asked. "I do feel bad about not being able to put you up. The facilities are yours."

"Oh, thank you, but no. I have paperwork waiting back at the motel. Actually, I wouldn't have taken the time to come out here at all if it hadn't been so important. Garrick doesn't seem to believe me, but he is this far from going to jail." She held up her thumb and index finger. They almost touched.

Cat just stared.

Janet offered no more details and left with Garrick right after lunch. When they were still gone two hours later, Cat rounded up the children and took them for a nature hike.

She tried to use the outing to take her mind off her worries, but she did not succeed.

When he finally returned close to supper time, he was withdrawn and pensive, uncharacteristically snappish and sarcastic. He sounded much like he had when she had first picked him up on the highway. She took it until after the evening camp fire, when all the kids except the Tanners were back under their parents' care.

"I want a word with you," she told him as he started to walk toward the cabin he shared with the boys without even saying good-night to her. He stopped, but didn't turn to face her.

"Not tonight, Cat. I'm beat."

"Tonight. Now. In my office."

When he turned, he was grinning tightly. "You're the boss, boss."

But nothing she could do or say could wring one word from him. "I *care* about you," she declared, pounding the desk. "Why won't you let me help?"

He spread his hands. "Cat, there's no problem, no need to help. I think Janet has simply blown a few things out of proportion. She's still grieving for Ann. She seems to think she'd feel better if I were home. She needs to learn to work through her feelings herself. If I went back, I'd just remain an emotional crutch for her."

"I don't believe that's all there is to it. She said you could go to jail."

"You don't go to jail for financial fraud, my love. You go to prison. The joint. Da big house."

"Don't joke with me, Garrick Drexel. I couldn't stand it if they took you away." Tears filled her eyes.

"Honey, don't cry." He came over and took her in his arms. "I haven't told you today how pretty you look without that damned cast." He raised her arm and kissed her pale wrist.

Cat knew full well he was deliberately distracting her, but his touch was irresistible. "My arm looks like a dead fish," she whispered as his lips moved along its sensitive surface.

"It'll tan." He reached the edge of her short sleeve and moved to her neck. "Say, I have an idea . . ."

"The twins?" Heat was building in her.

"I brought them back a stack of comics from town. They'll be busy for hours. What do you say?" His hands massaged the small of her back. "A real bed? No cast? What a deal!"

"Garrick, I—"

He kissed her and swept her up into his arms.

He undressed her and then himself with deliciously agonizing slowness and then explored her body leisurely. Love in bed, unencumbered by the cast, was everything the sexy huskiness in his voice had promised. His hands and lips drove all thoughts from her mind except thoughts of how to please him and make their joining more ecstatic. But it was the first time they had really been comfortable while making love, and the speed and intensity with which they reached the heights astounded her. Cat was taken far beyond anything they had known together and light-years beyond anything she had known with another man. When the experience subsided, she began to laugh and cry at the same time.

He gently touched her cheek, smoothing away the flow of tears. "I wasn't aiming to make you unhappy, love. Why the tears?"

"Just emotion. I'm laughing, too." She turned her head to look at him fully. "You reach me in places I didn't know existed. What's your secret?"

"I love my work." He sat up, grinning. "I'm dedicated to loving you, and I plan to keep on getting better and better at it." His expression suddenly turned quite serious. "I ought to be horsewhipped for not asking about this sooner, but you are protected, aren't you?"

She nodded, swallowing. So he really wasn't interested in children. When he hadn't checked with her the first time they had made love, she had wondered about it. He'd just been forgetful. Well, he didn't need to worry with her, that was for sure. "Garrick," she said, anxious to change the subject, "about your problems..."

He smiled again, but it seemed forced. "After what just happened, you can talk about my problems?"

"You know what I mean. New York. Janet. What are you going to do?"

"Not a thing. We talked. She calmed down and is going home tomorrow. I'm going to meet her for breakfast before she drives over to the airport, and I'm going to strongly suggest she make an appointment to see the guy who helped me so much, Peter Chance. He can straighten her out if anyone can. There shouldn't be a stigma attached to getting professional help when one loses perspective on one's life."

"But will she go?" Cat was sounding decidedly sleepy now. He leaned over and kissed her warm lips before making himself get out of bed and start to dress.

"I can't say," he replied. "All I can do is make the suggestion. Go on to sleep, love."

She was asleep before he was out the door.

Garrick was far less lucky in slumber. All night thoughts of New York, of what might actually be going on there and what really might be Janet's problem chased themselves around in his mind. By morning he had reached no solid conclusions and was testy and frustrated in spite of the memory of the love he had shared with Cat. He left to see Janet without trying to speak with Cat, thinking she might have trouble understanding that his mood had nothing to do with her.

That mood was downright ugly by the time he drove through town and turned off at the motel. By God, he was going to let Janet have it right between the eyes if she pulled any more crap on him about Sheldon and Jamison. A man couldn't have more loyal friends. And as for him needing to move back to be near Ann's grave... that was crazy. If he moved back it would only be because he found he couldn't be happy here. And at this point that seemed impossible.

He parked in front of the motel office to find out which was Janet's room. He had only dropped her off yesterday after an endless, pointless conversation and numerous cups of coffee at Sal's Café. Nelson Hendry's truck was parked in the lot, and Tom was coming out of one of the rooms. Garrick waved at the lawman and started for the office.

"Garrick!" The tone of Tom's voice made him turn. The younger man was becoming a friend of sorts; they often chatted when he came to court Abby. Garrick wondered if Tom just wanted to share some gossip about some goings-on in the motel.

But when he saw Tom's expression, he knew something far more serious was afoot. "It's about your sister-in-law," Tom said. "I think you'd better come look at her room."

CHAPTER ELEVEN

FOR A TERRIFYING MOMENT after he stepped into the motel room, Garrick looked around for Janet's body. When, to his intense relief, he saw no corpse, he began to take in the rest of the room.

And he was almost as terrified. The place looked as if a tornado had stormed through it. Pillows were ripped, the mattress slashed and the rest of the furniture smashed or tossed around. Nelson was on his knees by the overturned bureau, picking up bits of things and placing them in small plastic bags.

"'Lo, Garrick," he said. "You got some pretty strange relations, boy."

"S-she's my sister-in-law," he stammered. "Not exactly a blood relation. What the hell happened here?"

"You tell me." Nelson heaved his bulky figure upright. "Matt Herzog, the manager, said some folks started complaining about noise around two. He was gonna come check, then decided he was too tired, that he'd wait and see if things got really rough. It all seemed like it settled down and he went back to sleep. When the maid came to clean up this morning, she found the place like this. Your sister-in-law was gone."

"My God." Garrick ran a hand through his hair. "Do you suppose somebody attacked her, did all this?"

"Nope." Nelson handed him a note enclosed in a bag. Through the clear plastic, Garrick could read Janet's terse words of apology to the manager. She sounded as if she was apologizing for missing a tea party.

"Left a thousand bucks to cover damages," Nelson informed him. "Matt ain't too happy, but he figures it's cheaper than pressing charges. Me, I ain't so sure she ought not to be picked up. Looks like she's a few cans shy of a six-pack, if you ask me."

"Um." Garrick thought quickly. "Do you have to take legal action, Sheriff? Because I was planning on asking her to see a friend of mine in New York. He's a psychiatrist, a professional counselor. Helped me out of an emotional jam when my wife died."

Nelson frowned. "Think she'll see him?"

Garrick hesitated. "Honestly, I don't know. She came here with some crazy story about my old partner and my lawyer trying to frame me. I don't know what to believe. She seems pretty mixed up one minute and fine the next. Look, she didn't hurt anyone. It would be a big mess, trying to bring her back over a trashed motel room. Maybe...maybe she met someone at a bar or something. It's unlikely, but possible. And she did pay for damages."

Nelson eyed him. "You're kinda going out on a limb for someone who ain't a blood relative. You sure this is what you want to do?"

"I'm sure." He wasn't, but his conscience wouldn't let him give any other answer. As soon as he could, he would get to a phone and try to deal with her directly.

Finally, Nelson agreed to let the matter pass. He was, however, planning to keep the evidence and photographs of the mess. Garrick left him puttering in the room and muttering to himself about crazy Eastern females.

Tom followed him outside. "I know this ain't the best time," he said. "But could I talk to you for a minute? It's personal."

"Sure." Garrick leaned against the door of his car. "What's on your mind, Tom?" Maybe it would help to listen to someone else's problem for a change.

"Abby." The young man looked miserable. "I don't know what's going on with us."

"Hey." Garrick clapped him on the shoulder. "Welcome to the wonderful world of romance. It's usually like that, in my experience."

"That's really what I need to talk to you about." Tom edged closer and lowered his voice slightly. "Experience. You see, um, Abby and I... Well, we haven't...um."

"Fine." Garrick felt a little taken aback. "She's only seventeen, Tom."

"Yeah." He tilted his Stetson back and scratched his head. "But she's been real touchy-like lately, and I was wondering if she, you know, *wanted* to. How do you tell about a thing like that?"

Garrick groaned inwardly. Here he was, almost at his wits' end over Janet, being asked advice by a child in a sheriff's uniform! Not for the first time he wondered where old Nelson Hendry got off giving the boy the job in the first place. It was far too responsible a position for a kid who didn't even know if he should make love to his girlfriend or not. "Do you love her?" he asked.

"Oh, yes, sir!" The earnestness on his features was undeniable. "I want to marry her after she graduates. We'd only have to wait another year."

Garrick put his hand on Tom's shoulder. "Then wait another year for the other stuff, too, son. If she loves you, she won't mind. Fact is, down the line, she'll appreciate you more."

"Think so?" Tom had brightened considerably.

"Yes, I do." Garrick received Tom's effusive thanks, prayed he had said the right thing and headed home. On the way he asked himself just how hypocritical it was for him to advise abstinence for the young couple when he and Cat were setting erotic milestones with their lovemaking. It was, after all, only a matter of age.

But when he really thought about it, was really honest with himself, he knew he wanted to marry Cat. He wasn't at all sure Tom and Abby would get that far. The problems ahead of him and Cat weren't so insurmountable that he couldn't think about someday establishing a permanent relationship with her.

But would she want the same thing with him? So far, he was definitely playing second fiddle to the ranch. Could he stand to live the rest of his life that way? God, but life was complex! And he had come West seeking simplicity and answers. Whey were they so damned elusive? By the time he neared the ranch turnoff, he was in a highly volatile emotional state. And the sight that met his eyes triggered his temper before he could think about it. He screeched to a stop, leaped out of the car and yelled at Cat, "What the hell are you doing?"

Cat straightened and stared. The man who was standing by the sign in front of her had no resemblance to the sweet, thoughtful lover who had taken her to new heights last night. His hair was wild, his eyes were wide and high spots of color stained his cheeks. He looked like a man who had run a hard race. And lost badly.

"I'm fixing the sign, if it's any of your business," she snapped, stung and hurt by his behavior.

"You aren't fixing anything. You're *damaging* something, though." He strode over and jerked off the No Vacancy addition. "What's the big idea?"

"The big idea," she said, snatching the sign from his grasp, "is that everyone on this ranch, including the idiot I'm looking at, has been under far too much strain for the past few weeks. I'm shutting down except for guests who have booked in advance. We are all taking a break!" If her glare could have killed, she knew she would have incinerated him on the spot.

"You can't do that!"

"The hell I can't! It's my ranch!"

"Cat, you're making a sizable profit. In another month you'll be able to pay off the rest of the state loan. Two more months like this and you—"

"Two more months at this pace, and everyone will either drop dead or quit. I know my people, Garrick. They're loyal as the day is long and just as hardworking. I've been asking too much of them. I won't do it just for money.''

He glared at her for a moment, then, without a word, he turned and got into his car. The gravel spray his tires shot up when he hit the ranch road spattered around her like tiny bullets.

Well, hell, Cat thought as she watched the car disappear around a turn in the road. A plume of dust marked its progress. What kind of burr had he gotten under his saddle now? She sighed and forced herself to return to her work, refusing to give in to tears. How could he be so changeable? Which was the real Garrick Drexel? The lover or the hard-nosed money man? She had better be finding out soon, before it was too late, before her heart was lost once more to someone who would only stomp on it. After securing the No Vacancy sign to its chains, she took out a pair of pliers from her belt and squeezed the links shut. It would stay put even in a high wind.

She walked out to the road, wanting to give herself a small break from the madhouse that was Cat's Cradle. Then she trudged back, wondering at the fickleness of the human heart. Maybe it was already too late for her. If she wasn't in love with him, she was as close as she imagined it was possible to come. His arrogant, nasty attitude hurt far more than she cared to admit even to herself. But she wasn't going to let *him* know the power he had over her! Never again!

She kicked at dry clods of dusty earth laying beside the road. He had been fine the previous night. Fine and loving. In the interval, he had gone to see Janet off. Something must have happened to upset him. She squared her shoulders. He was *not* going to get away without telling her what was going on. She would get it out of him one way or the other!

The ranch would be relatively peaceful after noon, she reflected as she walked up to the yard around her house. Several families were leaving—the people in one group had already packed and were on their way. Others were loading suitcases for a late-morning departure. She waved and went into the ranch house.

Garrick was in the office. She could hear his voice, tight with tension, as she stood in the living room. Feeling strangely calm, almost emotionally numb, she went to where he was.

He was seated behind the desk, phone clamped to his ear. When she came in, he looked up, expressionless, and cupped his hand over the receiver. "You were right. I was wrong," he said. "Please don't leave. Sit down." He indicated the other chair in the room. Bemused and annoyed, Cat pulled it in front of the desk where she could watch him closely.

"Yes," he said into the phone. "Dr. Peter Chance. No, I don't want to leave a message. I'll hold. Just tell him it's Garrick Drexel and it's an emergency." His voice was as quiet and calm as if he was talking about the weather, but the knuckles of his fingers on the receiver were white. He cupped the phone again and spoke to Cat.

"I apologize for my behavior," he said. "I was upset to start with, and when I saw you with that sign, I came kind of unglued. I had no right to take out my frustration and anger on you like that."

"Garrick, what..."

He waved her to silence. "Hello, Pete. Yes, it really is me. I know. I am one for leaving without explanations. But it was the best thing that's ever happened to me." He glanced at Cat, and she saw all the warmth and love of the night before reflected in his eyes. "But that's not why I'm calling. Remember my sister-in-law, Janet Norton?"

Cat listened, horrified, as he described the destruction of Janet's motel room. It didn't take a professional to figure out that the woman was seriously disturbed. To Cat's relief, it now sounded as if Garrick was taking the situation seriously. And he was letting her know what was going on at last!

"No, I'm not coming back," he said. "I have no real control over her. I can only recommend she see you or someone like you. That's all I can do.

"No, the condition of the market had nothing to do with why I left, Pete. I wanted more out of life, and I've found it here. You need to see this country to believe it." He paused, listening. "Yes, there's a very special person here," he added, staring at her.

A tingle of excitement mingled with fear shot through Cat. It was already too late for her. She wasn't just in love, she *loved* Garrick Drexel, warts and all!

She had been in love with her ex-husband, so she knew the difference between the infatuation type of love and real love. Even now, she could objectively admit that Garrick's appearance was no match for Benny's Greek-god good looks. That man had the face of an angel, but she could only remember seeing him smiling. He had always been pleasant, passionate, accommodating. She had never seen Benny Jones angry, upset, confused or frightened—or any of the other ways she had seen the man in front of her look and behave during the past few days and weeks. Benny had been all false front. Garrick was showing her his honest heart! Good, bad and indifferent, she had been getting to know the real man in spite of his reluctance to discuss his personal problems. Awe and love filled her in the face of this realization. She felt she couldn't bear to sit still another second.

Garrick finally finished the call. Chatting with Pete had made him slightly nostalgic for the intellectual give-and-take he had enjoyed with friends and colleagues in the city. But in no way did he consider the conversation a tug back to his old life. Friends, he would miss no matter what. Not so the life-style.

When he hung up, he waited for Cat to verbally flay him for his rudeness earlier. She did have every right, he thought. It certainly hadn't taken him long to renege on his vow to learn to do without the bottom line. The first time she made a move he didn't like, what did he do? Blow his damn top! The muscles in his shoulders tensed, waiting for the explosion.

It didn't come. Instead, she gifted him with a beatific smile. "I love you, Garrick," she said. "You are emotional, exasperating, unpredictable and wonderful." She stood. "I am really sorry to hear all that about Janet. I hope she finds help and peace of mind. Now, excuse me. I've got to get lunch on.'' She walked out of the room, leaving him sitting at the desk with his mouth hanging stupidly open.

CAT PRACTICALLY SAILED into the kitchen. She hadn't expected or wanted a reaction from him immediately. He already had so much on his mind, it would only be right to let him think about her words for a while. She couldn't, however, keep from singing while she heated up the spicy chili she intended to serve.

Abby came into the room after a few minutes and stared at her. ''I left the kids with Ellen,'' she said, ''What're you in such a good mood about?''

''Life in general,'' Cat replied, sidestepping the truth. ''Did you get the empty cabin cleaned?''

''Not yet.'' There was more than a trace of rebelliousness and petulance in the teenager's voice.

''Well, never mind it.'' Cat popped a tray of corn-bread sticks into the oven for heating. ''I put up a sign this morning. We won't be taking any more drop-ins for a while. No one with a reservation is due until Friday. Why don't you two take the rest of the day off?''

''You're kidding.''

Cat smiled. ''Have I ever kidded about work? Get out of here. Call Tom and go for a ride. Have some fun.''

Abby's expression changed. ''I...I don't think Tom could get off duty. I mean, it's pretty short notice. Besides, I... I've been spending *all* my free time with him this summer. It's getting boring.''

''Oh.'' Cat took a large crock of coleslaw out of the big walk-in refrigerator. ''Well, then. Do whatever you want, Ab. Just take a break. You both deserve it.''

''Thanks.'' Abby shot her a grateful look, then went out onto the porch to set the table.

Too bad, Cat thought. She and Tom had seemed like such lovebirds. But they were both very young. If it wasn't going to work out, it would be better for the break to come before any serious public commitment had been made. She knew statistics on teen marriages were lousy. Granted, Tom was twenty-two and had a job, but goodness knows the young deputy was *not* a man of the world. She wasn't even sure he was a good deputy.

"Did you mean that?" Garrick's voice startled her out of her reverie.

"Hmmm?" She focused on the tall figure standing framed in the doorway. The light was behind him, and she couldn't see his face.

"Did you mean it?" He came into the room. "Because I couldn't stand it if you were just feeling sorry for me, Cat."

She put down the wooden spoon she was using to stir the chili. "Garrick, I don't think I've ever said anything to you I didn't mean. Even when it was unkind. Yes, I meant what I said in the office. Every single word of it."

Abby reentered the kitchen. Not noticing Garrick, she spoke to Cat. "I talked to Ellen. Could we borrow the Jeep and go over to Jackson? There's a lot more to do there, and we might meet some new people. We'll drive real careful."

Cat glanced at Garrick. He had assumed a casual posture against the counter. "Gee, Abby," she said. "I don't know about loaning out the Jeep. I don't care to be without a trail vehicle just in case something happens."

"Take my car." He moved over to Cat and stood close enough for her to feel the warmth of him. "It's got more power anyway. You'll need that on the pass."

"The BMW!" Abby shrieked. Then her expression fell. "Oh, I couldn't. I've never driven a fancy car like that."

"It's no different from any other car. After lunch I'll take you out on the highway for a spin. If you're comfortable with it after that, it's yours for the rest of the day and the evening." His fingers brushed Cat's shoulder.

Abby looked at Cat, who carefully kept her feelings off her face. Personally, she thought Garrick was out of his mind to entrust such an expensive vehicle to a youngster, but then, she trusted the girls to watch over the children on the ranch....

"You might want to give Tom a buzz and see if he wants to go, too," Garrick suggested, now full of compassion for the young lovers. It looked as if his relationship was going to work out, and he wished the same joy for everyone. "He was asking about you this morning in town."

Abby made a face. "He's always asking and never doing. Nothing personal, but sometimes guys can be a real pain, you know. Ellen and I'd rather go alone. If that's all right."

Both Cat and Garrick said "Sure" at the same time. When Abby left the room again to go tell Ellen the good news, Garrick explained what he and Tom had discussed this morning.

"Oh, my lord," Cat said. "I should have anticipated this. For someone willing to dive into the hay with her lover at the first opportunity, I have been very naive about Abby and Tom. And I'm responsible for that child!"

"Unless I misread what she was saying," he said in a wry tone, "Abby is far from a child anymore. It's possible the best thing for them just now is not to see each other so often. It'll be tough on Tom, though."

"Better for it to be tough on him than to have a little surprise nine months from now." Cat batted the spoon on the edge of the cauldron of chili. "Just in time for graduation!"

"Hey." He caught her shoulders in his hands. "It's not a problem until it's a problem, my love. No milk's been spilt yet, so don't fret over it. Think about what *we've* got. And how many years we had to live before we found it." He touched her face gently. "You don't know what it did to me when you said those words in the office. I've been hurting so bad. You made it all right."

"Garrick, the fact that I realize I love you doesn't solve a thing."

"Well, maybe not, but—"

"And the fact that I love you doesn't mean we have instantly wiped out all the differences between us, and in our attitudes."

"Of course it doesn't, but—"

"And even though I understand and forgive you, you were still way out of line out there on the road. This is my place. I will run it as I choose."

"Yes, boss." He tried to say it lightly, but her words hurt deeply. *Now* he was getting his tongue-lashing. Now, when his feelings were so vulnerable to her. "I said I was sorry."

She turned back to the chili. "I only hope you meant it," she said quietly.

It had been harsh, she knew, to hit him like that, but she knew the man. If she hadn't done some rug jerking, he'd have run haywire with his newfound knowledge of her love. What Garrick Drexel needed more than love, periodically, she reasoned, was a good slap of reality.

And she was just the one to give it to him.

Surprisingly, lunch was a pleasant affair. Garrick didn't sulk after her verbal plastering, and for the first time, he was willing to talk about his past profession, astounding the adult guests who had no clue to his background, and horrifying the Tanner twins. "You mean you was one of those nerdy sissies who dress up like they're going to church every day? And who don't do nothing but mess with money?" one twin asked. The other just made a disgusted face.

"Yep." Garrick spread a generous dollop of butter on his corn bread. "And you know what?"

"What?" the boys chorused. The adults looked as interested.

"I enjoyed it." He shoved half the corn stick into his mouth and chewed with obvious relish. Cat smothered laughter. Swallowing milk, he continued. "But I wouldn't go back to it for all the money in the world now." He stared at her pointedly. "I have everything I want or need right here."

Cat didn't smile, but she blushed. Whoops, he thought. Too fast. Too public. Her dressing-down had hurt, but it hadn't killed his euphoria, and he wasn't thinking clearly. She was liable to always have a sharp tongue, he reasoned. He might as well get used to it.

After the meal, he took Abby out as promised in the BMW. The teen proved competent, although she had to be cautioned against underestimating the power of the car's engine. By the time they headed back to the ranch, he felt all right about the loan. She parked in the yard, and he ceremoniously bestowed the keys on her. Her delight with the temporary gift warmed his heart and made him envious of those fathers who could do that sort of thing for their own kids. He remained on the front porch for a while, staring off into the distance, then he went into the office to think.

Cat had meant her words of love. He had meant his. Sure, there were still problems, but surely they could be worked out better under more comfortable, intimate conditions: in late-night talks before going to sleep—in the same bed—together. The more he thought along those lines, the more sense his idea made.

If they got married, she would have to believe he was happy to stay on the ranch the rest of his life. He drifted back to feelings of nostalgia his talk with Pete had brought on, but he dismissed them as unimportant. A more disturbing memory was Pete telling him he'd eventually grow restless as a mere hired hand, no matter how much control he might gain of her books. She would still always be the boss—always.

No, that wasn't important. They'd work something out. The important thing was to create the right atmosphere to do the working. The more he thought about it...

Then there was the matter of kids. In the weeks he had been the kiddie wrangler, the child ache in him had grown to almost unbearable proportions. It was a need he had denied for so long, and now there was the possibility it could be fulfilled. Neither of them was young anymore, but she could still have a baby. More and more women were putting off having a family until their mid-thirties. It was possible.

CAT SAW HIM COMING from the house just as she was finishing up a riding lesson for some of the little ones. He looked upset again.

He had to come to terms with his past, she thought. By running away, he was only compounding his difficulties. While she did love him, she wanted him whole, and she was painfully certain she would have to risk losing him to win him. She had almost forgotten how badly love could make her hurt.

When the kids left, he came into the corral to help with the horses. She noticed his hands were trembling as he unfastened a bridle.

"Are you still upset about Janet?" she asked.

"Yes. No." He didn't look at her.

"Well, what is it, Garrick? Yes or no? In any event, there isn't a thing you can do about it from here. If it's really bugging you, you ought to go back and deal with it directly."

"No!" He turned, and the intensity of emotion she saw on his face made her gasp. "Cat, I only want to stay here with you for the rest of my life. Will you marry me?"

CHAPTER TWELVE

"WHAT?" She could scarcely believe her ears. "What did
you say?"

"Marry me!" Impulsively, he sank to his knees, oblivi-
ous to the piles of horse leavings on the ground. "Become
my wife, Cat. I promise to do everything within my power
to make you happy for the rest of your life."

"Garrick, get up." She tugged at his shirt. "You're getting all dirty."

"I love you. You said you love me. Is there really any
reason why we shouldn't marry? Think about it, please."
His voice was calm now, but the entreaty in his eyes nearly
did her in. It would be so easy to say yes to him.

So easy and so wrong.

"No, Garrick. Get up. I can't marry you . . . won't marry
you. Not now. Not . . . yet."

"Damn it, Cat." He got to his feet. "You don't have a
single good reason not to, except your own doubts. And this
is the answer to those doubts." Before she could put up any
kind of struggle, he had locked her into an embrace and was
kissing her passionately.

Giggles, hoots and youthful laughter sounded jarringly in
her ears, and she managed to push away from him. About
half a dozen children were lined up along the fence, having
a great time watching the show. Cat blushed deeply.

Garrick, however, was unabashed. He kept one arm
wrapped around her. "Miss Cat and I are getting married," he said loudly. "Everyone is invited." That resulted
in squeals from the girls, boos from the boys.

That tore it! Cat jerked away from him. "This is a make-believe game," she said to the children. To Garrick, she hissed, "In my office. *After* you change your pants." Then she turned and stalked off, feeling his gaze on her back all the way to the house.

How dare he? She kicked open the door and slammed the screen shut behind her. It was quite one thing to have a private conversation and entirely another to parade themselves in front of the children, undoubtedly the worst gossips on the place! Nothing she could do now would squash the rumors about them. The more she thought about it, the madder she got. He was trying to maneuver her! Just like he maneuvered companies with his stock deals. She looked out the window, expecting to see him heading for the major chewing out she had planned. Right now she was just about angry enough to kick his butt off the ranch for good!

But he wasn't coming. She could see him clearly down at the corral calmly giving a bareback ride on the big red mare to two small girls who were giggling and clinging. His smile seemed genuine. Cat felt steam coming out of her ears. She was about to burst out the door after him when the phone rang. She counted to five before answering it.

The first thing she heard was the hollowness that indicated a long-distance call. She said hello and her name. The caller replied.

"This is Sheldon Sheridan, Miss Cantrell. Garrick Drexel's lawyer. I'm calling in regard to something very odd that's happened here, and I thought you might be able to shed some light on it for us, since you have him there in your employ."

"I'll be happy to help, of course." Alarms went off, sending a chill up her spine. "Is there a problem, Mr. Sheridan?"

"You might say. Janet Norton told us about her room, Miss Cantrell."

"Oh, yes. Hasn't Garrick's counselor friend been in touch with her yet?"

"With her? Why, no. I would think he ought to be getting in touch with Garrick, don't you?"

"Wait a minute. I think we ought to compare stories. Janet trashed her own room. Garrick is worried sick about her."

The lawyer was silent for a second. "May I speak to Garrick?"

"Hang on. I'll get him." She set the receiver down and took another deep breath. What was going on? She went to call Garrick.

He came immediately, unloading the children, securing the horse and jogging up the hill to the house. "This isn't about us, is it? Your tone of voice is entirely different."

Cat briefed him.

Garrick felt the edges of his personal sense of reality slipping as he listened to Sheldon. Janet had arrived back in New York with a story designed to paint him as certifiable. According to her, *he* had wrecked the room, descending on her in the middle of the night in an uncontrollable rage. Terror had forced her to flee, to leave the money and the note. She was insisting Garrick be returned to New York for psychiatric treatment.

"Do you believe her?" Garrick was starting to shake from indignation and incredulity. "Do you really believe I would do something that insane?"

"Garrick, it's not what I believe. This is prejudicing the investigation. You have got to come back now. You have no choice."

So that was her scheme—to do something that would force him to leave Cat and return to what would be a nightmare of arguing and legal gymnastics. But *why*? "No, I don't have to come back and yes, I do have a choice, Sheldon." He might have been shoveling manure for several months, but he hadn't lost his wits. "I can get a deposition from the sheriff and others who can testify to my whereabouts during the night." Sheldon sighed and asked for the lawman's number. Garrick gave it to him and, promising to keep him posted, Sheldon hung up.

Cat saw a bleakness in Garrick's eyes that reflected a new level of pain for him. All anger left her. "How badly can she hurt you?" she asked, putting her arms around him.

"I honestly don't know." He bent his head, resting it on her shoulder for a moment. "And I have no earthly idea why she did it." He stepped back and started dialing the phone.

"Who are you calling?"

"Janet. Please stay. I think it might be a good idea for me to have a witness." Cat complied.

"Janet. Yes, it's Garrick. Listen, I just had a very disturbing call from Sheldon Sheridan. Would you mind explaining to me..."

Cat watched his eyes get wider and his color deepen. He sat down abruptly as if the muscles in his legs had given out. "Janet, that's the craziest thing I've ever heard. I've got witnesses, damn it. Do you? I didn't go anywhere off the ranch last night, much less to your motel room." Cat felt a chill crawl up her spine. From what she could tell, Janet was actually claiming he had done the deed. He argued, but his remarks got shorter and shorter, until apparently he was cut off by her tirade. Cat could hear her high-pitched voice if not the words. It was a spooky sound.

Finally, he hung up while Janet was still talking shrilly at him. Then he just sat and stared at the phone.

"What did she say?" Cat went over and took his hand. "You look as if you've seen a ghost."

Seeking comfort from her nearness, he put an arm around her waist. "She seems absolutely convinced I did do the number on her room. She was upset, but sounded clearheaded. Her only concern, it seems, is that I get professional help." He paused, then slammed his palm down on the desk. "All I ever wanted was a chance to find happiness, to start over. I didn't plan on falling in love with you or with this country, but I did. Why can't I just be left alone to enjoy what I've found?"

She had no answers for him. It was his battle and he would eventually have to fight it. "I do love you," she murmured. "You can make me so mad I see red, but I do love you."

"About the marriage proposal." He stood and went over to the window. "I was serious, but this is clearly not the time to be making a commitment to you. Not until I get this mess straightened out."

Cat agreed, but was astonished at how disappointed his words made her. Logic, clearly, was not the operative mental activity in this situation. She was about to state her concurrence when one of the twins came tearing into the room.

"The sheriff's here," he announced. "And he looks real mad."

It wasn't Nelson, but Tom, and he wasn't there in an official capacity, but a personal one. "I was on my way over to see Abby," he said, "when I heard one of my ranger buddies calling on the box. He said he thought he saw her and Ellen tooling around Jackson Hole in some fancy, expensive car. Right away I figured it had to be the BMW. Is everything all right?" From his expression, it was plain he wasn't sure he wanted it to be.

"Everything's fine," Garrick reassured him. "I loaned the girls the car. They've been working hard and deserve some playtime."

Tom frowned. "I told her I was going to take some time off this afternoon to visit. Why didn't she wait for me?"

"Maybe she just needed a little time to herself, Tom," Cat said. "After all, even in the best of relationships, people need their own space."

This piece of advice seemed to make the deputy even more unhappy. Garrick decided a change of subject was in order and invited Tom into the office to listen to a recital of his latest trouble with Janet. Tom was immediately sympathetic and assured Garrick that none of the evidence collected indicated Garrick or any other man had been in the room. Garrick was surprised and gratified to learn that Nelson had sent the material down to the crime lab in Cheyenne. That would certainly help his case.

He was also somewhat surprised to learn Tom had had some junior-college-level education in criminal justice and that he had spent nearly two years at the community college down in Casper. Perhaps, he decided, there was more to the young man than met the eye.

Cat invited Tom to stay for supper, saying that Abby and Ellen might show up soon, and he accepted. While she prepared the meal, Garrick and he went out to occupy the kids. The kiddie wrangler organized a game of hide-and-seek, and Tom shed his romantic gloom and joined in the fun without a visible qualm for his dignity. Soon the ranch yard rang with excited shrieks and laughter.

Cat heard the ruckus from the kitchen and smiled to herself. Every hour she knew him, Garrick seemed to grow more dear. But marriage? He couldn't possibly be happy working on the ranch for the rest of his days. It just wouldn't satisfy a man who had been so in control of his life, as well as that of others. Eventually, she was sure, he would want to return to his old life.

And she was too selfish to give up hers to join him. They might love and care for each other now, but inevitably, sometime in the future, they would be saying goodbye. She warned herself to be emotionally ready for that day.

At dinner he brought up a topic that made her ever more certain she was right.

"I was thinking about something this afternoon," he said, addressing the gathering as a whole, but focusing on the kids. "You know I grew up in a city and never saw a wide-open space bigger than Central Park until after I was in my twenties."

"How big's Central Park?" asked a twin.

"Not very big compared to the pieces of land out here. Anyway, I was thinking about some other kids I know. They've never seen anything like this place."

Cat listened. He wanted to invite some of his old friends and their families out to the ranch. "Maybe then," he said, "they'd understand why I love it so much. Besides, I miss them and would really like to see them again."

He was, she thought, starting to get homesick. A bitter-sweet feeling rose in her and she realized that her feelings didn't matter: she wanted him to be happy whatever it took. "Do you think they'll come?" she asked with forced brightness.

There was a decided glint in his eyes. "I'm working on an unrefusable offer."

"Well, just don't ask anyone to get here the way you did. I don't think I'll ever forget the sight of you walking down the highway in your three-piece suit and Burberry raincoat." That necessitated a recitation of their first meeting. She was too close to her emotions, so she let Garrick tell most of it, and soon he had the entire group laughing and exclaiming sympathetically.

"And all I can hope," he concluded, "is that the bad guys gave my Burberry the proper respect."

"What's so special about that raincoat?" Tom had been morose throughout most of the meal. Now he seemed to perk up.

"It's a real status symbol," Garrick explained. "An East Coast, Wall Street establishment fixture of dress. It would look quite out of place on a Western road bandit." Tom seemed to mull over that information.

He left right after supper, plainly upset that Abby hadn't returned yet. Cat promised to tell her he came by, but her own mood kept her from encouraging him. When she went to look for Garrick, she found him in the office, engrossed in her records. "There's a whole week here in July when you don't have guests booked," he said. "Why?"

She braced herself for another tiff over finances and priorities. "That's the Fourth of July week. I always leave that free. Lone Tree has the Pioneer Festival then. I'm very involved with it."

"Good." He made some notes.

"Garrick, what are you up to now?"

He put down his pen. "A little defensive action. It seems after my rush for the West, I just don't have the credibility I need to counter Janet's attacks. I figure if I can get some key people out here to see I'm not really out of my mind, I can then try to tackle the problem from a position of strength. It's simple tactics."

"And how do you propose to get those key people out here? They aren't likely to just drop what they're doing and rush on out."

"They are all my friends. And I plan to offer a free week-long visit."

"Free? Garrick Bottom-Line-Drexel is going to offer *free* vacations?" She didn't believe it.

"I'm going to foot the bill." He held up a hand as she started to protest. "This isn't charity, Cat. This is to help me solve my problems. Will you do this for me? Please?"

"You have another motive, don't you?" She was reading his expression closely. "You miss these people and want to see them again." The smile on his face told her that she was right. "You know I'm going to be much too busy to be any help," she cautioned. "Do you think you can manage without me?"

"I'll work something out," he replied. She wasn't at all certain she liked the sound or implications of that statement.

LATER ON THAT EVENING they had a camp fire—the most moving one Garrick had attended. It was the twins' last night at the ranch, and that, plus everything else that had happened that day, made him unusually emotional. But there was real magic that night. The sky was clear and revealed millions of stars. A slight breeze made the pine trees sing and kept the camp fire blazing. All the guests seemed to be in a mellow, nostalgic mood, even the kids.

It was, however, the beauty and grace of the hostess and the wonder of her lovely voice that really made the night as far as he was concerned. Leading the group in classic folk and cowboy songs, she played masterfully on the emotions. In the particularly American experience of camp fire, fellowship and song, he realized, she was a genius. And he doubted if she had any idea of the extent of her talents.

The fire site was far enough away from any of the ranch buildings to be safe and was located just a stone's throw away from the creek. The tang of smoke filled the air, and later, when they all retired to bed, it was with the heady scent of wood smoke in their hair and clothes.

Since the guests had started coming and the camp fires established as a routine event, Jude had demonstrated a skill with the guitar that surprised Garrick until he thought of the long months of inactivity on the ranch during the dead of winter. The wrangler could make his old instrument do everything but turn handsprings. The guests loved it.

Finally, the last song was sung. Because the twins and another family were leaving in the morning, Cat had pulled the last few songs out of a schmaltzy repertoire of until-we-meet-again tunes. It was high theater, highly corny, and when it was over, the only dry eyes were the ones owned by small children already asleep on their parents' laps. Knowing this night the twins would demand Garrick's full attention, Cat only gave his hand an affectionate squeeze before saying good-night and heading to her house. The sense of melancholy weighed her down immeasurably. It seemed too much foreshadowing of future farewells.

But as she tidied up and readied herself for solitary sleeping, she mused philosophically that if it wasn't for the possibility of loss, love just wouldn't have the same savor. It was ironic but true that if you were too sure of a thing, it didn't seem as valuable. Would loving Garrick be as sweet if she knew she could have him the rest of her life? She wasn't sure.

She was starting to undress when a frightening realization came over her. It was well past eleven and the girls weren't home yet. Without thinking, she threw on a jacket and ran to Garrick's cabin. Knocking on his door, she called for him to wake up. When he appeared at the door, he was only wearing jeans and his hair was rumpled, but he didn't look as if he'd been sleeping. "What is it?" he asked softly, not wanting to wake the boys.

Cat grabbed his hand and pulled him outside. "Abby and Ellen. They haven't come home yet. Garrick, I'm really worried. What could have happened to them?"

"Just a minute." He went into the cabin and grabbed a flannel shirt. Slipping it on, he quickly pondered the implications of her coming to him with the problem instead of trying to solve it herself. *Interesting,* he thought. Outside, he tried to reassure her. "You didn't give them a curfew. They're young, and midnight doesn't seem so late when you're a teenager. Don't you remember? Heck, I used to stay up until dawn sometimes."

"Well, I had to work for a living," she said angrily. "I had to get up before sunrise every day of my life when we lived on the old ranch. Midnight seems damned late to me."

"I guess I could go... Wait, I see headlights coming down the road. I expect that's our girls." He glanced at his watch. "And it is not midnight yet, so don't go having a fit all over them." She gave him a furious look before running toward the car.

It was indeed the girls. And more. When the BMW pulled to a halt in the yard, four additional people piled out with Abby and Ellen—two men and two women. They spoke with accents that sounded British to her, but she was soon relieved of that misunderstanding.

"Aussies," said one of the men, holding out his hand for Garrick first, then Cat. "We're from Perth. My sis, Marilyn, her chum, Beth. I'm Jack O'Neill, and this's my mate, Charlie Winters. Abby and Ellen said you might be willing to let us tucker down in the yard for a day or so."

Jack was a tall, lean man with a tanned face that seemed to smile as a natural matter of course. The others were equally outdoorsy-looking and charming. Cat didn't normally allow camping on ranch property, but the sight of those pleasant eager faces won her over. "Of course you're welcome," she said. "And you can use the shower facilities in the bunkhouse, providing you can get past my wrangler. He's a bit touchy about sharing."

She was quickly assured that they wouldn't put anyone out. They had been traveling for weeks and were tired. All they wanted to do was rest a little while before moving on. Their ambition was to travel all across the country.

"That must be fairly expensive," Garrick commented. He sounded and looked thoughtful. "Have you found work along the way?"

"Now and again," said Charlie. "The best jobs have fallen to the girls. Waitressing and such. But we've managed."

Then Garrick dropped his bombshell. "How would you four like to hang out here for a few weeks and earn some decent wages under good conditions? I'm going to need extra help the week of July fourth. Can any of you handle horses?"

It turned out all of them could, and before Cat could get a word in edgewise, Garrick had offered them paying work after a few days of training. He was acting as if the place was all his, Cat thought angrily. Fuming, she excused herself, saying that she'd had a tiring day and needed her sleep, acidly indicating Garrick could certainly handle any details by himself. Then she headed to the house.

Ellen broke from the group and tagged after her. "You aren't mad, are you, Cat?" she asked. "We just couldn't resist them. Abby thinks Jack is really cute. And Garrick needs them, after all. I think that's just great. What's he doing the week of the fourth? I thought we'd have the time off."

"Talk to him. He seems to be in charge."

"You are mad. Cat..."

Laughter rounded from the others, and Ellen looked back. "Go on," Cat said. "Join them. I'll see you in the morning." Ellen hesitated, then obeyed, clearly happy to leave her angry boss. Cat entered the ranch house and closed and locked the door.

GARRICK WAITED until everyone else had settled down before going up to the house and trying the door. When he found it locked, he felt a wave of frustration and fury. She had given him command of the place for that week. Why was she so mad at his act of hiring help? It didn't make any sense. *She* didn't make any sense. He went to his own lonely bunk and lay there, still wearing his clothes and listening to the twins' youthful snores.

And his own gloomy thoughts.

Maybe he and Cat weren't meant for each other after all. Maybe it had been purely accidental that they had met and hit it off. Maybe this was only meant to be another phase in his life. Everything certainly indicated that right now.

She was dictatorial and unreasonable. She spoke of love one minute, then kicked him in the teeth the next. Could he ever be sure where he stood with a woman like that? He closed his eyes, and his mind immediately flooded with pictures of her—working, talking...loving him. God, why did it have to hurt so much and be so hard!

He tried to look at the situation as if it were a business operation. The thing to do was to go ahead with his plans and invite his friends out, show them he wasn't crazy, then go back and straighten out his life—let the future take care of itself without Cat as a consideration. It was pretty clear she didn't want him. All that mattered to her when it came right down to it was the damn ranch. She was married to a place, and it was doubtful a man would ever usurp the position of spouse.

But, oh, how he wanted to.

And hadn't he given until he was blue in the face? He had given his time, his talent, his love. He had been the best he could be for her, and what had he gotten? He'd been locked out at midnight over some silly snit of hers. Did she have to make every decision about this damn place? he wondered angrily. A quiet voice kept trying to tell him it was *her* place, but he chose deliberately to ignore it. She was stubborn; he could be just as stubborn.

He'd improved. When she had closed the place to extra guests, hadn't he agreed it was a good idea to give everyone a little rest? Maybe it had taken a while, but he *had* agreed.

He was going to use his own money for the Aussies and for the week of the fourth. Didn't that prove he had learned to move beyond the profit margin? He smiled. Hell, he could go back to Wall Street a much stronger, more confident investor now.

So why did the idea make him queasy?

Just habit, he told himself harshly. *Get used to the idea of leaving, Drexel. Because it sure looks like you're going to have to. Sooner or later.*

CHAPTER THIRTEEN

CAT SLEPT VERY LITTLE that night. Morning found her itchy-eyed and irritable, and she only remembered while preparing breakfast that it was the Tanner boys' last day. She hurried to fix pancakes. When they came into the kitchen, they looked as sullen and unhappy as she felt. But the stack of steaming goodies seemed to revive their spirits. "If we gotta go home," one said, "at least we get to eat good before." She let them eat in the kitchen a few minutes before everyone else assembled on the eating porch.

"I expect you eat just as well at home," she chided. "Don't make a big deal out of my cooking or your mom will get her feelings hurt."

"Garrick got his feelings hurt." A twin speared a pancake and plopped it on his plate.

"What?" Cat nearly dropped a pan of sizzling sausages.

"He said so this morning." The other twin eyed the sausages. Cat gave him two. "He was real grumpy, so we asked why. That's what he said." The meat vanished.

When Garrick came onto the porch with the others, it was abundantly clear to her that if his feelings weren't hurt, he was at least as angry as she had been the previous night. He grunted good morning to everyone but her, took only a cup of coffee and disappeared into the office. Cat managed things herself until Abby and Ellen dragged themselves in. Rather curtly, she ordered them to handle the rest of breakfast and to introduce their Australian friends. Then she went after Garrick.

He was hunched over some papers, making notes. She shut the door and he looked up. "Oh, now I get to be on this side of the locked door," he said dryly.

"I'll lock whatever doors I want. I still own this place." She faced him, determined to remain calm and in control.

He put his pen down. "And that's the issue?" His expression was cold and grim.

"I think so."

"Well, you're wrong, Cat." He got up and came around the desk, looking like thunder. "You want to know what the real issue is?"

"I can't wait to hear what you *think* it is, Mr. Financial Advice." Her heart was beginning to beat rapidly, but she wasn't sure it was from anger.

"The issue, Miss People First, is materialism." He pointed a finger at her. "You really had me snowed with all that crap about how good you were to your employees and devil take the money. There's money and there's money. Yours just happens to be in the form of a crummy little piece of acreage and a few lousy buildings. You're as wedded to this joint as I ever was to the profit margin. Probably more, because I was able to walk away from my ball and chain. You can't. Not even long enough to let me hire a few nice kids who need the work to do some things for me. Damn it, Cat, you're a hypocrite of the worst kind."

"And you're a manipulator! You think just because you walk in here with experience you can jerk us all around to suit yourself. You charmed me. You made me love you. You've used my place to settle your spirit. And now you're getting ready to leave it and me. What do you call that, you snake?" It was impossible not to cry and yell. His words hurt so badly—partly because she knew in her heart they had a ring of truth to them. "I swore I'd never let love hurt me again. And look at me."

"You don't love me." He turned his back on her.

"Oh, but I do. I must. It couldn't hurt this badly if I didn't. Not even Benny—"

"Don't bring up your ex-husband to me!" He turned suddenly, rushed at her and grabbed her shoulders. "I have *never* done anything that wasn't in your best interests. Not since the first day I met you. I cared for you, I worked for you, I loved you. Why are you treating me worse than you'd treat your barn cats?"

"I'm . . . I'm not!"

His dark gaze probed her eyes. "You don't think you are, do you? You don't even have the sensitivity to know how much you can torture me." He stared at her so long she began to tremble. Then his lips closed over hers.

Cat shrieked with outrage, but couldn't get free. He continued to kiss her, gently but firmly, until she started crying again and threw her arms around his neck. He embraced her tightly and bent her back so that their bodies touched along almost every inch. Her rage changed to desire, and she melted against him.

Her reaction both aroused and infuriated him. Garrick had intended to prove one last time that she was only a cool little landowner, willing to enjoy and use him until she felt threatened or crossed. If she had resisted his embrace and kiss, it would have convinced him for once and for all to leave as soon as he could. Now, he was more confused than ever. He released her so quickly, she staggered to keep her footing. "The boys leave in a few hours," he growled. "I'll stick around to say goodbye, then I'm heading for town. I need to think." He pushed past her before she could say a word and left the house, slamming the door behind him. It was not a particularly satisfying gesture.

Cat stumbled over to the desk and sat down carefully in the chair. Her leg muscles were trembling violently. A timid knock on the door got her attention. Abby stood there. "Is everything all right?" she asked fearfully.

"No," Cat said. "It is not."

But she gave the girl instructions for the Australian women regarding the kitchen and cleaning routines. She also told her to tell Jude to tell Garrick that he was in charge of the two men. He had hired them; he should train them. Shortly, a curt message came back via Jude.

"He ain't gonna start today, Cat." The wrangler looked extremely ill at ease. "Never seen a man so riled."

"Okay." Cat sighed. She was just a millimeter away from another flood of tears, but she was darned if she would subject poor Jude to it. "Why don't you run them through the livestock routine." She gained further control of herself. "I will run a trail ride this afternoon. We'll see how they do then."

The twins left late in the morning. Garrick turned them over to their parents reluctantly after giving them vigorous handshakes, then hugs. Cat felt a lump in her throat as she watched the scene. His affection for the boys was genuine, and it was sad to her that a man capable of those feelings had never had children of his own—might never have them in the future, either.

Thinking of the future brought other sad thoughts. No matter how much they might desire and love each other, she and Garrick couldn't go on much longer like this. They were both too strong and opinionated.

Garrick drove away not five minutes after the twins had gone.

Cat did lead a trail ride that afternoon. Jack and Charlie declared their determination to learn the ropes and prove themselves useful. She found them to be entertaining companions and noted the other guests warmed to them almost immediately. If they did catch on to Western-style horsemanship and ranch work, she decided, Garrick would have made an extremely smart move in hiring them. Of course, it would only have been dumb luck. If she'd needed hands, she would have sought them by word of mouth or even advertising. That way, she would have gotten already trained professionals.

After the ride, Jack expressed a specific interest in learning how to care for the tack. "My old man was quite the one for the ponies," he informed her as they carried saddles into the tack room. "I guess I've developed a fondness for the beasties. And I really do love the smell and feel of good leather." Cat explained what had to be done, watched him work for a few minutes and left, satisfied that the young man was serious about doing a good job. As she walked toward the house, she saw Ellen and the two new girls playing a game with some of the children. Garrick's car wasn't back. At the front door, she ran into Abby.

"Sheriff Hendry called," the girl said, her tone indicating it had been Nelson, not Tom. "I think you'd better call back. He sounded . . . funny."

Cat ran to the telephone.

"'Lo, Cat." Nelson answered the phone on the second ring. "There's a situation here I thought you oughta know about."

Her heart raced. "It's Garrick, isn't it? Is he hurt? Is he all right?"

"Well—" Nelson drawled the word "—so far, he is. I'm gonna try keeping it that way."

"Nelson! What's wrong?"

"He's been down to Chuck Benson's place for a couple of hours now, puttin' 'em away. Chuck called me about thirty minutes ago, and I wandered down. Politest drunk I ever did see. Gave me his keys without a fuss and swallowed another one of those god-awful martini things Chuck says he's been drinking steady. Wouldn't talk to me about anything but the weather and baseball. I mentioned you an' he acted like he was deaf. Honey, you got a problem with the man." It was a statement, not a question.

"I know. I'll be right in."

"No, that ain't the thing to do, Cat. You let him get good and sloshed. I'll take care of him. He's got something in his craw and needs to wash it out. You trust me?"

Cat felt sick and scared. "I guess I have to. Nelson, don't let him get hurt. He used to box when he was young. I don't know if he'd get into a fight or not, but if he's been drinking a lot—"

"I won't tell you not to worry, but I will baby-sit him as best I can, okay?"

"I guess it has to be. Please, Nelson, keep me posted."

"That I will do. You take care now, honey."

Cat promised to, but when she hung up, her hands were shaking violently. Had she actually driven him to drink? Or was it more than his relationship with her that had to be washed out of his craw, as Nelson had put it?

She moved through the rest of the day and evening in a daze of confusion and sorrow, keeping up a front for all but those who knew her best. Jude, Abby and Ellen watched her closely, as if she were an invalid. The Aussies and some of the kids asked after Garrick and she managed to say brightly that he was away on business. The business of washing *her* out of his craw, she thought dismally.

Later, lying alone in bed, she gave herself over to the tears she had held in all day. Nelson hadn't called, and she found her mind filled with the worst scenarios: Garrick falling down drunk, Garrick in a barroom brawl, Garrick deathly ill from alcohol poisoning. Garrick, sobered and hung over in the morning, receiving custody of his keys from Nelson and heading his BMW back to New York. Would her love force her to follow him if he fled? Would it be worth it, or would he just tell her to kiss off?

Was the ranch worth losing the love she might find with him? a still, small voice whispered inside her. But she managed to ignore it and tell herself that she would face tomorrow when it came. Like Scarlett, she still had her beloved land.

Just before she fell into a troubled sleep, something quietly reminded her that she had it only by virtue of Garrick Drexel's brains and skills. Without his intervention, she thought, she would be out job-hunting—the ranch only an issue in bankruptcy court. Knowing how indebted she was to him only made matters worse, however, and she did her best to force the thoughts from her mind. She was moderately successful.

"WHATCHA DRINKING, DUDE?" The big man settled onto a bar stool next to Garrick. "Looks like water t'me."

Garrick glanced at his new companion. The burly cow-boy had been eyeing him from across the barroom for some time. Garrick's muscles were relaxed from the amount of gin he had ingested since noon, but he put his reflexes into the ready state. "It's a martini," he said pleasantly. "Want one? I'm buying."

"Hell, no." The other man signaled the bartender. "I'm drinking bourbon. That's a *man's* drink."

"For some men." Garrick drained his martini and pushed the long-stemmed glass forward for a refill. He hadn't had enough yet. His heart still hurt.

"F'r any man," the cowboy said belligerently. "Look at that sissy glass you's using. They teach you how to hold that thing back East in some fancy college?"

Garrick smiled. *Whoa,* he thought. He hadn't come here to relate *mano a mano* to a local gunslinger. He had come to drink and think. To drink until he could think instead of feel. "Actually," he said in a gentle tone, "I learned to drink these things in the Marines. I'd match my buddies martini for beer. Wanna try?"

The cowboy looked at him. "You was in the Marines? What unit?" Garrick told him.

NELSON HENDRY GATHERED UP his barroom-fight equip-ment—nightstick, sap and handcuffs—and raced to his truck. Chuck had just phoned in panic, telling him that Roscoe Petersen from the Star Ranch down the road had picked Garrick as his target of the night. The big Swede usually waited until the weekend before heading to Lone Tree or Jackson and picking a fight with the biggest man he could find. This week, it seemed, he'd started early. Nelson felt a rise of panic. The cowboy was an experienced brawler, and Drexel wouldn't stand a chance against his dirty tactics if he was only trained as a boxer. Cat would have his hide if something happened to the man! She loved him, there was no doubt about that in Nelson's mind.

He drove as fast as possible to the bar and screeched to a stop. Things looked quiet, but Chuck had called....

Inside, it was quiet, too. Except for the boozy laughter coming from one booth in the corner. Nelson looked questioningly at Chuck. The bartender shrugged and indicated the corner.

Garrick and Roscoe were facing each other across the table, a bottle of gin on the Easterner's side and bourbon in front of the cowboy. Garrick was drinking from a fancy, fluted glass; Roscoe, a plain shot glass. Both bottles were nearly empty. It was clear from the eyes of the men that these were not the first bottles they had consumed. They stopped laughing and grinned at Nelson.

"Hey, there, Sheriff," Roscoe said. "This ol' boy was in the Marines division fought with mine in 'Nam."

"Told him I wasn't in combat," Garrick said. "But we're buddies anyhow."

"That's good." Nelson relaxed a little. This was hardly what he had expected. "Boys, your bosses know where you're at?"

Garrick's expression darkened. "Who the hell cares," he growled, reaching for his bottle.

"She does." Nelson dragged a chair over and sat down at the end of the table. "Lady's right worried."

"Good."

"Didn't know you worked around here," Roscoe said. "You got a *female* ramrod?"

Garrick burped. "I'm th' kiddie wrangler over at Cat's Cradle. Catherine Cantrell's my...boss."

Roscoe laughed. "Kiddie wrangler! A Marine, even an Eastern dude one, a *kiddie wrangler*? Lady musta scrambled your brains, man. 'Course, I heard she's the kind who could scramble any man's—" That was as far as he got. Garrick was out of his seat and over the table, grabbing the bigger man by the lapels of his shirt.

"Not one word about Miss Catherine Cantrell," he snarled, his face inches from the Swede's. "Not one damn word about that lady, or I'm wiping up the floor with your butt. Understand?"

Nelson loosened his nightstick, readying for action, but it wasn't necessary. Roscoe looked totally astonished, nodded and subsided into his seat. Garrick released him, glared for a moment, then settled back himself. His expression softened, and Nelson could have sworn he saw a glint of moisture in the man's eyes. Garrick swore in a whisper, reached for the gin bottle, upended it and turned to the sheriff. "Hendry," he asked, "you got a drunk tank?"

"No, but I can accommodate you in a regular cell if you want."

"Think you better." Garrick got unsteadily to his feet. "I'm sure drunker than I've been in about twenty years. Hey, Roscoe, no hard feelings." Roscoe nodded. "I just...I just..." Garrick didn't finish the sentence. He collapsed in a sodden heap at the sheriff's feet.

Roscoe gazed down at his erstwhile drinking buddy. "For a greenhorn," he said in an awed tone, "that old boy can sure drink. We was matching drinks, but after a while I started cheating. Couldn't keep up. He's some kind of man."

"Yeah," Nelson agreed. "He is."

GARRICK DIDN'T END UP in the jail. Nelson took his inert body over to Doc Turner and explained the situation to the sleepy physician. Doc promised to give Garrick the best of care, especially after Nelson explained that the reason for the binge was love.

"You know how it can be with kids," he said. "Neither one of 'em showing a lick of sense. Well, Cat and her friend here may not be kids, but they ain't any smarter. See what you can do with him when he wakes up, all right?"

"I'm no shrink," Doc said good-naturedly as he eased Garrick's clothing off. "But I'll give it my best shot."

Predictably, Garrick awoke late in the morning with the worst hangover of his life. Sue Futrell, kind but not entirely sympathetic, nursed him through the worst of it. Then, when he was convinced he wasn't actually dying, Doc came in to his room.

"Feeling right rocky?" the white-haired man asked.

"I've been better," Garrick croaked. "How long was I out? Your nurse wasn't exactly a storehouse of information."

"She doesn't care for drinking. You weren't out nearly as long as you deserved, considering the amount Chuck tells me you consumed. Been drinking like that long, son?"

Garrick laughed, then stopped and groaned as his head threatened to come apart. "I haven't had so much as a beer in months. But you're looking at the product of the three-martini lunch. It's becoming passé, but the ability to drink and conduct business used to be a real asset. I guess I still have a hollow leg. So to speak." He reached down as if to check and make sure his legs were still there.

"It's no way to solve problems, son." Doc looked concerned.

"I know." Garrick struggled and managed to sit up. "It was a damn fool thing to do. I just . . . I just was at my wits' end. Is Cat all right?"

"Worried silly. But she's okay. You ready to go back to her?"

Garrick stared out the window. "I'm not sure she really wants me. I *know* she doesn't need me."

Doc swore silently about the idiocy of people in love. "Maybe she doesn't. But she's called every five minutes since Nelson told her you were here, asking if she should come in. Asking how you are. Crying some. Think about it, son. What do you want? Someone who needs you? Just needs you? Or someone who's ready to make themselves sick worrying about you when you go off and make a fool of yourself?"

At this point, Nelson Hendry knocked on the door and entered the room. At the sight of the big sheriff, Garrick felt a rise of anger. "Did she send you to escort me home in handcuffs?" he asked testily. "I wouldn't put it past her."

"Cat didn't send me nowhere." Nelson sat heavily on the only other chair in the room. "I came over to see how you managed to keep from getting your head beat in last night. Remember the cowboy you was drinking with?''

"Big guy. Yeah.''

"Well, you can ask Doc here if I'm telling you the truth, but old Swede Roscoe has laid up more men than I care to count. And I don't care if you was a Golden Gloves fighter when you was a kid. He'd 'a near killed you if he'd 'a mind.''

"No." Garrick spoke confidently. "He wouldn't have. He came over, spoiling for a fight. I used my head and turned him. If the Marine bit hadn't worked, I'd have come up with something else. It's a matter of brains over brawn. I would not have had to fight him, Sheriff. I've got more sense that that. Hell, I'm forty years old.''

"Yeah? Then how come when he started saying stuff about Cat you practically challenged him to a death duel? I ain't never seen a man lay hands on Roscoe like that and be conscious to tell of it the next day. You got some kind of special guardian angel or something?''

"I did that?" Garrick's voice broke slightly. "I...I don't remember.''

"I ain't surprised." Nelson got to his feet. "Next time, I might not be around to bail your butt out if Roscoe takes offence. He was almost as drunk as you, and he let you get away with it. This time. A man can't be so lucky twice in a lifetime. Anytime you feel ready, you can have the keys to your car back. Just come on down to the jail." He settled his hat on his grizzled head. "Don't know if Doc told you," he said, "but after you left, Roscoe kind of took the bar apart. He didn't hurt nobody bad, but he's sleeping it off down at the jail until Chuck can decide if he wants to press charges. You did rile him. It just took a little while for your words to get from his ears to his brain." The sheriff left the room.

"I need to think," Garrick said to Doc Turner.

"About time." The doctor smiled and left also.

CAT STOOD IT as long as she could, which was until after supper that night. Garrick still hadn't shown up, and the reports from Nelson and Doc had been highly cryptic—not satisfactory at all. Finally, she convinced herself they were both lying to her, and that her lover was either in jail or the hospital, seriously injured. She left Jude and the girls in charge of the camp fire and headed for town.

Garrick was not at Doc Turner's, and the good doctor swore that his patient had left on his own steam, if none too steadily. "He's down at the jail," Doc told her. "Had a little unfinished business from last night." He explained about Garrick's prodigious drinking bout. "Why don't you go on back home—"

"I've been *home* long enough," Cat snapped. "I need to see for myself that he's all right. If he tells me to take a hike, fine, I will. But I have to know." She got in the Jeep and drove to Nelson Hendry's place of business. As she got out of the car and prepared to go in, her heart began beating rapidly and her palms became so sweaty, no amount of wiping them on the sides of her jeans would dry them. He *had* to be all right.

When she entered the office, she saw Tom and Nelson at their desks. Both men rose immediately to their feet, obviously astonished to see her. "Where is he?" she asked, putting all the authority she could muster into her voice. In fact, she wanted to cry.

"In there." Tom pointed toward the cells.

"No!" In anguish, she flung herself against the barred door leading to the jail section. He *couldn't* have been arrested! Nelson didn't say a word or offer an explanation. He just unlocked the door and stood back. She ran to the cell where Garrick sat behind the bars, talking to another man— a cowboy she recognized. Both men stared at her in astonishment as she reached through the bars to him.

"Whatever you did," she said, her voice husky with unshed tears, "I will bail you out or get you the best lawyer in the state. I don't care what it costs!" She turned her attention to the cowboy. "Listen, you bastard, if you've hurt him, I'll make sure you never see the light of day again. Oh, Garrick." She looked at her dumbfounded lover. "I'm so sorry for the things I said. You were right. I've been acting holier than thou, and I was as hypocritical as you said. Whatever our differences, whatever has happened here, I love you too much to drive you away because of my stubbornness. Can you forgive me?''

Garrick listened to the plum of self-denial dropped right into his lap. There was no doubting the sincerity of her words. No doubting her love. At this moment, he could take complete advantage of her, extract any promise he wanted. It could be like the easiest hostile takeover in the history of business.

"Nothing's the matter, love," he said, getting slowly to his feet. "Mr. Petersen and I were just concluding some negotiations about a bill this gentleman ran up last night because of some stuff I said and did. I—"

"Your old man threatened to beat the crap outa me," Roscoe Petersen said to her. "On accounta I kinda said some stuff about you I didn't really mean, ma'am. We was both pretty drunk."

"I was defending your honor, Cat," Garrick Drexel said. "On accounta I love you, no matter how mad you make me. And the last thing in the world I want is for you to make concessions on the way you think or run your business. I love you just the way you are."

CHAPTER FOURTEEN

IT SOUNDED TOO GOOD to be true, and to a certain extent it was. To a certain extent, however, it was not. Cat learned that deep into his binge, Garrick had indeed risen to her defense in a ridiculously macho but nevertheless admirable way. He had then passed out. On regaining consciousness the next day, he had still been angry at her, but he had known that if his subconscious had put him in the position of getting his brains beat out in her behalf, something had to be going on in his heart that he would be foolish to deny.

Since it had been his belligerence that had sparked Roscoe's belated rage, he had felt partly responsible and had offered to pay for the big man's damages to the bar. This had mollified the bartender, who had agreed not to press charges. Roscoe was grateful, pledging lifelong friendship even though Garrick was an "Eastern dude."

After Tom promised to return the BMW the next day, Cat and a subdued Garrick returned to the ranch. Neither had much to say to the other. Embarrassment, even shyness, hung between them, keeping feelings and words locked inside. Cat gave him a brief summary of how the Australians were working out, but she was still unwilling to openly praise Garrick for his choice. For his part, he was tempted to gloat, but he knew doing so would be in bad form. After all, he really had lucked into the foursome.

"Abby seems quite taken with Jack," Cat said as they turned on to the ranch road. "When Tom comes out tomorrow, I hope that doesn't cause any problems."

"What if it does?" Garrick's tone sounded strained. "Would that make their relationship any different from so many others?"

Cat didn't have an answer to that.

She turned him over to Jude for the night, explaining his hung-over condition in general terms. Garrick wouldn't kiss her for fear, he said, of inability to perform well. "Give me a rain check," he said curtly before disappearing into the bunkhouse. Cat returned home, wondering if anything had been solved by the events of the past day or if she and Garrick were just politely returning to square one.

By morning Garrick's physical condition had improved considerably. He greeted everyone cheerfully, didn't explain his absence and wolfed down a huge breakfast. He was pleasant to Cat, but not overtly affectionate, and he disappeared into the office almost immediately after eating. He was, he declared, going to start issuing invitations for the week of the fourth. Reluctant to start anything so soon after the last blowup, Cat stayed away.

Tom arrived around the middle of the morning with Garrick's car. He was off duty and dressed in civilian clothes, and his happy demeanor soon faded when Abby begged off being the one to drive him back to town. After introducing him to the new hands, Cat undertook the task herself, planning on grabbing a bite of lunch at Sal's and dreading what Tom might ask her about the tall, tanned Australian named Jack. But he was as silent as Garrick had been the day before. Maybe it was a communicable disease, Cat mused. The Condition of the Silent Male. Maybe it was a good thing.

And maybe it wasn't. She would have given a lot to have known what was going on in Garrick's mind.

But he wasn't giving. The office door was closed when she returned, and she chose to spend her time on chores and riding lessons for the kids rather than storming the castle. If the giant wanted to come out, he was on his own.

On his own, Garrick was doing all right. Peter Chance couldn't make it—a disappointment to both men. But Jamison Pratt could and was bringing some of his family. And two men and one woman from the law office down the hall had said yes. With their families, the number was brought to ten people so far. He was pleased.

That is, he was pleased strategically. Emotionally, he was a basket case. All morning he had expected Cat to break in on him and demand that they talk, work things out. Hell, he had half expected her to follow him into the office as she had the day they'd had the big fight. He itched to see her face, hold her, watch her eyes as she talked. But she had not afforded him either the pleasure or the opportunity.

Well, two could play the game. He'd heard her in the jail and knew that at the moment he had the upper hand. She was in a conciliatory mood, and the smartest thing he could do was let her sweat and then press his advantage—just as he had done so many times in business transactions. It was basic battle psychology.

Except he didn't want to be at war with Cat Cantrell. He wanted to be at peace.

He realized he was very confused and suspected she was, as well. His drinking stunt had been dumb as hell, but it had served the purpose of shaking both of them up. He was no longer sure what he wanted, but the idea of living without her was untenable. He wondered if she felt the same way. God, he thought, they were two mature adults, and you would think they could figure out a way to overcome their differences. He *had* to get her to sit down and talk to him.

But she was more elusive than a legal inside tip. At lunch Abby informed him that Cat had driven Tom back in the BMW and that the boss was going to eat in town instead of barreling back for lunch. The meal seemed cheerless and empty without her presence, and he scuttled back to the office as soon as he could.

Later, through the window, he saw her working with the kids in the riding ring, but pride kept him from running down as he had before and declaring himself with his knees in manure. Right now, he found it a little difficult to believe he had actually done that.

But he had, and it hadn't been such a bad idea. At least he had gotten a reaction. How could you get a reaction from someone who was plainly avoiding you?

He planned, outlining the activities he wanted his friends to enjoy. He organized, cataloged and estimated the supplies he would need to order. It was mindless, empty activity, but it filled the time. After dinner, he thought, he would finally get her to himself.

But she managed to surround herself with people. Garrick's need for her and his frustration level grew with each passing minute. He had completely recovered from his hangover, and she had never looked so desirable with her flowing gold hair, flashing eyes and a figure that combined trimness and lushness in such a special way. By the time the camp fire was over, he was sweating bullets. When she started back to the house with only a general good-night to everyone, he grabbed her arm.

"Cat," he said, his voice thick with emotion and passion, "we need to talk."

"I couldn't agree more." She gazed at him steadily, and he saw none of his own feelings reflected in her calm eyes. "Perhaps tomorrow after breakfast."

"Now."

"Garrick, I don't think—"

"Don't. Cat, were you lying to me when you said what you did last night in the jail?"

"No." Cool as ice.

"Then come on. Let's go." He started to lead her, drag her toward the house.

"Miss Cantrell, you have a problem?" Jack and Charlie appeared suddenly. They carried cigarettes and had been smoking a last one down near the creek in obedience to Cat's stricture against smoking near or in any of the buildings.

"By God," Garrick swore, releasing her arm. "I'm gone one day and you turn my own hands against me, and into your personal bodyguards. No, she doesn't have a problem, boys. Not yet, anyway."

"It's okay, guys." Cat was having trouble deciding whether to laugh or get mad again. It was clear, however, that Garrick was ready to get rid of whatever had driven him to the bottle and whatever he had kept bottled up since. Her patience and pretended coolness had paid off at last. "Garrick and I do have some personal business to discuss. I'll see you in the morning."

"Yes, ma'am." The two gave her sloppy salutes and went back to their smokes. But she could sense they were watching as she and Garrick made their way into the house.

"You do inspire loyalty," he said when the door was closed. "If we could combine my business sense with your people sense, we could own the world."

"I'll settle for a little piece of it, thanks. What did you want to talk about?"

"Just this." His kiss was sudden and searing. Cat didn't fight it, but yielded and responded instantly and eagerly. Her whole body and soul ached for him, and if this was the only way they could start knocking down the barriers, it was all right with her.

He held her so tightly it almost hurt. "Oh, my God, Cat. How could I stand it without you? I've never needed someone so much in my life. Even when I was blind drunk and mad as hell at you, I still wanted you." His breathing was ragged, passionate. "Cat, do you really love me?"

"I do. I think we're both crazy, but I do love you." Her breath was starting to come rapidly.

"Lovers aren't supposed to be sane," he said, and scooped her up into his arms.

Succumbing to his particular brand of insanity brought only delight. He undressed her with adoring hands and made love to her with kisses and touches before his desire reached the point where it couldn't be denied. For once, she was almost able to read his mind and heart, and she gave him love so generous and passionate that it seemed nearly to tear him apart. He gasped and cried out, clutching her with hands that seemed as if they would never let her go.

As he moved over and in her, his strength surrounded her and engulfed her, calling from her a more primitive female response than she had ever felt. The heat of the summer day had lingered into the night, and soon they were both bathed in the clean sweat of passion, which made their contact all the more sensual. His arms gripped her like iron bands and his mouth worshiped the skin of her face, neck and shoulders gently until his passion reached its height. Then his teeth closed on the sensitive area at the juncture of her neck and shoulder and without hurting her, made a primeval claim on all of her body.

She experienced a physical and emotional release like nothing she had imagined. After that, she had no thoughts except the sure realization that she could never live without the kind of madness and love he brought.

Although he was gone when she woke up in the morning, his looks at breakfast demonstrated that he had been as deeply affected as she had been. But they had little time to spend exploring this new level of their relationship.

Nelson called with the news that he had another witness for Garrick regarding the Janet Norton situation. Sal had been at work around three on the morning in question. She had started early in order to get out a fresh batch of her famous cinnamon rolls before first light and had seen Janet driving her rented car through town like all the devils of hell were on her tail. Sal was willing to testify that no one else had been on the street until around five. If Garrick had indeed gone to the motel, she would have seen him either coming or going.

But a call to Sheldon proved disappointing. Neither the testimony of Garrick's lover, a couple of kids and a café operator, nor the evidence from the crime lab at Cheyenne held as much clout in New York as the personal testimony of a respected member of the financial community. Gossip, Sheldon told him, favored Janet by a far margin. Garrick did get two more acceptances to his free vacation offer, but he wondered if the two investment bankers who agreed to the deal weren't merely curious to see how crazy he was and how far he had fallen. Not even Cat's renewed affection could restore his spirits completely, although he genuinely appreciated her efforts to cheer and support him.

By unspoken mutual agreement, they put off any serious discussion of their relationship problems in the face of Garrick's personal ones. While they shared love when they could, the silent barriers, doubts and questions were still there, big as ever and shadowing the delight and happiness they found in one another. Days passed with no real communication other than conversation about business.

Then there was the matter of Abby, Tom and Jack.

Cat tried, subtly, to defuse the situation. "You know," she said to Abby as they were preparing dinner, "Jack's a nice-looking, pleasant young man, but he is in his twenties. Isn't that a bit old for you?"

"So's Tom." Abby doggedly peeled potatoes. "Nobody minded him."

"Nobody minds Jack." Cat tossed handfuls of floured meat into a gigantic stew pot, stirring the chunks so that they browned quickly. The meat was mostly elk and deer and for some reason the strong gamy smell made her feel slightly sick. "But Jack will be moving on in a few weeks. Are you going to be ready to face that?"

Abby turned on her with a look that would have curdled milk. "Could you?" she asked.

That ended the discussion as far as Cat was concerned. The girl was determined to pursue Jack O'Neill at the emotional expense of her devoted Tom, and Cat just didn't have the energy to fight it out with her on any level.

Soon another burden was laid on her, although this was one she welcomed. The Pioneer Festival was an event she had attended as a youngster when her parents had ranched south of Lone Tree. It was a combination Fourth of July celebration, rodeo, outdoor theatrical event and church social all rolled into one. The partying and performances lasted an entire week. The talent was all local and, as a result, uneven, but no one ever seemed to mind. Lone Tree always enjoyed a much-needed shot of prosperity during the week, and though she would be the last to agree, Cat's talents were currently the strongest drawing card of the event. She sang and acted in the pageant, barrel raced in the rodeo, fixed food for the barbecue and generally acted as goodwill ambassador to visitors.

"You *are* the Pioneer Festival week," Garrick exclaimed when he learned all this. "Why didn't you tell me?"

"No, I'm not." They were down by the creek. She was teaching the fundamentals of fly-fishing to some guests, and Garrick had burst onto the scene with his information and comment. Cat told her students to keep practicing and led him out of earshot. "Don't you dare go around saying that, you hear? There are dozens of people far more involved and committed than myself. You'll cause feelings to be hurt if you aren't careful."

"But, Cat, you're missing a major marketing opportunity here!"

She groaned. "I don't want any major marketing opportunity out of this. I want to have fun."

"That's a lousy attitude."

"Well, tough. It's *my* attitude." They had squared off like two prizefighters, and Cat saw an end to the tentative treaty that had existed between them since the last fight. But to her surprise, he didn't pick up the gauntlet.

What he did was much worse. His eyes grew dark and cold, his expression withdrawn. "Fine," he said and turned and stalked up the hill, reminding her of the times she had done the very same thing. Part of her wanted to run after him and try to get him to talk, to understand her position. The other part of her wanted to tell him to go to hell with his superior attitude. She returned to her fishing lesson, saddened by the encounter and hoping she had heard the last of this particular disagreement.

She hadn't.

Garrick, convinced that she was only being narrow-minded and stubborn, included her professional history in the information he sent to his prospective guests, knowing that the chance to hear her sing would be a good lure. Cat found out about this in an indirect way.

The daughter of one of the stockbrokers called her, begging for a chance to do a feature article on her for a small magazine she had just gone to work for. "I was a journalism major," Barbra "Call me Barbie" Durham explained. "And you'll be my first real reporting assignment, if you'll agree." She went on to say that the magazine was circulated in the Rocky Mountains and the Southwest, mostly out of convenience stores and gas stations, but that lots of tourists read it and that it would be great publicity for Cat. She agreed to the interview for one reason—she remembered what it was like to be young and hungry for success. After making the commitment, Cat hung up the phone and sought out the culprit responsible.

He was out behind the barn, chopping wood. The sight of his sweat-streaked bare torso made her throat tighten, but she forced herself to ignore her libido. He was concentrating so hard on his work she had to yell three times to get his attention. He stopped, his broad chest expanding and contracting with the breaths of his exertion, and the ax held across his body with both hands. "What is it?" he asked, a concerned expression forming on his face. "Did Sheldon call again?"

"Nope. A little number by the name of Barbie Durham. Guess what she wanted?"

"I don't know, Cat," he said impatiently. "Come on, I'm too busy for guessing games."

They hadn't made love since the argument about her unwillingness to exploit her importance to the festival. That was days ago. "I'm just real damn sorry you're so busy," she snapped. "I got a request from this woman for an interview, you louse! I told you not to make a big deal about my past or what I'm doing for the festival. What if she writes something offensive to the other people involved?"

He grinned slightly. "So, you're going to do it?"

"Only because I felt sympathetic. She's just starting out. Anyone else would have gotten the bum's rush. Which is what I ought to be giving you for disobeying my explicit orders!''

"Disobeying?'' His laughter was sharp. "Cat Cantrell, I never promised to *obey* you.''

"Much less to honor!'' She was truly furious now. "I think that when this week of yours is over, you ought to plan to move on. You've worn out your welcome here, Garrick Drexel.''

"Leave? You want me to leave you?''

Cat was treated to a disquieting sight of the big, strong man suddenly looking like a little boy who had been told that not only was there no Santa Claus, but no one else was going to take his place. Her heart softened and started to break, but she fought for control. "Isn't that what you were planning anyway? Isn't that why you invited all your friends here? So you could exonerate yourself and go home with a clean slate?''

The muscles in his bare arms bunched and flexed. "No,'' he said hoarsely. "I'm doing it so that I don't *have* to go back. So I don't have to leave you.''

The look on his face and the tone of his voice finished her off. The tears came. "Oh, Garrick. What are we going to *do*? We can't go on like this, and we can't not go on!''

He didn't move toward her, but his knuckles whitened around the ax handle. "I honestly don't know, Cat,'' he said, looking as if he was close to tears himself. "I honestly don't know.''

Cat turned and ran as fast as she could up the road, not stopping until she was out of his sight. Then she slowed to a walk, sobs still lingering in her chest and throat. The sky was clear and impossibly blue, as only the Wyoming heavens could get in summer. No breeze blew through the trees, and she could hear the birds singing clearly. She thought of her flute, long neglected during the tourist season. Maybe she should slink off into the woods and commune with it and herself for a while, she mused. Doing so usually helped her gain a perspective on things. And God knew she needed perspective now.

She stumbled over a clod of dirt and kicked at it viciously. *Damn him!* she thought angrily. He did what he wanted, then made her feel like a heel for coming down on him for it. She was boss at Cat's Cradle, but she was rapidly losing control. He was like a steamroller, crushing everything in his path that didn't suit him. Was that right? Was that fair?

He didn't understand life in Wyoming. He didn't know how sensitive people could be over a silly thing like the festival. Some of the participants lived year to year just to have their moment in the sun that week. What would they think if she started strutting around like a prima donna? He was a fish out of water out West, just as she had been back East in spite of all her successes. He'd lived in the city all his life. There was no way he could adjust to the realities of small-town living.

But when she had told him he had to leave...

She was almost at the main road, so she decided to go ahead and pick up the mail. Usually she did that by Jeep early in the morning, but she hadn't today. She wasn't sure if it was due to the emotional roller coaster she had been riding or advancing age, but it seemed this year that she was more tired than usual. *Pressure and stress,* she told herself. She certainly had plenty of that!

The box was jammed with mail—mostly junk. There were a few bills, several personal letters for her, one for Jude and a sizable brown envelope that felt as if it had been stuffed full. She tucked the rest under one arm and opened the mysterious envelope as she started home. There was no return address on the front. Puzzled, she peeked inside. Then she stopped, scrabbled for the contents and let the other mail fall to the ground unheeded.

The envelope was full of clippings, all of which dealt with illegal activities of people involved in finance. She read through a couple quickly. The stories were taken from newspapers and magazines published around the country. But what brought first a chill to her heart and then a white-hot flood of rage was the fact that in each article the name of the real offender was marked out and Garrick's name was scrawled above it. She felt frozen with fury and horror.

GARRICK RUMMAGED in his bunkhouse locker until he found his car keys. She had run off toward the highway, and there was no telling how far she was going to go. He had been too stunned by her words to follow at first. Now he figured his best chance of catching up to her was with wheels. The woman could move when she had the wind at her back!

And he had blown her a wind and a half. He didn't bother with a shirt, but got into his car, cursing his shortsightedness. He had only been thinking of her stubborn attitude about her old profession—not about the impact his action might have on her relationship with her community. How stupid! he berated himself. Of course it would embarrass her to have her name held above those of the other participants. She had told him that, but he hadn't listened. He gunned the engine and headed up the road, hoping she hadn't hit the highway and run into trouble with some yahoos like the ones who had burglarized her Jeep.

She hadn't. She was standing near the mailbox, holding some papers. Relieved to the core, he slowed and stopped. She didn't look up. Relief turned to alarm. Had bad news come in the mail? He knew she had a brother and sister living somewhere in the southern part of the state. He didn't think she was close to them, but even so... "Cat," he yelled. "What's wrong?"

She looked up and saw him. Her expression was frozen and horrified. She said nothing, but held out the bundle to him. Puzzled, Garrick got out of the car, approached her and took the packet from her stiff fingers. He didn't look at the papers. "Cat." He touched her face. "I am so sorry. I wasn't thinking..."

"Forget me." Her voice was raspy. "Look at those papers. Look!"

He looked. "Oh, my God. Who do you suppose...?"

"Janet." She was starting to shake. "Your crazy sister-in-law. She must have sent them." Cat finally moved, grabbing him by his bare shoulders. "Garrick, forget what I said about your leaving because I was kicking you out. Forget all that! You have got to go back now. Don't you see? This time it's poison-pen stuff. Next time it might be a letter bomb! She hates you, Garrick. She hates you! And, God help me, I love you!"

CHAPTER FIFTEEN

"SHE DOESN'T HATE ME, CAT." Seeing how upset she was, he put his arms around her. She came into his embrace without argument. "If anything, she's just confused. Or trying a rather unfunny joke."

"This is no joke." She wanted to push away, but her muscles relaxed against her will and she rested on his chest, smelling his sun-warmed, sweaty skin. His natural scent was more sensuous than any cologne. "Garrick, she's getting to a dangerous edge. I can feel it." Tears started again.

"Now, Cat." He stroked her hair.

"Don't 'Now, Cat' me!" She managed to push away. "What are you going to do about it?"

"Nothing. When my friends get here in a few days, I'll get a better perspective on what's up."

"What's up is there's an enemy out there setting up to skin you! She's nuts, Garrick." Cat waved the papers. "Just look at this scrawl. She must really hate your guts. Maybe...maybe she'll hire some Mafia hit man or something."

"Will it make you feel any better if I give this stuff to Nelson? He can get in touch with his counterpart in New York."

"Oh, yes." She smiled through her tears. "That's the first sensible thing I've heard you say in a long time."

"Good." He put his arm around her again, thinking that the last thing he was going to do was show the papers to the sheriff. Janet was family, and he would handle the situation without the intervention of the law. "Now, about my leaving after next week..."

"Forget what I said. You're arrogant and shortsighted but you're *my* arro—'' His kiss cut off the rest of her words.

THE DAY OF THE ARRIVAL of Garrick's guests came much too soon. In the interim, he and Cat had enjoyed a time of peace and love that had served to bandage some of the wounds they had opened in each other's hearts. Nothing had actually been solved, but they felt better and closer than they ever had before.

They arrived in a caravan to pick up the arrivals at the Jackson airport: Cat in her Jeep, Garrick in his BMW and Jude in a van Cat had borrowed from a friend. The New York contingent was stunned and openmouthed at the Wyoming scenery—particularly the magnificent Tetons. The weather had cooperated, and the vista was cloudless. Cat explained to her passengers that while they had no view of the mountains from the ranch, spectacular scenes could be found within a short horseback ride. The entire drive back across the pass, she was beseiged with questions, most from the fledgling reporter, Barbie Durham. By the time Cat turned into the driveway, followed by Garrick and Jude, she felt that Barbie had collected enough information to write a biography, not just an article.

The days that followed were strange for her. Now Garrick really was the boss, and she was only a part-time employee. He took on all responsibility for his guests and for the management of the ranch, and he did it all with consummate skill and obsessive attention to detail. They now slept together openly, agreeing that to do otherwise would send the wrong signals to his friends, but he was always so tired at night that he passed out before his head hit the pillow.

She got along well with his friends. Jamison Pratt had clearly come intending to dislike her; he obviously resented her for keeping his partner away from the Street. But she won the man over with her frank and easy manner. The silver-haired investment advisor showed a particular interest in learning to fly fish, and she tried to spend a fair amount of the little spare time she had instructing him in the finer points of the sport.

"You know," Pratt said as he practiced casting under her watchful eye, "I'm going to do everything I can to persuade Garrick to return to the firm, Miss Cantrell. I like you and I like this country, but it's not the real world. A man like Garrick belongs where his talents can best be utilized." He puffed on the pipe he smoked incessantly.

"I'm not in competition with you," she said easily in spite of the tightness his words brought to her throat and chest. "Garrick's a big boy, capable of making his own decisions. I care too much to squabble over him. If he'd be happier back at his old job, well and good."

Jamison eyed her skeptically. "You mean that? I thought you were, well, planning on netting him and getting him to settle down as your manager."

Cat laughed. "Mr. Pratt, the last thing I need is Garrick Drexel managing Cat's Cradle. New York methods just don't work out here. Like you said, it is a different world."

Pratt's eyebrows rose. "Young lady," he said in an admiring tone, "there is definitely more to you than immediately meets the eye."

"I hope so," Cat replied. Then she showed him how to cast with delicacy, causing the fly to land at a precise spot on the water. Jamison Pratt became so intrigued with the process he let his pipe go out.

Despite the tentative friendship she achieved with his friends, however, she did not discuss Garrick's professional problems with anyone, trusting him to take advantage of the opportunity to listen.

Garrick tried. The best he could do was to get his colleagues to agree the ranch was a wonderful place and Cat a wonderful woman. But no one gave him encouragement about his situation. It was becoming more and more apparent that he was actually going to have to compromise his principles and possibly his relationship with Cat to go back and chip down the edifice that was rising up in front of his good name.

Jamison was upset about the poison-pen notes. "Garrick," he said one evening as they strolled the grounds, "don't you see that this is just further justification for coming back and confronting whatever devil is doing this? I don't for a minute believe it's Janet. She doesn't have that kind of twisted mind. You have an enemy, son, and the sooner you find out who it is, the better."

"I made my share of enemies in the business," Garrick conceded. "But I never worked anyone over so badly that they would set out to destroy me. Willis Kent has a few bullets with my name on them, but he's a professional lawman. I can't see him doing something crazy like those notes. He'd nail me in a minute if he found solid evidence, though."

"He would." Jamison puffed on his pipe. "And the fact that he hasn't yet is in your favor. But facts aren't as weighty as gossip, you know that. Janet's account of your tearing up her room in a rage has made the rounds. That, plus your abrupt departure, doesn't look good."

"I didn't do it."

"No one knows that for sure. Oh, I believe you," the older man said as Garrick turned angrily toward him. "I have seen these past few days there's nothing wrong with your mind. Just your sense of direction."

"What's that supposed to mean?"

"What really is out here for you, Garrick?" Jamison pointed around the ranch with the stem of his pipe. "This is a fairyland, a playground. The real world is where you came from. It's time to come home, son."

His words and advice ate deeply into Garrick's fears, doubts and confusion. He began to seriously think about returning, not only to take care of the rumors about himself but to see if he really did belong in the world in which he had lived for four decades.

He considered asking Cat to go with him. Every day she grew more beautiful to him, and he longed to beg her to give up everything, marry him and follow him where he had to go. But he couldn't. This was her life, and he couldn't take it away from her for any reason. What had seemed a selfishness in her to him for a while now seemed only a natural symbiotic relationship between her and the land. To remove her from her environment would be as cruel as to cage and remove the wild cat that had stalked him that snowy night. In his mind the mountain lion came to symbolize Cat—wild, free, untamed and, in her own way, not a little dangerous. She had taken his heart and soul as easily as if he had been helpless prey.

The week went well for him, though he was exhausted by the end of it. Then came the night of the Pioneer Festival pageant.

Garrick was emotionally keyed up to the snapping point. He and Cat had made love once during the week, but instead of relieving his tension, the lovemaking had actually increased it, leaving him wakeful for hours afterward while she slept soundly in his arms. He couldn't live this way, he realized. He couldn't be in conflict with her and be a proper lover or husband. Was he really a fish out of water here? he wondered. Doubts assailed him, but desire for life with Cat was equally strong. He was a man torn.

Then he watched and listened to her perform in the pageant.

She played the part of a frontier wife who had given up a life of luxury in the East to come with her man to a wild frontier. The play was a bit hokey and the musical score amateurish, but the message to Garrick was clear: love brings sacrifice and sacrifice can bring happiness. He struggled not to cry openly as she sang this message. His heart aching and on fire, he decided recklessly to take the greatest risk.

AFTER THE PERFORMANCE, Cat was as high as a kite, flying on leftover adrenaline. Her body was wearier than she could remember it being, but her spirit still sang. Nothing, she felt, could go wrong tonight. She kept her upswept hairstyle intact, and stayed in her gingham gown to socialize with an admiring entourage consisting largely of Garrick's New York crowd. Barbie Durham's attitude was almost worshipful, and Cat made it clear that she wanted to see and approve a draft of the article before it was sent on to Barbie's publisher. No toes in Lone Tree would get stepped on if Cat could help it. The only shadow over the evening was that Garrick had kept himself at a distance. She didn't even see him at the barbecue, at which she ate enough to feed an army. Her appetite had returned with a vengeance after a period of barely picking at her food, and she put it down to relief that Garrick's rule over the ranch was almost over. Things would soon return to normal, she told herself.

Then Garrick appeared by her side and whispered that he needed to speak to her in private. His voice was shaking slightly, and she could feel a trembling in his hand when he touched her arm. Puzzled and a little concerned, she agreed to talk to him.

His heart beating with trepidation, Garrick led her to a relatively sheltered place near the creek under some trees. She sighed and leaned against him, making his spirit soar with hope. "Fame and fortune too much for you?" he asked, teasing the stray hairs that fell down her neck.

"I'll say." She laid her head on his chest. "Once a year is plenty, believe me."

"More than one of my friends is saying you ought to go professional again."

She looked up, her eyes gleaming in the moonlight. "You know how I feel about that." He remembered his lioness image.

"Yes, I know," he said. "But I need to talk to you about something else. Will you please listen to me?"

"Of course." Cat drew back. His tone and expression told her whatever he had to say was important. Very important. "Go ahead."

He didn't mince words. "I want you to marry me. I have to go back to New York. I'm not asking you to come. You belong right here. No place else. Will you marry me?"

She caught her breath. "I can't...can't leave the ranch."

"I'm not asking that. I have to leave, but you don't. Will you be my wife?"

"Garrick, you can't have it both ways! We can't live at two different ends of the country and still have a relationship, much less a marriage. You haven't been hitting any of the home brew being passed around, have you?"

"I'm as sober as a judge, love. And I'm not talking about living in New York forever while you stay here. I didn't want to worry you this week when you were so involved with the festival, but things are far more messed up than I even dreamed. I have to go back."

"Oh, Garrick, then all this trouble you went to with your friends has been a waste of time?"

"Not by a long shot. They've had the time of their lives. You ought to have seen that yourself. Several have already booked for next year. If you aren't careful, I may make a fashionable vacation spot out of Cat's Cradle."

"At what cost?" She touched his face tenderly.

"What do you mean? Wouldn't it be good to have some customers who could spread the word in another part of the country?"

"I mean, my dearest, sweetest friend, that you have practically killed yourself this week." She kissed his cheek. "You would burn out in a month if I left you in charge. This isn't for you, Garrick. Go back to your Wall Street office. That's where you belong."

"Cat, no!" He couldn't believe she could dismiss him so easily, so casually. Not after all they had shared.

Cat forced herself to smile. "I want what's best for you. It isn't here, Garrick. You're still searching, just as much as you were the day I picked you up. I hope—"

"Damn it, woman!" He grabbed her by the waist and pulled her to him. Her hair sprang loose from its pins and spilled down her back. "I want you to be my wife, have my kids, grow old with me."

Tears now. "Garrick, I can't have children."

"You aren't so old . . ."

"No, listen. I cannot have children. There's something wrong with my plumbing—nothing the doctors in New York could explain, but they said it would be a miracle if I ever conceived." She watched the terrible disappointment she had feared appear in his eyes. His grip on her loosened.

"Well, okay," he said uncertainly. "That doesn't matter, but—"

"Shh!" She put a warning hand over his mouth. "Do you hear that?"

"What?" He stiffened, thinking again of the mountain lion. She had told him the few animals of that species in the vicinity rarely neared the population centers. But there was a first time for everything. Then he heard the noise.

It was a strange, squeaking, bubbling sound, but he recognized it. A female was crying and trying her best to muffle it. "Where's it coming from?" he whispered, trusting her tracking ability far more than his own.

"Farther down the creek." Cat took his hand. "Come on. She may be hurt."

She was, but not physically. They found Abby Springer crouched under some red willow bushes, sobbing her eyes out. Cat knelt down and took the girl in her arms.

"Come on, honey," she said. "What's the matter? It won't hurt so bad if you talk about it."

Garrick got down on one knee nearby. The sight and sound of Cat comforting a suffering child made his heart ache. He couldn't bear to watch. He couldn't stand to walk away.

The story came out in gasps and sobs. Jack was leaving. They were all leaving after the weekend, but he was taking her broken heart with him. They had all gone to the dance at the school gym together, and Jack had danced with her, told her she was a lovely little sheila, but that he had a girl back home. She thought he might have been lying about that, but it didn't change the fact that he was leaving and she would never see him again. "He...he kissed me good-bye," she sobbed.

Terrific, Cat thought. *Just a taste. Enough to make her long for more.* Men had very little sense when it came to letting women down easily. She glanced at Garrick. Under her calm exterior, her own heart was breaking just as thoroughly as Abby's, if not more. "Would you mind leaving us alone for a few minutes, please," she said to him, warning him with her eyes not to dare refuse.

He got up without a comment and disappeared into the dark. Cat turned her attention to Abby. "Where people are concerned, you can't always have what you want," she said. "You're old enough to know that."

"Yes." She was sniffling now. No longer sobbing.

"Look around. Think of your friends who broke up this summer. Or think of Tom. He was crazy about you." That was hard, but Cat figured it was necessary.

"He hates me now." Fresh tears started down Abby's cheeks.

"I doubt that. But he has been hurt. Now, just in case you think it gets any better—" the words stuck in her throat for a moment "—Garrick told me tonight he's going back to New York." She left out the proposal of marriage. It made so little sense, there was no point in mentioning it.

"Oh, Cat!" Abby turned a horrified look on her. "He just *can't.*"

"Yes, he can. But I still have my ranch and my friends. It isn't the end of the world for me. Nor should Jack's leaving be for you. We women are stronger than that."

Abby dried her eyes and straightened her shoulders. "I've been pretty silly, haven't I?"

"No. I expect I'll have a good cry or two when Garrick leaves. But I won't wallow in self-pity. Will you?"

"'Course not." She tossed her red hair. "That would give him too much satisfaction. I'm going back to the dance to have a good time." She got to her feet and dusted off her jeans.

"That's the spirit." Cat got up, too, wondering if she would recover as easily. She seriously doubted she would. She still had to deal with Garrick's senseless proposal, and she wasn't sure she could say no to him without coming apart and confessing that she loved him enough to follow him anywhere—a decision she knew she would come to regret eventually. No, it would be better to make a clean break, even though it would hurt worse than anything she had done before. For the rest of the evening, she steeled herself to be strong when the time came to say goodbye. She wouldn't hold him back from seeking his own truth.

AT THAT MOMENT Garrick was not thinking about the "truth," but was panicking. He had wandered along the streambed, knowing he could use it to find his way back. His emotions had driven him, however, and when he came back to reality, his watch told him he had been walking for more than an hour. He couldn't see one light, not one sign of civilization.

He was angry. Mad as hell at Cat for dismissing him so casually when he *knew* she didn't feel casual about him. She was fooling herself if she thought they could get along apart. They were meant to be together for life! He grew angrier and crashed heedlessly through the brush along the creek. When he caught the heel of his boot on a root, he stumbled and cursed loudly.

The silence that followed his shout seemed suddenly menacing. He glanced upward, mentally apologizing for his language. Then he froze when he heard a rustle in the bushes on the other side of the creek. The moonlight was bright, and he had no trouble seeing what had caused the noise.

"Oh, God," he said, meaning it. The sleek mountain lion paced lazily out of the shelter of foliage. It stopped and looked across the water at him. Its huge golden eyes blinked once.

Water, he thought. It wouldn't cross water to get him. He was safe as long as the creek was between them. Relatively safe. He started to walk in the direction he had come.

The lion paced him, keeping just a few feet ahead or behind as he hurried along. After a while, Garrick's fear subsided and his curiosity grew. Was this the same animal he'd met in the woods? Did it recognize his scent? Then a really crazy thought occurred to him.

Was this some kind of sign he wasn't to mess with Cat's mind? To be perfectly honest, that was exactly what he had planned. He knew he could cajole and manipulate her into agreeing to marriage. He was going to bring on the heavy artillery until she did things his way. He was the weaker one! The less noble. The longer he thought about it, the madder he got, not at her but at himself.

"You've made your point," he said loudly, stopping and addressing himself to the animal. It looked mildly interested, stopping and settling back on its haunches. "I wasn't going to treat her honestly. I'm glad we had this talk. You can go home now." To his astonishment, the animal stood, yawned and disappeared into the night without another sound. Garrick stared dumbly at the spot where it had sat.

Then he headed to town. Three days later he was on a plane to New York. He had made no further demands on Cat, but had parted from her with a declaration of his love. She had put up a cool front with him, not trusting him.

But he was beginning to trust himself.

CAT SAT AT HER DESK, going through the morning mail. It had been three weeks since Garrick had left, and every day had been a living hell for her. Nothing took his place—not the ranch, not her social life. She was heartsick and miserable. She had received a letter from him every day, which was somewhat heartening. When he had left, he had whispered with his last kiss that he would be back. He had even left his car and most of his belongings at the ranch, as if they were proof of his intentions. She yearned to believe. But it was so hard!

Cat's Cradle was running smoothly without him. At first his physical absence had been sorely felt. Then Jude had hired a young cowboy from a dude ranch over in Jackson Hole. Bart Hansen was a strong, willing and experienced hand with the same laconic style as the wrangler. Cat approved.

Abby had settled down, obviously matured by her experience. Tom dropped around from time to time, but they just talked. There was no dating. The deputy seemed permanently melancholy. Cat understood the feeling.

She was deep in unshakable melancholy herself. Since Garrick had gone, she had been dragging herself around at half speed. Lovesickness, she told herself. But it bothered her since she ordinarily had the constitution of a horse. She would have to find the time to make an appointment with Doc Turner, she thought, just in case she had a real physical problem. But time wasn't in rich supply of late, so she waited.

The mail produced the usual letter from Garrick, which she set aside to devour at her leisure. A brown envelope held the galley proof of Barbie's article. Cat read it, approved and wrote a short note giving her go-ahead for the piece. Then she turned to ranch business.

But her heart was not in it.

GARRICK READ THROUGH the article about Cat. She had written that she liked it, and he agreed that it was accurate and flattering. What he wouldn't have given to be able to share the fun of reading it with her in person!

He had spent the most frustrating weeks of his life pounding the pavement, going from office to office in the combined August city heat and frigid air-conditioned buildings. He had made some progress toward clearing his name and had acquired a cold in the process. His temper was short and his feet constantly sore. He longed for his comfortable boots and the clean, healthy air of the mountains.

He and Sheldon had hired a private investigator, a police veteran specializing in white-collar crime, and Garrick was confident Booth Callahan would eventually put together the pieces that would exonerate him for good. The sad part was that it had become clear Janet was at the bottom of the whole scheme. Booth had counseled against confronting her until he had more evidence, and the waiting was driving Garrick nuts.

Cat wrote him, and from time to time they talked on the phone, but it wasn't the same. He treasured every moment they communicated, but he felt she was still keeping herself distant. Something was different, and he couldn't put his finger on it. That was driving him even crazier than the business with Janet. He cursed softly and let the magazine with the article about her slip to the floor. Sooner or later this mess would end, and he would be back to her so fast her head would spin!

JUST THEN, NORM RUNGE took a bite of his candy bar and absently rubbed his fingers on a magazine lying on the counter of the east Arizona gas station. A name caught his eye, and he stuffed the thing in his pocket without paying for it. The proprietor didn't notice.

In the car with Bob, he pointed the article out. "Looky here. Ain't this about the rancher lady was so kind to us last spring?"

"So 'tis." Bob studied the article. "She's doin' okay. Got a bunch of rich New York guys at her place. How much cash we got?"

"A thousand left from the guy with the Chevy."

"Well, then, Miss Cat can wait for a while. What say we head south again for a while? I kinda miss them cantina ladies. What say?"

Norm agreed enthusiastically. He tossed Garrick's raincoat in the back seat of the car and whooped as they raced out of the parking lot.

CHAPTER SIXTEEN

CAT TAPPED THE PLANE TICKET on the edge of the counter
at the travel agency in Jackson Hole. It represented so
much, it might as well have been written in solid gold. *New
York*, she thought, *here I come.*

The decision hadn't come lightly. She had wrestled with
herself into the small hours of the night, making herself
nauseated by morning. She lost weight, she gained weight,
she cried even in front of Jude. It was the old wrangler,
probably her most loyal friend, who finally sat her down
and talked sense to her.

"Known you for longer'n either of us'd care to tell," he
said. "And I ain't gonna sit here and watch you kill yourself over that man. Get outa here, Cat. Go to him. We can
manage."

"But hunting season..." she began, protesting weakly.

"Ain't no problem. Them boys don't expect the kind of
treatment you give 'em, anyways. Alls they want is a chance
to get some meat and a trophy or so. Me and Bart can handle it. Sal said she'd be happy to come cook, and Abby and
Ellen will drive out with her after school to clean. Tom and
a couple other men said they'd like to help, too.

"Really?"

"You know it, gal. Not a soul in town ain't been telling
me they're worried about you. And Garrick, he made a few
friends himself. They all want you to bring that boy back.
He belongs here now. You listening to me?"

Cat was listening. What it amounted to was that in her
hour of need, her friends were rallying. The realization of
that, the depth of caring the townspeople showed, almost

overwhelmed her. Because of the economic crunch that had squeezed everyone, they hadn't been able to help in May, but now it was different. It didn't cost money to cook or clean or care. And she knew in her heart she would have done the same for every one of them. She accepted the community offer.

So here she was, picking up the ticket, only a few hours from flying to meet an unsuspecting Garrick. She had decided to keep her plans secret, thinking he might say she ought not to come. She suspected he wouldn't understand about the help she had received. The only thing remaining was for her to go home and pack. That and make a quick stop at Doc Turner's. Sue Futrell had called and declared that an appointment was not optional and she was to come in or be dragged in bodily. Ellen had been reporting on Cat's physical problems, and Doc wasn't going to take no for an answer. Furthermore, Nelson Hendry had told her that he was willing to use handcuffs if necessary. Cat grinned. It was nice to have everyone so concerned about her, although she wasn't really worried. Once she was with Garrick, she believed, all her weird symptoms would disappear.

Packing was mildly depressing. She had no fashionable clothing, but made do with the classics she had saved after moving back. She hoped she remembered how to put on makeup. After tossing in a few unread paperbacks, she headed into town and the doctor's office.

TIME WEIGHED HEAVILY on her as she waited in his office for the exam results. He had been unusually silent during the process, and Cat had grown worried. When he finally appeared, there was a strange expression on his face.

"What is it?" she asked, now fearful. "What's the matter with me?"

"Nothing." He sat down at his desk and played with several medicine bottles he had carried in with him. "Nothing abnormal, anyhow."

"Doc!"

"You got a doctor out there?" he asked. "Somebody who treated you before? Someone you like and trust?"

"Yes. I did go to a physician for some female troubles. Patricia Shaffer. She couldn't help me, but I liked her."

Doc made some notes on a sheet of paper. "Well, I think the lady can help you now, Cat. Just give her this and tell her your old country doc said you were just shy of two months pregnant."

"Pregnant! I can't be! It's impossible." Doc just grinned at her.

GARRICK STRODE ANGRILY down the street that had been his territory for so many years. He no longer felt at home on it, and today he had donned a pair of boots and a cowboy hat as a gesture of defiance. He looked ridiculous, he knew, but he didn't give a damn. It didn't matter that Booth's fine hand was beginning to unravel the web Janet and the unwitting Willis Kent had woven. It didn't matter that one by one his old business colleagues were admitting they had no real reason to believe the rumors about him. What mattered was he was stuck here until something broke. And he most emphatically did not want to be here. He wanted to be in Wyoming with Cat.

Lately, it had become a serious obsession. Every leggy blonde he saw had her face. He woke in the night, sweaty with the aftereffects of erotic, romantic dreams with her as his co-star. He'd taken up jogging, daring muggers to challenge him. Cold showers, he had learned, didn't work. He wanted Cat!

But it was more than just Cat. He wanted to be where the sky wasn't obscured by pollution and concrete. He realized he had been spoiled for the city forever. Maybe he wasn't cut out to be a ranch hand or even manager for the rest of his life, but he would find his niche. He'd find a way to live in the country he'd come to love—with the woman he knew he'd love the remainder of his days.

See, he thought, slowing his pace. There she was again, this time in the guise of a slender blonde in sunglasses who was leaning dramatically against the famous street sign. This one looked out of place in her navy suit with unpadded shoulders, high heels instead of Reeboks, her hair pinned up in an old-fashioned, vaguely familiar...

He stopped and rubbed his eyes. The crowd surged around him, unheeding. He really had gone crazy. If he wasn't certain he was absolutely out of his loving mind, he would have sworn...

She took off her sunglasses and stared at him. Garrick started to run.

They embraced in a joyous frenzy, paying no mind to the sea of humanity around them. He pinned her against the Wall Street sign and kissed her thoroughly and passionately. She responded as enthusiastically as she had in his wildest dreams. Her body strained to his, and Garrick knew that even if he had lost his mind, he had never been happier.

Finally, they both became self-conscious. He pulled her back from the sign and the crowd and found them shelter in the doorway of an office building. "What in the world are you doing here?" he asked, grinning like an idiot.

"Looking for you." Her own smile was wide but tremulous. "Garrick, I can't stand to live without you. I left the ranch in good hands and came out here to find you and tell you that."

He stared at her. "What have you done to yourself? You look... different."

"No—nothing." She had decided on the long plane trip not to tell him about the baby right away. It would seem as if she had run to him only when she had found out that she had a problem. Her pride would never stand for that. He would know eventually—by now it was a sure bet her closest friends in Lone Tree knew. But Garrick would know only when she was sure he understood she had come for him and him alone. "I just have makeup on," she said. "You aren't exactly used to that."

"Well, whatever, you look great." He stepped back a bit. "And you've put a little meat on your bones. Not pining away for me, I see."

"Oh, yes, I have been." She touched his face. "You've lost weight, and you look so pale. Are you all right?"

"I am now. It's restaurant food and being indoors all day long. Cat, I've got to get out of here. I've got to get back home. I . . . Oh, damn." He looked at his watch.

"What's wrong?"

"I have a meeting. Sheldon and Booth. They said they had some new information, but it can wait. Let's go back to my place."

"Time enough for that," she chided. "Let's go hear what they have to say. The sooner you get this cleared up, the sooner . . . Did you say you wanted to get back *home*?"

"Home is in Lone Tree with you, Cat. If you don't want to marry me, okay. But I'm going to live there anyhow. I've renewed my acquaintance with the city and found it wanting. Check out the hat." He tipped it back on his head. "Not very Wall Street, is it?"

Excitement filled her. They had so much to talk about. "No," she said, eyeing him critically. "But it would be all right with a Western-cut suit. We'll have to buy you one in Casper when we get back." He hugged her tightly.

SHELDON SHERIDAN and Booth Callahan were not what she had pictured from Garrick's letters. The lawyer was a lean, spare man who didn't look old enough to have the smarts Garrick claimed he had. When he spoke, she changed her mind. Booth was a graying little Irishman who chain-smoked. He didn't say much at first. When Garrick introduced her, both men were stiffly courteous, but they warmed to her as time passed.

They were in Sheldon's office. Cat recognized the symbols of success: paneled walls, thick carpet, oak desk. The lawyer tapped a thick folder on the polished wood surface of the desk. "Here's the bottom line, Garrick," he said. "Booth and I have documented enough evidence to bring a case of harassment against Kent. I've shown it to a friend down at Justice, and he agrees you've been a victim of a personal vendetta, beyond doubt."

"That's great. Now I can get out of this town." He squeezed Cat's hand.

"Not so fast. I said we could bring a case. It could take years to win the thing."

"Then no suit," Garrick said firmly.

"There is an alternative in this situation." Booth stubbed out a cigarette and reached for another. Cat suddenly worried about the secondhand smoke hurting the baby. Funny, she hadn't thought that way about the child until she had seen Garrick.

"We can try to get him to admit publicly what his little game was," Booth went on.

"How?" Garrick sat forward in his chair.

"How did you keep the lion from attacking?" Cat asked softly. All three men stared at her.

"Lion?" both New Yorkers asked at once.

"Just a small cougar," Garrick said, enjoying himself. He had not told Cat about the second encounter. "She was a real pussycat, actually. And what I did was confront her, cuss to beat the band and generally make it known that I'd be more trouble than I was worth. Is that what you had in mind?" They nodded.

The war council regarding Kent concluded with the decision to confront him in his office with the evidence of his activity and threaten him with the civil suit Garrick didn't intend to bring. With hope, the man would crumble and retract his accusations.

Janet Norton was also discussed.

"I doubt if threats will work with her, even if you were willing to use them," Booth Callahan said. "The lady is severely disturbed, and I think it's clear her condition has something to do with your marriage to her sister. I just can't for the life of me figure why she hates you so much or what her root problem is."

"I have some thoughts," Garrick said somberly. "I'm going... *we're* going to meet with Peter Chance tonight to talk about it." He looked fondly at Cat.

They discussed strategy for a little while longer, then Garrick declared the meeting over. His private reunion with Cat had been delayed long enough. The elevator that took them down to street level was empty except for them. Garrick took the opportunity to embrace her again. He still couldn't believe she was really here. "Tell me, love," he murmured against the soft skin of her neck, "how did you know where to look for me in the middle of New York City?"

"Easy." She grinned at him. "I checked into a hotel, then went hunting. You see, darling, it's not so different from the forest. This is your range, your territory, and I knew I'd find you somewhere in it." He started to laugh, then kissed her until she was breathless. And then they hurried to her hotel room to continue what they had started....

Later in the day, Cat dressed carefully for their dinner meeting with Peter Chance. This was a man who knew Garrick in some ways more intimately than she did, and she wanted to make a good impression. Makeup was a problem because her lips were swollen from the passionate lovemaking they had indulged in most of the afternoon. She winced a little as she passed a lip brush across them.

"I don't think I'll ever get used to you with lipstick." Garrick came up behind her and kissed her bare shoulder. "But you look beautiful any way."

She smiled. He had been overflowing with tender praises all day, and it seemed he wasn't ready to stop yet. She had worried that the changes in her body would be apparent to him, but he hadn't commented on them; he'd just loved her.

"I'm only applying protective coloration appropriate to the environment," she teased. "You won't find me in a dress on the ranch, nor blue jeans here."

His sexy gaze in the mirror seared her. "I prefer you in nothing at all." He turned her to face him.

"Don't," she protested. "You'll ruin the paint job."

Some time later, she managed to repair it, and they set off to see Peter Chance.

He was exactly as she had pictured him—a nice-looking man with sandy hair and an engaging smile. He greeted her not with a handshake, but a hug, and she liked him immediately. "I'm glad to finally meet the lady who's turned this character's life in the right direction," he said. "It's a good thing you came out, because he's been on my consulting couch a couple of times, climbing the walls because he missed you so much."

"Oh, really?" She glanced at a grinning, reddening Garrick.

"Really," Peter said.

After they ate, over coffee, the subject of Janet was reluctantly raised. "I'd like to get her in therapy before I forward a diagnosis," Peter said, "but from everything Garrick has told me, it sounds as though she's suffering from guilt transference. Her guilt about Ann has changed into hatred for you, since she can't deal with it directly."

"Why in the world should she feel guilty about her sister?" Cat asked.

"It's not uncommon for a child to feel guilty when a sibling dies," Peter said. "In the most balanced of minds there's a sense of competition and jealousy that can lead to guilt if the object of those emotions is removed in some way. I have no doubt that Janet loved her sister very much, but it would be natural for there to be some resentment. This must have turned pathological after Ann's death."

Garrick looked worried. "But that was over five years ago. Why get on my case now?"

Cat took his hand. "You didn't give her an opportunity before. You were here where you could defend yourself. When you disappeared without warning, you were wide open for attack."

"It may be even more complicated." Peter fiddled with his coffee cup. "She may see your leaving as a final desertion of your wife. You told me she said some things about your needing to tend the grave and such. That indicates a serious break with reality.''

"Poor woman," Cat said, suddenly feeling sorry for her. "She's almost as much a victim as Garrick.''

"Maybe more. She can't help herself.''

They talked a while longer, but concluded that unless something were to drive Janet to seek help in therapy, the situation was not going to be resolved for a long time.

Both Garrick and Cat were thoughtful and quiet during the ride home.

The phone was ringing when they entered Garrick's apartment. He went for the instrument, Cat for the bathroom. He greeted the caller.

"Drexel?" The voice was gruff, deep. "Nelson Hendry. Cat there?''

He glanced up. The bathroom door was still shut. "She's here, Sheriff. But she can't come to the phone just now. Can I take a message?''

"Sure thing. We got some good news about those highway robbers who took her cash. Seems one of them was wearing your coat. Gassed up at a little station down in Arizona, and the owner thought the coat was a bit fancy for the guy. Plus he lifted a magazine. Mentioned it to a local lawman, and the cop ran the plates. Turns out the car was stolen, and the driver robbed. This time they took a few thousand he had in the glove compartment and roughed him up some. These boys are not good citizens.''

"Have they been caught?''

"Nope. Disappeared again. It's a safe bet over the border. But it's the best lead we've had. Thought she'd like knowing. By the way, congratulations about the kid. Hope you two'll wait till you get back home to get hitched, though. Folks'll want to throw a big party.''

"Uh." Garrick stood at the bathroom door. "Thanks. I expect in that case we'll wait." He listened, dazed, to the rest of Hendry's conversation, then hung up. As he did, the bathroom door opened.

"Good news, I hope." Cat was straightening a lock of hair. "You weren't on very long."

"Long enough." He stared at her. Now he could see the changes, but why she hadn't told him immediately was a question that cut him deeply. "That was Nelson. It seems your road bandits are making a living at it. They were spotted down in Arizona."

"That's terrific." She came over and put her arms around his neck. Her warmth and perfume enveloped him like a soft, erotic cloud. "Are they going to catch them?"

"Maybe. They hurt a guy this time. It was a good thing we didn't stay with your Jeep after all, I guess." He looked into her eyes, willing her to tell him.

"I wouldn't be afraid with you around," she said softly. "You could take on dozens of bad guys."

"There are situations where muscle only gets you into worse trouble." He brushed his hands over her enlarged breasts and settled them on her waist. It was still as slender as ever. His hands trembled slightly.

She sighed, closed her eyes and drew herself against him. "Yes, but you have brains, too. You proved that when you were faced with good old Roscoe in Chuck's bar. You'd figure out how to save us."

"Let's talk about us, Cat."

"Okay." It was a seductive sigh of a word.

"Cat, Nelson told me. Apparently everyone in Lone Tree but me knows."

Her eyes opened and she pulled back, a blush staining her cheeks and throat. "Knows about w-what?"

"About the baby. Cat, why didn't you tell me? Don't you want our baby?"

The hurt in his eyes was so intense she wanted to die. "Oh, Garrick. I want this baby more than anything in the world. I just didn't want you to think it was the only reason I finally came to you."

"I would never believe that." His voice was husky, and his dark eyes grew misty. "Cat, I know you love me."

"I didn't find out about it until a few hours before I flew out. Please believe me."

"I believe you." He started laughing, but tears filled his eyes. "You and your damnable pride, Catherine Cantrell. What am I going to do with you?"

She started to laugh and cry, too. "I guess you'll have to begin by making me Catherine Drexel. I think the kid would appreciate it."

"And you?"

"*I* would love it!" She fell into his arms, and they laughed and cried together all the way to the bedroom.

He made love with such tenderness it almost seemed he was worshiping her. And he was so gentle and careful she finally had to explain loudly that she was not going to break. She had been just as pregnant that afternoon during their marathon sex session. After that he relaxed and behaved naturally, passionately.

Later he said, "I'm going to make a great daddy."

"I know." She snuggled against him. "And I'm going to make a great mom."

GARRICK WASTED NO TIME getting the word out that he and Cat were not only marrying, but were also starting a family. His news was met with delight by all his colleagues and friends.

Save one.

Janet responded by loading her father's gun carefully. Her fingers didn't shake at all. He had betrayed Ann. He would pay. She slipped the weapon into her briefcase and calmly left her apartment. She knew exactly where he would be and at what time.

"WELL," WILLIS KENT BLUSTERED. "I'm sure I have no idea what you people are talking about. I never engaged in any conspiracy with your sister-in-law, Drexel. I simply followed leads—"

"*False* leads." Sheldon Sheridan leaned over the agent's desk. "Leads that Miss Norton put in your way. Leads that, if you'd been the least bit objective, would have easily been proven untrue." He had slapped a thick folder on the desk when the four of them had first entered the room.

Cat stood back, watching the process of intimidation. The men had rehearsed it, agreeing that Sheldon would be the spokesperson. As a lawyer, he was the one most likely to scare the lawman. Although Kent was frightened of Garrick's physical strength, it was a professional fright they really wanted to induce. Garrick took third place to Booth Callahan, another lawman. Kent was clearly cracking.

"Maybe I have been a bit hasty on this case," he said, rubbing his lip. "It just seemed—"

"So easy," Booth interrupted quietly. "So pat. Right? Think about it, Willis. Your reputation, even your job will be on the line if Drexel presses this civil suit. And remember, the man is retired by choice. He has the time and resources to pursue this as far as it will go."

Kent looked decidedly worried.

Garrick put an arm around Cat's shoulders. "But I'm not in a vindictive mood these days, Willis. Cat and I are expecting our first child. Of course, she'd get much better care here in New York, so I suppose I wouldn't mind staying around for a trial."

"Now, now." Kent held up a hand. "Let's not let this get out of hand. I—" He turned his head as the door to his office opened suddenly. "Oh, hello, Janet," he said, relief in his tone. "We've got a bit of a problem here. Perhaps you can help. After all, it was from you that I got most of the incriminating material against Mr. Drexel."

CHAPTER SEVENTEEN

WHAT HAPPENED NEXT astonished even Cat. A warning bell went off in her mind as clearly as if she had heard it with her ears. Everyone else in the room seemed frozen, but her muscles bunched and warmed, ready for action.

To Garrick, the scene unfolded as if it were being played out in slow motion. Janet entered the office, shut the door behind herself and smiled at everyone. Then she focused on him. Her eyes seemed glazed. "Garrick," she said, rolling his name off her tongue as though intensely satisfied with the sound of it. "Say goodbye to these people. It's time for you to join Ann. Before you have a chance to be even more unfaithful." She pulled an enormous pistol from her briefcase and pointed it at him. He stared at the black hole of the muzzle and saw all his hopes and dreams sucked inside and destroyed.

Then a lioness launched herself from beside him. Cat shrieked, an unearthly, chilling sound, and pounced on Janet, bringing the smaller woman to the floor. The two women rolled across the carpet, screaming and yelling and fighting for control of the gun. Garrick felt terror far greater than what he had felt for himself a moment ago and started to go to Cat's aid, but arms like steel bands closed around him, imprisoning him in a hammerlock. "Leave her be," Booth yelled. "She knows what she's doing!"

Janet fought with the strength of the insane, but Cat was using her brain. It wasn't long before she had the weapon, tossed it to one side and pinned the other woman securely to the floor. "Any of you big-shot lawmen have a pair of handcuffs?" she asked, panting. "I could sure use a pair."

Kent rummaged in a desk drawer, withdrew some cuffs and came around to help. Soon Janet was lying on her side on the floor with her wrists behind her. She was sobbing brokenly. Cat knelt by her side and stroked her hair.

"Janet," she said gently. "Can you hear me? Why did you want to kill him?"

"Ann. He... he belongs to her. He killed her and has to pay." She stopped talking and started crying again. Cat looked up at Garrick. Booth had released him, but he was as white as a sheet.

"Get Peter Chance," he ordered hoarsely. Sheldon grabbed the phone and started dialing. Then Garrick went over to Cat. "If you ever take another risk like that, I'll skin you alive," he said fiercely. "Cat, my life is not worth yours and the baby's." He drew her up and embraced her so tightly the breath left her lungs for a moment.

"She wasn't risking anything," Booth said, lighting a cigarette. "Your lady's got a fine head on her shoulders, Drexel. You're a lucky man."

"I'm missing something." Garrick looked at his future wife quizzically.

"You all did. Except maybe Booth." Cat extricated herself from Garrick's embrace and went over to pick up the gun. "See," she said, displaying the weapon. "Safety's on. She could have pulled the trigger from now until doomsday and nothing would have happened." She looked down at the now quiescent Janet. "I have a feeling she never really meant to kill you. Just scare you to death."

"She did that." He took her in his arms again.

Peter arrived shortly with a paramedic, who sedated Janet. The cuffs were removed, and everyone agreed to allow Peter to admit her to a small, private psychiatric hospital for observation and treatment. "She's very ill," Garrick said sadly. "The last thing I want to do is press charges. Pete, if there's any problem with money, I'll pay the bills." Peter asked for a quick rundown on what had happened, then left with his patient, promising to let Garrick know as soon as he had a handle on Janet's condition.

Willis Kent was back at his desk, obviously shaken to the core. "Gentlemen," he said, "I believe I owe all of you, especially Mr. Drexel, an apology. I confess that I was using information provided by Ms Norton as the basis for my investigation. It's clear now that as a source, she is not to be considered reliable."

"I think that's one hell of an understatement," Sheldon said sternly. "The grounds for a defamation-of-character suit against you are growing by the minute, Mr. Kent."

Garrick had helped Cat into a chair. After the bravado she had exhibited following her fight, she was experiencing trembling muscles and had whispered to him that she had best sit down or she was liable to fall down. "I'll be willing to forget the whole thing, Kent," Garrick said, his hand resting protectively on Cat's shoulder, "if you'll issue a formal apology and retraction to me. In print."

"Well, it's hardly policy..."

"Policy be damned." Booth blew a cloud of smoke at the investigator. "You and I both know that if Drexel sues you, your career is down the toilet. What's a little loss of pride compared to your pension? Think about it."

Kent did. Eventually he agreed, paling when Garrick insisted the note be published in a prominent place in the *Wall Street Journal*. "That's my condition," Garrick stated. "Take it or leave it." Kent took it. A celebration followed, marred only by Garrick's sorrow over Janet.

A few days later, Peter reported on her condition. He met with Garrick and Cat at his office. In contrast with Sheldon's office, it was a place of bright colors and pleasingly designed furniture. They sat in chairs around a small coffee table.

"She blames herself for Janet's death," Peter said. "She believes deep down that she killed her sister by giving her strep throat when she was a child. The strep developed into rheumatic fever and led to her heart condition. And the guilt was buried so far down in her psyche, she wasn't even consciously aware of it."

"So she had to pick a scapegoat," Cat concluded.

"And I was the logical choice," Garrick said.

"Right and right." Peter folded his hands together. "The illness came on her gradually. It had been building for years, but when Ann died, it began to really fester. Then when you left, it became a full-blown disease. She was ready to do anything to get you back here, not even realizing that what she really intended to do was punish you for Ann's death in order to keep from facing her own feelings. When she learned Cat was going to have your baby and that you might never return, it tipped the balance."

"But was she really going to kill him?" Cat wanted to know.

"That's debatable. I think your observation that she neglected to remove the safety catch was a good one, but she did load the thing. Garrick had a close call, I don't mind telling you."

Cat reached for her lover's hand. "What are her chances for recovery?" Garrick asked.

"I won't know that for a while." Peter smiled. "But they're a whole lot better now that she's undergoing therapy willingly. I think she does want to get better. With that attitude there's always hope. She's also aware how lucky she is that you're a forgiving man. There's nothing wrong with her thinking except in the area of her relationship with her sister. She told me, grudgingly, that she thanks you for not putting her in the slammer. It is just possible that at some time in the future, she will be able to tell you herself how she feels."

"But not yet."

Peter smiled again. "Not yet. But as I said, there's hope."

"For now," Garrick said, "that's enough."

When the dust was settled, Garrick insisted that Cat make arrangements to see her doctor. Although she was feeling fine, she did as he asked and was gratified by Pat Shaffer's post-exam report. "Despite your age, Cat, you're one of the healthiest first-time moms I've seen in ages. The outdoor life in Wyoming must agree with you. And I don't know how you did it," the doctor said. "The chances of your getting pregnant were astronomically negative. But I foresee no problems. My only warning is not to expect this to happen again. You might be disappointed.''

"I'm hardly worried," Cat assured her. "This child is like a gift, and I am so happy to have it. One or a dozen, I love the man I'm marrying enough so that it doesn't matter. I'll be content with him whatever the circumstances.''

The issue of where and how they would live came up later that day. Garrick took her to lunch at an Italian restaurant up a side street near his office building. The proprietor welcomed him like a long-lost brother and made certain they were served only the best of everything. Cat's now ravenous appetite actually came close to being satisfied by the time she dug into the spumoni ice cream. As she ate, she watched him fidget, then clear his throat. "Come on," she said. "Out with it. You've been wanting to say something to me ever since I came out of the doctor's office. What is it?''

"Um." He fiddled with his fork. "It's about New York, Cat."

"What about New York?" She gestured broadly. "I honestly never liked the place until now. But with you, it's different. I almost feel comfortable. Like I was home.''

He stared. "Then you don't hate it?''

"How could I hate any place when I'm with you?" She covered his hand with hers. "I knew I loved you enough to marry you when I decided to come here. You'd make the far side of hell bearable. Not that I'm ready to turn in my jeans and boots permanently, but I am ready to talk compromise.''

"Wonderful!" He looked extremely relieved. "After the publicity following Kent's apology, I've had some interesting offers. Those that would tie me here permanently once more, I've refused outright. But there are others I'm considering: portfolio counseling, general financial advising for people who have imagination and a willingness to work with a less-than-orthodox kind of financial planner. The only thing is that no matter which position I decide to take on, it would involve spending a certain amount of time in the city every year. And I don't relish spending time away from you."

"I don't ever want to be separated from you, either. Those weeks we were apart were the worst of my life. But at least they made me realize how much I need and love you."

He lifted her hand to his lips. "Well, what about it? Do you think we could work out some kind of compromise that would let us have the best of both worlds? I think you know that eventually I was going to have to find something to do besides work for you, much as I enjoy it. And I don't want to give up my work around the ranch for good. It's healthy and better than letting myself get old and soft. But I'm an expert. Like Jamison says, its wrong for me to just throw away all my years of experience."

"Your experience is one of the most endearing things about you. Yes, if we put our minds to it, we can work it out. I don't want to deny you the satisfaction of doing your job. You should know that by now."

He grinned. "Does this mean I'm finally more important to you than Cat's Cradle?"

She felt a small twinge of doubt. "Of course you are," she said as firmly as possible.

But she hoped she would never be put to a test.

They remained in New York long enough for Garrick to become something of a social news item. The public apology by Kent had captured media imagination, and the day Cat saw their picture splashed across the cover of a national tabloid was the day she decided enough was enough. It was time to go home.

"This is awful," she complained to Garrick, waving the paper in his face. "Scarcely anything they printed is the truth. Listen to this: 'The beautiful owner of a fabulous guest ranch in the remote mountains of Wyoming and a dashingly handsome millionaire financier—'"

"Sounds true enough to me, love." He enfolded her in a warm embrace. "You can always sue if you don't approve."

"Don't be silly." She relaxed against him. "I just don't enjoy being public property. Garrick, I want to go home."

"We're out of here tomorrow, then. I'll make the arrangements. Besides, there is the small matter of a wedding that should have taken place a few months ago."

"Funny." She nuzzled his neck and looked around at his apartment. "I feel married now."

"Well, you aren't. How long will it take to make the arrangements in Lone Tree?"

"Not long. Once I set the date, we only need to go through a few formalities, then go to the justice—"

"Hold it. You aren't talking quickie civil ceremony, are you?"

"It would be a lot less trouble."

"Listen, Cat. I want a formal wedding with all the trimmings. Besides, if we don't give the town a bang-up wedding complete with a party, I don't think we'll need to go back at all. No one will forgive us."

"You really think so?" She thought about the people who had volunteered to help out at the ranch. He was right.

"I really think so." He kissed her. "Now, get packing. We've got a plane to catch!"

Cat set to work with a will. Judging from Jude's regular phone reports, it seemed the ranch had been running well without her, and she was satisfied the laconic wrangler had been straight with her. Jude was not overly endowed with imagination, but he was scrupulously honest. She knew she had no cause to be concerned.

But she was concerned. The longer she'd stayed away, the more she'd missed the place. It was going to take more effort than she had thought to compromise with Garrick, no matter how much she loved him. She only hoped that their love could stand the stress. Right now, it was as if the ranch was the lover from whom she was parted and for whom she longed.

Fortunately, they were soon flying west. She was almost as excited as she had been when she had flown in the other direction to find Garrick. He seemed to sense her mood.

"Cheer up, little mother," he said, taking her hand. "Just a few more hours and we'll be back with your first love."

"Reading my mind?" she asked, a bit afraid he was doing just that.

"Not at all." He kissed her fingers. "I know the way you think, that's all. Frankly, I'm amazed you stayed away with such good grace for as long as you did. I figured you'd be hanging from the walls in a week."

"So there's hope?"

"I know so."

"I am finding other priorities in my life, but it's been so long..." Surely she was telling the truth. Surely a place couldn't be as important to her as he was, as their unborn child was. But she remembered his bitter accusations of that long-past argument. Had she really outgrown her own brand of materialism?

"Don't rush it, Cat." He kissed her fingers again. "You've been Cat Cantrell, boss and owner of Cat's Cradle, a lot longer than you've been my lover. Cut yourself a little slack, okay?"

Emotion seized her to the point where she could barely speak. "You know me so well," she whispered.

"No, I love you so much." This time, he kissed her lips.

"Excuse me." Both looked up at the strange voice and saw a stewardess smiling down at them. "I don't mean to be rude or interrupt you, but I just have to ask you something."

"Sure." Garrick didn't move away from Cat. "What is it?"

"Aren't you two famous? I mean, I'm sure I saw your picture in a newspaper. You're the millionaire, and you're the lady with the big ranch out in Colorado."

"Wyoming." Cat kept a smile in place with difficulty. "And it's not such a big place. Just a beautiful one."

"Oh, I'm sure it is." The young woman gushed on for a bit more, then clinched it by asking for autographs. When she left, Garrick finished his intended kiss.

Cat barely responded. "Enough is enough," she hissed. "I want to go back to just being me!"

"And so you shall, love." This time his kiss met with more satisfactory results. "So you shall. Soon all this ugly fame-and-fortune stuff will be only so much water under the bridge."

Cat fervently prayed that he was correct.

WHILE CAT AND GARRICK flew west, their picture in the tabloid was causing excitement in two road thieves. Bob and Norm Runge studied the photo, laboriously read the article, counted up their dwindling funds and decided it was time to head north. . . .

JUDE MET THEM at the airport with Cat's Jeep. "Ran your machine once a week," he told Garrick as he piled their bags in the rear of the vehicle. "Sounds like it's got no problems."

"Thanks," Garrick said. Then he asked the question Cat had been holding back. "How's everything else?"

"Runnin' smooth." Jude swung behind the wheel, clearly expecting them to take the back seat together. They obliged. "Even had Roscoe Petersen over one afternoon helping with the corral fence. That boy can sure handle a sledgehammer."

Garrick rubbed the back of his neck. "Glad I didn't know about that talent before." Cat snickered as quietly as possible, but got a dirty look anyhow.

Abby and Ellen were at the house to meet them, and both cried when they hugged Cat. "Oh," Abby said tearfully, "it's so wonderful about the baby. Don't you ever worry about getting baby-sitters. Even if we get married and have kids of our own, we'll always be available. It's so wonderful." She was almost sobbing. Cat assumed from her demeanor and tone that all was not well with Tom.

This turned out to be the case. Tom was giving a little of what he had gotten by dating a waitress over in Jackson occasionally. It was impossible to keep it a secret in such a gossipy community, and Ellen confided to Cat that Abby was eaten up with jealousy, but that she would die rather than let Tom know. They saw each other from time to time, but shared none of the closeness they had enjoyed last spring. Cat wasn't sure that was actually a bad thing, but she kept her counsel. Most of her energy was spent renewing her reign over Cat's Cradle. She fell on the place like a doting mother returning to a beloved child.

Jude had not misled her. The ranch was running as smoothly as a top. All she needed to do was pick up the reins, which she did eagerly after effusively thanking everyone who had helped out while she'd been gone. Details about the wedding she left to Garrick.

Garrick went about the business of setting the date, renting the school gym and making arrangements with the minister without complaint. Cat had already made enormous personal sacrifices for their relationship, he realized, and because of her pregnancy she was forgoing leading hunting parties this year—a job she confessed she loved. Garrick wasn't too thrilled with the prospect of his future wife ever being out on the trail with a bunch of guys armed with rifles, but it was just one more thing, he told himself, that he would learn to adjust to. He could do it. He loved her enough.

He had no illusions, however, that she loved him enough to willingly abandon her old life-style. He would work his visits to New York around her seasonal schedule. It would put a cramp in his business style, but he would manage. Many of his problems would be solved when he got around to opening an office of his own in town. An office with the proper communication hookups. The idea had come to him out of the blue one day, and he planned to get going on the project right after the honeymoon.

But when he brought up the subject of a honeymoon, he hit a brick wall. "I can't take the time," Cat said. "Maybe after Thanksgiving."

"Damn it, Cat!" Garrick felt his hold on his temper slipping. "You said you were willing to compromise. Are you backing out?"

"No, of course not. But—"

"You sit at that desk all day, or putz around the kitchen, cooking. Or supervise Jude and Bart and the girls. You do get around to me by evening, but I don't like being a poor second!"

"Darling, you sound like a neglected housewife." Cat spoke teasingly, but she felt guilty. He was speaking the truth far more clearly than she cared to admit. "Once the ranch is closed for the season, I'll be glad to go anywhere you want. What's wrong with that?"

"It's wrong because I've been compromising my fanny off, and I'd like to see some similar action from you!" He picked up his hat and coat and started for the door. "I'm going for a ride. Don't worry, I'm not going to get drunk this time, but I am mad. You think about it. I'll be back in a little while, and we'll talk this out." With that, he was out the door. To Cat's relief and surprise, he didn't slam it.

She pushed back from the desk and regarded the gentle curve of her lower abdomen. She didn't really look pregnant yet, just a bit out of shape. But another month, and she would definitely be showing. She would get bigger and bigger and then the baby would come. There wouldn't be an opportunity for a honeymoon after that.

She owed it to them both to go immediately. It was likely to be the last time in their lives they would truly be alone, without anyone else to worry about. He was right to be mad at her. She had behaved poorly.

The sound of a car made her leap to her feet. He was back and she would apologize immediately, agree to go wherever he wanted for however long he wanted. The ranch could get along without her a little longer. She would teach herself to put him first in her life! Deep down, in spite of her ambivalent feelings, she knew he was the most vital element in her life.

But it wasn't Garrick. Tom had come by to pick up Abby. Cat thanked him again for his help around the ranch and asked him how things were going. "She ain't sure about her feelings," he said. "And I ain't sure I trust her. But we still care about each other. Know what I mean? Maybe there's a chance for us down the line." The deputy looked older than he had even a few weeks before, and Cat decided it was an improvement. He didn't seem so much like a kid dressed up to play cops and robbers anymore.

"That's good to hear." She offered him a cup of coffee and some cookies while he waited for Abby to finish her chores and fix herself up for the date. "Did you by any chance pass Garrick when you drove in?" she asked, anxious to know how much longer it would be before she could make her apologies.

"Nope." Tom took a sip of the coffee. "Just some out-of-state heap driven by two guys. Probably hunters." Cat smothered her disappointment and they chatted about nothing in particular until Abby was ready.

But several hours later, when Tom and Abby came back from the date, Garrick still wasn't home. Cat spent the night in turmoil, and first thing in the morning, she called Nelson.

"I'm sorry, Cat," he said. "But unless he's gone for longer than one night and a day, I won't get any cooperation from the state boys. No reports of car accidents have come in. I can check the jails and hospitals in the area, but I think you'da been called by now if he was in one of them."

"I know. But I feel something terrible is wrong. This isn't like the last time he walked out. He said he was coming right back."

"Don't always know what a man will do when he's got his dander up, honey."

"He wasn't that mad!"

"My advice is to wait a while longer, Cat. Likely he'll turn up in a few hours. He's a grown man and can take care of himself. Don't you fret so. It ain't good for you."

Cat had to admit the truth of his words. She hung up the phone with a heavy heart and resigned herself to waiting.

But she didn't have to wait long. Just a few minutes later, the phone rang. She knocked over the desk lamp getting to the instrument.

"Miz Cantrell?" The voice was male, gravelly and unfamiliar.

"Yes. Who is this?" Her heart was pounding. Garrick had been hurt and someone was calling to tell her about it!

"Never you mind that. What this is about is we got your boyfriend, and it's gonna cost you plenty to get him back!"

CHAPTER EIGHTEEN

CAT LISTENED IN HORROR as the kidnapper spoke. Garrick was in the clutches of men who would harm him, maybe even kill him, if she didn't come up with a million dollars! "But I don't have that kind of money," she cried. "If I did, I swear I'd give it all to you in a minute if you promised to let him go!"

"Don't try lying to me, doll. I can read. I know you got a pile of dough. And me and my brother better be getting a pile of it soon, or you ain't got no boyfriend no more. Understand?"

"I understand." The words caught in her throat. Some way, somehow she would have to get her hands on some money. Then a terrible thought occurred to her. What if they had already killed him? Garrick would certainly be a handful for kidnappers. It would be a lot easier to dispose of him, then make the demand. "But how do I know you really have him?" she asked, unwilling to give the caller any bad ideas in case Garrick was still all right.

"Oh, he's right here, doll. Only he ain't being real cooperative. Maybe you can talk some sense into him." There was a pause on the phone.

"Cat?" His voice sounded muffled.

"Garrick! Where are you? Are you all right? Have they hurt you? I'll *kill* them!"

"Slow down, love. I'm not hurt much. They wanted me to write you a note, and I wouldn't. We had a little discussion about that. Then they decided to call. Listen to me, Cat. Don't give these creeps a damn... Oof!" The sound of a fist hitting flesh cut his voice off. Cat started screaming into the phone.

"Shut up!" The kidnapper's voice was back on the line. "Don't listen to him if you want to see him alive. Get the money and stay by the phone. I'll call back this afternoon with more instructions."

"I cannot get any money by this afternoon. I don't know why you think I'm rich. All I've got is the ranch. You've got to give me more time!"

There was a pause. "The newspaper said he was a millionaire."

"I don't know. Maybe he is. But I'm not his wife yet, and I can't get my hands on any of his money. It's all locked up in stocks and stuff anyway. Don't you understand?"

"Okay, doll. Sell your ranch. We'll give you until tomorrow afternoon. If you don't have the money by then, we'll start shipping lover boy back to you in pieces." Before she could shout her outraged reply, he hung up. For a long moment, she couldn't move. She just stood there with the buzzing receiver in her hand.

"Cat!" Abby came rushing in. "What's the matter? I thought I heard screaming!"

"It's Garrick," Cat wailed. "He's been *kidnapped*!"

"I'll call Tom." Abby took the receiver from her hand. "You sit down. You look as pale as a ghost."

Cat obeyed. Her legs were too shaky to support her, anyway. She listened, dazed, as Abby talked to Tom. Then the girl handed her the phone. "He has to ask you some questions," she said gently.

Cat would have preferred to talk to Nelson, but she didn't have the strength to argue. She told Tom exactly what had been said, her voice breaking when she described the abuse Garrick had received. The deputy was all business and didn't attempt to reassure her with stock phrases. She appreciated that, at least. "Of course," she concluded, "there is no way on earth for me to get that much money. Ever. Much less by tomorrow afternoon. Why don't they know that?"

"Don't sound like they exactly got their act together," Tom said. "Might work against them and for us. You stay put. I'll get right on this."

"But the money. What if—"

"Cat, you know they ain't gonna let him go even if you do get the money." Tom's tone was gentle, far more mature-sounding than usual. "They can't. He's seen them."

"Oh." Dark spots formed in front of her eyes. "I...I hadn't thought of that."

"Sorry, but I thought you ought to hear the truth. Let me talk to Abby again, please."

Cat handed the receiver back. Her hand was trembling violently. She wasn't ready to give up hope. She couldn't give up hope—couldn't just sit and wait for someone else to do something. She had to act!

Abby caught up with her as she was opening the door to her Jeep. "Tom said for you to stay here, Cat," she said. "Where are you going?"

"Into town." Cat slid behind the steering wheel. "I have to at least try to get some money. Maybe even a little will keep them from hurting him right away."

"You won't help anything by doing this. If you couldn't get the money for the ranch this summer, what makes you think you can get money now? No one's going to loan you cash to pay off a kidnapper."

"I'm not going to try for a loan." She started the car. "I'm selling the ranch."

"What?"

"One of Garrick's friends told me if I ever wanted out of here, he'd take the place off my hands in a minute. I'm going to talk to Betty Johnson over at the real-estate office. She can handle the deal. I won't get a million, but I'll get a fair amount. Once they see I'm sincere, I know they'll give me time to let the deal go through."

"That's crazy! *You're* crazy. I'm not going to let you do this!" Abby raced around the Jeep and got in the passenger seat.

Cat hit the gas, causing a cloud of dust to rise behind the vehicle. "Don't try to stop me, Abby. I will not let Garrick be harmed!"

But Garrick wasn't being harmed at the moment. He was being infuriated. The idea that these two creeps could capture him was bad enough, but to have to listen to them threatening Cat was beyond what he could handle sanely.

They had got him with the old flat-tire routine. He had stopped to help and the big one had drawn a gun on him. Thinking they only wanted to rob him, he had surrendered relatively meekly. If he had suspected their actual plans, no gun would have stopped him!

But now he was hog-tied and helpless. They had bound him and shoved him into the trunk of his own car and driven for what seemed like hours before unloading him at a cabin out in the middle of nowhere. The place had all the amenities—lights, telephone, running water. But he sensed he was far from civilization. There was no way he would be found even if someone was looking for him. It was up to him alone.

And he ached for the anguish he knew Cat must be feeling....

WHEN CAT AND ABBY returned to the ranch, Nelson and Tom were there, along with a couple of men in suits who said they were with the FBI. When Cat expressed surprise that they had come, she learned they were from Jackson Hole and that kidnapping was a federal crime.

"We want permission to put a tap on your telephone, Miss Cantrell," one of them said. "That way, when they call again, we'll have a chance to trace the number."

She agreed readily. Under mild pressure, she admitted what she had been up to in town. Advised to cancel the deal, she stood firm. "I have to do something. This was a thing I could do."

Nothing happened until late the next afternoon. She refused to take to her bed as everyone suggested and threw herself into her work, hoping that by keeping extra busy, she wouldn't go crazy with worry. It didn't work. When the phone rang at four, she nearly jumped out of her skin.

"Keep him talking as long as you can," the FBI man told her as he dove toward his equipment. "Argue with him, make him angry. Anything. Just keep him on the line."

Cat tried. But the kidnapper wasn't having any. He curtly told her the money had better be at hand and cursed when she said it wasn't. Fearing he would hang up and kill Garrick, she hastily explained that she was selling the ranch. "It will take a little time. I can't have anything for you until the deal goes through."

"No more games, doll," he growled. "You get your fanny down to the bank and get the dough. If I don't see you in town tomorrow, the guy gets it. You got that?" When she gulped and said yes, he hung up abruptly.

"Not enough time." The agent hung up his receiver. "But he said he would see you. That means he'll have to be in town, too."

Cat sat down and put her head in her hands. "Terrific."

So the next morning she went obediently to the bank. There, she received another surprise.

"The community knows and is rallying behind you," Don Jeffers told her. "We're keeping it all quiet because we don't want that scum to know what's up, but last night I went door-to-door with Nelson, explaining your troubles. Cat, I raised nearly five thousand in donations. The bank will put up another ten against your livestock, more if you want to lay the whole ranch out as collateral. But you can leave here with close to fifteen thousand in cash right now. That ought to keep them from killing Mr. Drexel right away. Especially if you make them think he's sort of a goose with golden eggs. The longer they keep him alive and in one piece, the more money they might get."

She was speechless. This was the man who had coolly denied her an advance in May. And he had spent hours of his personal time making an effort to save her lover! "Don, if

I weren't so upset, I'd hug you. I really don't know how to thank everyone.''

"You just do whatever you can to help the FBI boys catch those crooks,'' Jeffers said. "Humane considerations aside, I want Drexel returned to this community in one piece myself. The man's a financial genius. We spent some time talking business and investments the other day, and I know he would be a real shot in the arm for Lone Tree if he set up an office here. He was talking about building a state, even a regional network of investment-advice centers that would cater to the average person and would support local enterprises. Frankly, I think it's an idea that's come of age, and Drexel is just the guy to pull it off. God knows, he has the experience and the guts to do it. He's a fine man, Cat. And we don't want anything bad to happen to him.''

She expressed agreement, although this was the first she had heard that Garrick's ideas about working in town had gone any further than talk between the two of them. It made the future look even brighter.

Provided he was still around to share it with her.

She and the money bag got home without incident. The streets had been crawling with federal agents—the ones from Jackson had called in reinforcements overnight and had pushed Nelson and Tom more or less politely to one side. Cat wasn't too happy about that, but she knew she was well-protected by the seasoned professionals, and that was a comfort. After all, she told herself, the FBI had a great deal more experience in these matters than did the local lawmen, even if she was more comfortable with the two she knew. In her office, she settled in for the agony of waiting and spent much of the time thinking about the kindness and generosity the people of Lone Tree had exhibited. Hours passed slowly, and it was almost dusk before the telephone shrilled again.

"You was a good girl,'' the harsh voice said. "Seen you with the loot. Also seen all them cops. Tell 'em to get lost, honey. Otherwise your boyfriend is history.''

"I can't tell them just to go," she cried. "They're FBI agents and they won't listen to me." She looked pleadingly at the agent by the phone tap.

"Do it! And wait by the phone. When they're all gone, I'll call you and tell you how to get us the money." He hung up sharply.

Cat expected the agents to argue with her, but they left willingly, telling her not to worry—they would keep a watch on her from a safe distance. The kidnappers, they assured her, would never know they were still around. She prayed they were correct.

The ranch was cleared, as well. Jude moved into town with a friend, the girls returned to their own homes and the hunters farmed out to other dude ranches in the area. If she hadn't been so terribly worried about him, Cat would have found it funny that Garrick himself had caused a considerable loss of revenue for her. Tears filled her eyes as she thought about how they could have a knock-down-drag-out argument over the situation.

But what did profit or anything else matter when his life was at stake?

The sudden roar of heavy vehicles coming down the road brought her racing to the front door. Four huge pickup trucks pulled to a dust-raising stop in her front yard. Cat went outside. Roscoe Petersen got out of the first truck and lumbered over to her.

"Miz Cantrell," he said, holding his big hat in his hands, "I brought some of the boys over from the Star. We gonna comb these here woods for your man. If he's here, we'll find him," he said firmly.

Cat surveyed the small army of large, grim-faced cowboys. "Roscoe," she said carefully, "I can't tell you how much I appreciate this. And Garrick will, too, when he learns about it. But if you go looking for him, you could get him killed." She looked the big man right in the eye. "You men are cowboys, not trackers. The kidnappers would spot you in a minute, and Garrick would die. Is that what you want?"

"No, ma'am. But—"

"Roscoe, please go back to the ranch and wait. If there's anything you and your friends can do, I promise I'll call you immediately. But I can't take the risk. Do you understand?"

Roscoe looked vastly disappointed. It was clear he wanted nothing more than to bash some heads. "I guess so," he said. "How about guarding you, Miss Cantrell?" he asked brightening.

"They said if anyone stayed around me, they'd kill him. It's for the best that you all go home and wait. That's what I'm having to do. It isn't easy, Roscoe."

"No, ma'am." He put his hat on his head. "Well, if there's anything, anything at all we can do for you, you just give a yell, y'hear?"

"I hear, Roscoe. And my deepest thanks to you all."

The convoy left in a cloud of dust and gravel, and Cat went inside to ponder the meaning of loyalty and neighbors.

A little after eight she got the call. In the morning she was to ride up to a ridge she knew about five miles from the ranch in the national forest. She was to bring the money, and she would be met. She consumed a meager supper and went to bed shortly afterward. She scarcely slept.

GARRICK DIDN'T SLEEP, EITHER. When Norm had gleefully informed him of Cat's plan to sell the ranch, he had almost torn his arms out of their sockets trying to get loose and get at the grinning man. That she would even *think* of selling her beloved place astounded him. That these men had made it necessary angered him beyond belief. He *had* to get free!

He struggled for what seemed like hours against his bonds. The ropes grew slippery as his skin abraded and bled. Still he struggled on, every nerve screaming and every muscle aching. Finally he was rewarded for his efforts when one wrist came free. Elated, he increased the tension on the other.

And then Norm sauntered into the room. His gun was tucked into his waistband, just under his slightly bulging belly. "Just checking on you before we turn in," he said. "This is your last night, you know. Any final requests?"

Garrick was about to answer abrasively when a horrible sound cut the night air. The scream was hoarse and loud. After the first instinctive rush of fear, he felt a strange kind of excitement. He knew that sound!

Norm clearly did not. He raced out of the room without another glance at Garrick. "What the hell was that?" he yelled to his brother.

"Damned if I know," came the reply. "Get the flashlight. Something's moving out there. Something big!"

Garrick worked his ropes.

"Can't see a damn thing," Norm said.

"Right over there," Bob said. "By that clump of trees."

Garrick got the other hand free. He bent until he reached the bindings on his feet.

Suddenly Norm cried, "There's a goddamn *lion* out there. And it's looking straight at me!"

Garrick moved as quickly as he could, listening to the two kidnappers panicking over the sight of the cougar. *His* cougar. There was absolutely no doubt in his mind it was the same animal that had confronted him twice before. Only this time it was coming to his rescue. He told himself he was insane, but he believed it, anyway.

He stripped off the rest of the ropes and sneaked over to the door. The brothers—they had introduced themselves early in the game—were standing crowded close to one another at the front door, clutching rifles and a flashlight. Garrick weighed his chances and decided it would be suicidal to try rushing them.

"Where'd it go?" Norm peered into the darkness.

"I don't know," Bob replied. "Why don't you go out there and find it?" They started bickering again.

He slipped back into his room as the argument accelerated. He had no choice. He had to go outside. He could only hope that the luck he'd had so far with the big cat would hold one more time. The problem was that this time he smelled of blood.

There was a window that opened easily under pressure. The night was cold, and he had no jacket. But, hell, he thought, he was more likely to be eaten than frozen to death. He vaulted through the opening and hit the ground at a run, not caring about the noise he made, only determined to put as much distance between himself and the cabin as possible.

Shouts and gunfire followed him. Calling on training from decades ago, he dodged through the trees, ducking low and moving as quickly as he could. He was almost out of sight of the cabin when something slammed into the side of his head and sent him crashing to the ground.

He clutched dirt and pine needles and struggled to rise, but his muscles wouldn't obey him. Something warm and wet bathed the side of his face, and his eyes refused to focus. Garrick realized he had been shot. His only emotion was stark regret that he wouldn't be able to marry Cat and see their child born.

"I got the son-of-a-bitch!" Footsteps pounded the ground.

"Make sure he's finished. Then let's get out of here!"

Garrick rolled onto his back, unwilling to die with his face in the dirt. What he saw next confirmed his belief in a benevolent universe.

Norm was standing about ten feet away from him, aiming the business end of his rifle right at Garrick's chest. But before he could pull the fatal trigger, he was knocked down by a large, tawny body. The rifle went off and the bullet buried itself in a tree trunk.

The cougar didn't wait around to study the situation after the explosion. With a startled yowl, she raced past Garrick and disappeared into the night. He got one good glimpse of her golden eyes as she flew by him. He swore he saw a flicker of recognition in them.

Then he saw Norm reach for the rifle. Garrick struggled to get to his hands and knees to fight for possession of the weapon, but it wasn't necessary. Another man appeared from out of nowhere and put his booted foot on the rifle. With a great rush of relief and gratitude Garrick heard Tom Hendry say, "I think there's been enough gunplay for one night, mister. Don't you?" He had the kidnapper on the ground and cuffed before Garrick could blink twice. Then he came over, worry all over his young face.

"I got here as soon as I could," he said apologetically, kneeling by the wounded man. "I shouldn't have stopped to take out the guy in the cabin. How bad is it?" He took out a clean handkerchief and pressed it to Garrick's scalp.

"Not so bad I can't say thanks for my life," Garrick said sincerely. "Just a graze, I think. How's Cat?"

"Worried sick." Tom slipped an arm under his shoulders. "Think you can get up?"

"I can sure as hell try," Garrick growled. "And if I make it, why don't you just step over there by the trees for a few minutes and let me have a little conversation with old Norm there. I have a few things to discuss with him."

Tom chuckled. "Can't do that, man. Wish I could. God, do you know how lucky you are he tripped?"

"You didn't see the mountain lion?"

"What lion?" Tom eased him to a sitting position. "I heard one earlier tonight. But I never saw one."

"He didn't trip. My lion knocked him over."

"Yeah. Now see if you can stand. A head wound can make you real dizzy."

Garrick made it to his feet and was about to defend his story when the world turned black around the edges and he fell softly into oblivion.

CAT HELD HER LOVER'S HAND. He lay so still on the white sheets of the bed in Doc's clinic it was hard to believe he was only sleeping. When Nelson had come for her at three in the morning and had told her what had happened, she had

"I wasn't babbling! The lion knocked Norm down and saved my life. She ran off into the woods right after. Then Tom appeared. He saved my life a second time."

Cat and Doc looked at each other. Doc shook his head with a barely perceptible motion.

Garrick knew when it was politic to shut up.

TOM WAS THE HERO OF THE HOUR. With all the FBI agents running around, it had been he who had spotted Norm in Garrick's Burberry raincoat and he who had carefully, cautiously stalked the kidnappers, biding his time until he saw Garrick make his break. Then he had stepped in and disarmed and captured first Bob, then Norm. He had not seen the cougar, and Garrick said no more about it. He knew the truth, and no amount of patronizing talk about his head wound would convince him otherwise. His lioness existed, and she had saved him, if not deliberately, then by a special fate. He was content to treasure the memory and let Tom have his days in the sun.

And to Tom's delight, those days included a renewed relationship with Abby. She was far more impressed than anyone else with his accomplishment and confessed that she wished she could erase all the months of misunderstanding and distance between them. Tom assured her that he had long since forgiven her, and that it was probably a good thing they had cooled it for a while, whatever the reason. But if she was interested in getting serious again, it was okay with him. His prospects had improved considerably with Nelson's recommendation to the county commissioners that his nephew be given a raise and considered for the post of sheriff in a few years' time. Abby started calling herself Tom's girl again.

With Doc's permission, Cat moved the invalid to the ranch and then almost decided to move him back because of the flood of visitors and well-wishers. Roscoe Petersen came by every day and would sit with Garrick on the porch exchanging military lies until Cat chased him off. "You have your very own Swedish puppy dog,'' she remarked wryly after one such visit.

"I could do worse." Garrick grinned and pulled her down onto his lap. "Do you still think my story about the cougar is just a figment of my imagination, love?"

"Well . . ." She stroked a lock of his hair. "It does seem a little far out, you have to admit."

"It's true." He nuzzled her neck. "And some day, something will happen to make you realize it. Mark my words."

She laughed and started marking something else.

CHAPTER NINETEEN

THEIR RELATIONSHIP ADVANCED to a new level of openness and trust after the kidnapping. "You were right," she said one evening shortly before the wedding. They were sitting in front of the fireplace, enjoying the warmth of the fire and their love for each other. "I really was a slave to this place." She indicated the ranch. "It took knowing I'd give it up in a minute for you to make me realize how unimportant it is compared to my love for you."

"We were both slaves," he said, putting his hands behind his head. "Only I ran away from my prison. Now I know I can control my work rather than it control me. I think you've reached the same plateau. And I don't mind at all that you were willing to give the place up to save my skin, wildly furious as it made me at the time. I think it proved you weren't really so materialistic after all." His tone was teasing, but she understood the seriousness of his words.

"I think you're right." She lay down, putting her head in his lap. "It's been so easy to let Jude and Bart run the place. Of course it's more like an old-fashioned hunting camp now, not the glorified motel I was running before. But I think the guys are happier."

"They still like your cooking, love."

"Well, I can't bow out entirely. I do have this reputation to keep up."

"Yeah." He bent over and kissed her teasingly. "I know."

The issue of a honeymoon had been easily solved. Cat had announced that she was willing to go anywhere for any length of time. Garrick had said two weeks in Tahiti would be enough, that they both had responsibilities. It had been a joyful compromise!

Neither had there been any trouble over the deal she had started to sell the ranch. Garrick's friend had understood completely, although he declared he was disappointed and that if she ever changed her mind, his offer still stood. Cat expressed gratitude.

Both of them expressed gratitude to the community of Lone Tree, which had opened its purse and heart to help save Garrick. He announced he would be offering discount counseling to all the people in town who wanted help with their investments, to show how much he appreciated the effort. This met with adulation, especially by people already in finance like Don Jeffers.

"When we get back from Tahiti," Cat said when Garrick let her up for air, "I'll start decorating your new office. That place is depressing as all get out."

"Oh, Lord. A domesticated office. I won't live it down if any of my old buddies see chintz pillows and gingham curtains."

"That's not what I had in mind, but if you insist..."

"I'll show you what I insist on," he said, standing suddenly, causing her to fall off his lap. Then he bent down and gathered her up in his arms.

It was a long, long time before they finally settled down to sleep that night.

EVENTS TUMBLED SWIFTLY and smoothly along toward the wedding day. Sheldon and Peter were able to come. Booth was regretfully involved in a case, but he sent his regards and a lavish gift of a Steuben glass ashtray. "When I do manage to come out there," he wrote in the accompanying note, "I want a class ashtray to put my butts out in. Best Wishes, Booth."

Cat wrote him a special thank-you note and enclosed a small sprig of sagebrush, saying that the air out here was so clear not even his habit could pollute it.

Jamison Pratt also extended his regrets. His gift was even more generous. He provided Garrick with a complete computerized communications system for his office and gave Cat a smaller system that would suit the ranch business and tie in to the office in town. She groaned at the prospect of learning to use a computer, but was pleased with the gift, nevertheless. It was time she entered the last part of the twentieth century in her business systems, she realized. And she would better understand what Garrick did if she could operate a system of her own. Garrick said sarcastically that maybe she would finally emerge from the Dark Ages. He was rewarded with a pillow thrown in his face. He followed by throwing the pillow to the floor—among other things.

They picked Peter and Sheldon and their families up at the airport and drove them along the front range of the Tetons for a few miles before turning for the pass to Lone Tree. Once more the weather was perfect for the Eastern visitors, with clear skies and that extraordinary state called Indian summer in the Rockies. "This is incredible," Peter said to Garrick as he stared out the window. "I've seen pictures, but nothing prepares you for the real thing, does it?"

"Nope. It may be remote, but it is paradise. And you ain't seen nothing yet," Garrick promised.

Sheldon and his wife, who were riding in the Jeep with Cat, were equally awed. "I can't imagine why you ever left here in the first place," Mable Sheridan said to Cat. "To have been born and raised here must have been wonderful."

"It was," Cat admitted. "But I had ambition. I had to see if I could make my mark. I could, I did, and I found out nothing was worth the kind of life I could lead here. I don't think it's for everyone," she added quickly. "But it sure is for me."

"And for Garrick," Sheldon said. "The man looks ten years younger. Mable, do you think we ought to look into retiring out here?"

"After the children are all through college, dear," the well-groomed woman said. "Until then, I think you'd better continue working."

Cat laughed. "If that's the criterion, I guess Garrick and I will be working for the rest of our lives. He'll be nearly sixty when Junior here is ready for college."

"So?" Sheldon turned to look at her. "How old do you think I'll be before our last one is through?"

Cat didn't guess, but she smiled as she got the point.

The New York guests settled into the somewhat primitive conditions of the ranch in late fall with equanimity and good humor. The cabins were heated by fireplaces only, but the water was hot, and Cat made sure that everything was spotlessly clean and the food was the best she could prepare. Her guests seemed content and happy.

Then, two days before the wedding, Garrick got a telephone call. Cat was in the office, going over some last-minute details, when the phone rang. She picked it up and answered absently, "Cat's Cradle, Cat Cantrell speaking."

"Cat, *darling*!" It was a cultured contralto voice she did not recognize. "This is your future mother-in-law, Elizabeth Drexel. Would you please get my son on the phone for me, dear?" Cat stared at the receiver for a moment, then mumbled an affirmative and scurried out of the office to find Garrick.

He was down by the corral, shooting the breeze with Peter. "It's your mother," Cat exclaimed. "And it doesn't sound like long distance!"

Garrick made it up to the house in record time.

Contrary to her fears, Cat found Elizabeth Drexel to be a delightful person. Having received a note from her son about his upcoming marriage, she had wasted no time and had gotten on the first plane out of Palm Beach to Denver with a considerable amount of luggage. She had then taken the commuter flight up to Jackson and called from there. "I wanted to surprise you," the small, energetic lady said. "And I didn't want Garrick to worry about me. His father never believed I could take care of myself, much less travel alone, and I was afraid he would feel the same way.''

They were seated in the kitchen, just the three of them, having coffee. Cat had tried to get Elizabeth to take her own room, saying that the cabins were far too primitive for someone used to luxury, but the older woman had refused. After the air-conditioning of Florida, she had declared, a little nip in the morning air would be no hardship. Garrick promised to be up before sunrise to light a fire in her fireplace. ''Mother,'' he said, ''I don't doubt you can do anything you set your mind to. If I didn't believe in the capable and independent woman before I met Cat, I certainly do now. She can do things that would turn your hair white!''

Elizabeth patted her silver curls. ''I doubt it. But I am so glad to hear you say you trust me to take care of myself and my affairs without help. It is such a good feeling. When I think how long I let myself be caged in—not that I minded at the time, of course—I can't believe it. Darlings, it is so nice to be free of any obligations but my own. You must keep that for yourself as much as you can even after you're married, Cat,'' she advised.

''Well...'' Cat toyed with a spoon resting in her coffee mug. ''I've had my time of freedom, Elizabeth. I've enjoyed independence in two professions, and now it's time for me to dedicate myself to my family.''

''Family?''

''Mother, Cat's going to have a baby. We didn't think it was possible, but—''

''A baby!'' Elizabeth's hands flew to her face. ''My God, Garrick. Am I to be a grandmother?''

''Guess so.''

Tears rolled down Elizabeth's cheeks. ''Oh, I had given up hope. I thought after Ann died—'' She looked quickly at Cat.

''It's okay,'' Cat assured her. ''I revere Ann's memory, too. After all, she helped shape the man I love.''

"Oh, my dear. Does my son really realize what an extraordinary wife he's getting?"

Cat grinned. "He'd better, hadn't he?"

THE DAY BEFORE THE WEDDING Cat declared she had to get out into the fresh air and away from the endless plans, phone calls and mail. At breakfast she announced there would be a picnic trail ride and anyone who was game could come along. Only Elizabeth and Mable begged off, pleading bones too old and muscles too out of shape to take the punishment of several hours in a Western saddle. The rest of them took off around ten with Cat in the lead on Sam Spade and Garrick bringing up the rear on Grace.

The air had that special blend of heat and chill particular to autumn. While they were in the shade under the trees, everyone was bundled up in jackets, gloves and hats and conversation was at a minimum. Frost lingered on the ground and the brown, quarter-sized leaves that had fallen from the aspens a week earlier after the first killing frost were patterned delicately with the white crystals. It was a somber but beautiful sight. They emerged into the bright sunlight of the upper meadows.

The temperature shot up, and coats came off. Garrick felt a particular surge of excitement because they were near the spot where he had first made love to Cat. The spring and summer flowers were gone, and the tall grass was golden, not green. But the view was still as spectacular as ever. "My God," Peter whispered, looking at the magnificent vista. "It's even more awesome from here than it is close up." Sheldon wasn't speaking, just staring.

"Beginning to see why I don't ever want to leave this place?" Garrick asked. Both men nodded, not taking their eyes off the mountain view. Their faces reflected almost religious awe.

Cat called a halt on the far side of the meadow where the sunlight was strongest and the temperature warmest. There, they spread out blankets and ate lunch, enjoying the surroundings and the fellowship. After lunch the majority opted for naps in the warm sun. Garrick had another suggestion for Cat.

"Let's take a walk," he said. "It's likely we won't get back up here again until late spring next year, and I'd like to absorb the ambience of the place. It might sustain me through the winter."

"Good idea." She took his arm. "Especially if we'll be spending part of the time in New York. I know I'll need some sustenance there." She laughed and squeezed his arm, taking the potential sting out of her words.

They headed west, walking out of the meadow and into the trees. It was only a few degrees cooler under the shelter of the pines by now. When they were out of sight and earshot of the others, Garrick stopped and pulled Cat to him. They kissed lingeringly, but when he grew more insistent, she pushed him away with a smile. "Let's keep going," she said softly. "I've got something to show you."

"So do I," he quipped, but he followed her lead.

She guided him through the trees until they came to an area where the forest gave way to rocky outcroppings. Great chunks of silver-gray rock thrust up through the soil, and across the valleys and smaller mountains, the Tetons rose majestically. About thirty feet from the edge of the trees, a cliff fell away to a stream-cut valley hundreds of feet below. She led him near to the edge.

"Oh, my sainted Aunt Sadie," Garrick said, clutching her comically. "It's a good thing I'm not afraid of heights."

"Your office building's probably taller, sport." Cat leaned over and kissed him. "But isn't this a sight?"

He put an arm around her shoulders and she felt a sudden tension in him. "It sure is," he said in a strange tone. "Cat, don't move real suddenly, but take a look over to your left."

She did so and nearly exclaimed aloud.

On some flattish rocks not so very far away lay two cougars, sunning. The smaller one raised her head, stared at the humans, yawned and returned to her nap. Her mate never bothered to look up, although Cat knew the male had to be acutely aware of their presence. "Which one is your cougar?" she asked in a whisper.

"The little one, I think. If that big guy had clipped Norm, he wouldn't be alive to stand trial. I didn't tell you, but I met the female once again after the first time. It was just after I'd made a jerk out of myself during the festival by trying to pressure you into marriage. I wasn't ready, and neither were you. I think my little lion happened by to make sure I knew that. She scared some common sense back into me."

"You really believe that?"

"I don't disbelieve it. Say, are these guys safe from your hunters? I'd probably skin anyone I saw shoot a cougar after all that's happened to me."

"As long as they don't start hunting cattle or sheep, they're as safe as any wild animal can be. It bothers me, though, that they don't seem afraid of us. If they're that way with humans in general—" She broke off as the sound of Peter's voice calling them disturbed the stillness.

"Oh, there you are," the psychiatrist said as he came out of the clump of trees. "Hey, what a view. Do you ever run out?"

"Shut up, Pete," Garrick warned. "Look over to your left, and you'll really see something."

Peter looked. "I don't see anything. Just some more rocks."

"They're gone," Cat whispered. "Were they ever actually there?" The rocks were bare. No sign of the mountain lions remained.

"They were," Garrick said firmly. "And I don't think we need to worry about them being too casual about humans. I think it's just us they tolerate."

"You are getting mystical on me," she teased. "But I like it."

"Believe me now?"

"About the lion saving your life? Maybe."

He gave a low, warning growl.

"Yes! I believe!"

THE WEDDING was the social event of the year. Friends and relations Cat hadn't expected to show up did, filling the motels to capacity. Townspeople close to Cat and Garrick opened their homes to those who couldn't find regular lodging, and she noted another debt of gratitude she owed to families like the Hendrys and the Fullers. When Garrick commented on the incredibly generous nature of those people, she simply reminded him that hospitality was just one of the special touches he could expect if he continued living in Lone Tree.

"For the rest of my life," he promised.

He got to meet her sister and brother, both up from the southern part of the state. Daniel Cantrell was a stockily built man with a permanent farmer's tan on his face and neck and pleasant lines around his eyes. Her sister, Norma, was a slender blonde not quite as tall as Cat. She had the pale complexion of a person who worked indoors. Both were older than Cat.

"Mom and Dad would be so happy," Norma said, "to know you'd finally found someone to love for the rest of your life, Sis. We're so happy for you."

"Only thing I'm upset about," said Daniel, "is that you didn't call on us when you were having so much trouble. We would have wanted to help, if we'da known."

"I know," Cat said, hugging them both. "But I just had to work it out by myself. I wouldn't have even taken Garrick's help if he hadn't forced me. In a nice way, of course."

"She's stubborn," Daniel told Garrick. "Always has been."

"I know. It's one of her more aggravating and endearing qualities." Garrick could sense he was going to like his new brother-in-law and sister-in-law. They were plain, contented folk who had found life to be good.

Peter's report on Janet's progress had been optimistic, but guarded. A few months, he said, maybe a year or so, and Garrick could see what renewed contact would bring. But her psychosis was not a thing that would rush to be healed. Garrick accepted that. His friend's words certainly pointed to a happier ending than that which would have come had Janet been allowed to continue on the way she was.

Elizabeth Drexel took over the job of preparing Cat for the ceremony. With Abby and Ellen acting as assistants and go-fors, she transformed Cat from a pretty ranch owner to a stunningly beautiful bride. Even Cat was amazed at what the matron's practiced hand accomplished with her face and hair. The teenagers were speechless for once in their lives.

"I never thought I'd live to see this day," Elizabeth said, standing back to survey her handiwork and dabbing at her tears. "You don't know how happy you've made me, my dear. I think I'm the happiest woman in the world." Cat didn't correct her, but she knew Elizabeth was wrong. Catherine Cantrell was the happiest woman in the world!

And the moment she walked up the aisle on Nelson Hendry's arm and saw Garrick waiting for her in front of the altar, she wanted to shout it to the world. He was splendidly handsome in a gray morning coat—he had insisted the wedding be formal in spite of spirited objections from almost everyone else involved. The dreaded prospect of wearing a tux had kept Jude from participating as anything but a spectator. Finding one large enough for Nelson had been a problem, but a friend of Garrick's in New York had come through. Beside Garrick stood Tom, acting as best man. The young deputy didn't look as if he minded being in what his uncle had scornfully called a "monkey suit." In fact, he looked completely content as he watched Cat's maid of honor, Abby.

Garrick had eyes only for his bride. He had known his mother was going to work her considerable skill on his love, but the results were astonishing. His bride was undoubtedly the most beautiful woman ever to walk down an aisle!

As the ceremony continued and he took her hand, he felt a joy so great he wondered if his mortal frame could contain it. He felt strong and wise and powerful and more in love than he had ever dreamed possible. Cat was an absolute vision in ecru lace and satin. Her hair was curled and hung to her shoulders. There was no doubt in his mind that this woman was capable of making the transition from a hot, dusty day on the trail to a cool night on the most sophisticated town in the world. She was as near perfection as possible. And she was his!

In a few moments the words spoken by the minister made that possession—and the one making him hers—legal in the eyes of the world. Garrick believed they had been legal before God for much longer—maybe even from the first time they had met. But he took full advantage of the legalities and managed to kiss his new wife with tender passion before they both turned and walked proudly and happily down the aisle and out of the church. They were husband and wife at last.

Cat smiled through tears of joy and waved at the crowd of friends and neighbors who, not having been able to squeeze into the small church, had waited patiently outside. Roscoe Petersen and a bunch of his buddies were sitting in pickups parked on the periphery of the crowd, and they began honking their horns in celebratory cacophony. She laughed delightedly as Garrick grabbed her and laid a dramatically passionate kiss on her for the benefit of the heckling cowboys.

Her life was now complete, she decided, her happiness at its greatest peak. After all the trials and struggles and fears, this was her finest moment. She had her love, her friends, her ranch and a wonderful future to look forward to. Things just could not get any better!

But of course, things did get better. Six months after the wedding, Cat Drexel was delivered of a healthy baby boy. Thanks to Garrick's special touches, a year later, Garrick

Thomas Drexel had a baby brother. And the year after that, a sister. And the next year...

Within a decade there was no need to hire extra help at Cat's Cradle in the summer. Her children, under the aging wrangler's tutelage, became expert cowboys and wranglers themselves. The boys tended to gravitate to ranch work, while Garrick's daughters demonstrated a precocious ability and interest in finance. Within two decades the Drexel Corporation was one of the most powerful financial forces in the Western United States, and Cat's Cradle was still a pleasant place to spend a holiday.

And the patriarch and matriarch of the clan were as much in love as they had been the day they had wed.